was born Katherin~~~~~~~~~
ary 8, 1851, of a prosperous Irish-born merchant
father and an aristocratic Creole mother. She studied piano, wrote poetry, and read Dickens, Austen, Goethe, de Staël, and the Brontës. Despite her
free spirit—she was once nicknamed the "littlest
rebel" for yanking down a Union flag—Kate grew
to be a leading social belle, admired for her wit
and beauty.

In 1870 she married Oscar Chopin. Matrimony
did not quell her independence: she dressed un-
conventionally, took long unchaperoned walks,
and smoked cigarettes. In their twelve years of
married life, she bore six children, and upon Oscar's
sudden death in 1882 she took over the management of the Chopin family plantation in Natchitoches, Louisiana. She turned seriously to writing
shortly thereafter, publishing stories in *Vogue* and
Atlantic Monthly. She wrote a novel, *At Fault*
(1890), *Bayou Folk*, a collection of stories (1894), *A
Night in Acadie*, a second collection (1897), and
her masterpiece, *The Awakening* (1899), which
aroused a national scandal for its "indecency."
Banned by libraries, it even prevented her admis-
sion into the St. Louis Fine Arts Club—even though
Kate Chopin was famous for her literary salon,
which attracted distinguished artists and writers
from all over the country.

Always sensitive to criticism, Chopin was devas-
tated by the furor that surrounded the publication of *The Awakening*, and its harsh reception
ultimately caused her to stop writing. When she
died in 1904, she had been denied the recognition
she desperately wanted and richly deserved.

Bantam Classics by Women Writers
Ask your bookseller for titles you have missed.

EMMA by Jane Austen
MANSFIELD PARK by Jane Austen
NORTHANGER ABBEY by Jane Austen
PERSUASION by Jane Austen
PRIDE AND PREJUDICE by Jane Austen
SENSE AND SENSIBILITY by Jane Austen

JANE EYRE by Charlotte Bronte
VILLETTE by Charlotte Bronte
WUTHERING HEIGHTS by Emily Bronte

A LITTLE PRINCESS by Frances Hodgson Burnett
THE SECRET GARDEN by Frances Hodgson Burnett

O PIONEERS! by Willa Cather
THE SONG OF THE LARK by Willa Cather
THE TROLL GARDEN AND SELECTED STORIES
   by Willa Cather

MIDDLEMARCH by George Eliot
THE MILL ON THE FLOSS by George Eliot
SILAS MARNER by George Eliot

THE CUSTOM OF THE COUNTRY by Edith Wharton
ETHAN FROME AND OTHER SHORT FICTION
   by Edith Wharton
THE HOUSE OF MIRTH by Edith Wharton

THREE CLASSICS BY AMERICAN WOMEN
LITTLE WOMEN by Louisa May Alcott
THE AWAKENING by Kate Chopin
THE YELLOW WALLPAPER AND OTHER WRITINGS
   by Charlotte Perkins Gilman
THE STORY OF MY LIFE by Helen Keller
IN A GERMAN PENSION by Katherine Mansfield
THE SCARLET PIMPERNEL by Baroness Emmuska Orczy
FRANKENSTEIN by Mary Shelley
UNCLE TOM'S CABIN by Harriet Beecher Stowe
THE VOYAGE OUT by Virginia Woolf

A Matter of Prejudice and Other Stories
by
Kate Chopin

Introduction by
Roxana Robinson

BANTAM BOOKS

NEW YORK · TORONTO · LONDON · SYDNEY · AUCKLAND

A MATTER OF PREJUDICE AND OTHER STORIES
A Bantam Classic Book / May 1992

PRINTING HISTORY

"A No-Account Creole" *published in* Century, *January, 1894;* "A Rude Awakening" *published in* Youth's Companion, *February 2, 1893;* "Love on the Bon-Dieu" *published in* Two Tales *July 23, 1892;* "After the Winter" *published in the New Orleans* Times-Democrat *April 5, 1896;* "Old Aunt Peggy" *published in* Bayou Folk *January 8, 1892;* "The Lilies" *published in* Wide Awake *April, 1893;* "Loka" *published in* Youth's Companion *December 22, 1892;* "At the 'Cadian Ball" *published in* Two Tales *October 22, 1892;* "In and Out of Old Nachitoches" *published in* Two Tales *April 8, 1893;* "Mamouche" *published in* Youth's Companion *April 19, 1894;* "Madame Celestin's Divorce" *published in* Bayou Folk *May 24, 1893;* "A Matter of Prejudice" *published in* Youth's Companion *September 25, 1895;* "In Sabine" *published in* Bayou Folk *November 7, 1893;* "Tante Cat'rinette" *published in* Atlantic Monthly *September, 1894;* "A Dresden Lady in Dixie" *published in* Catholic Home Journal *March 3, 1895;* "Regret" *published in* Century *May, 1894;* "Ozeme's Holiday" *published in* Century *August, 1896;* "Odalie Misses Mass" *published in the* Shreveport Times *July 1, 1895;* "Dead Men's Shoes" *published in* Independent *February 11, 1897;* "A Night in Acadie" *published in* A Night in Acadie *March, 1896;* "A Family Affair" *published in* The Saturday Evening Post *September 9, 1899. Grateful acknowledgment is made for permission to reprint the following:* "The Storm," "A Little Country Girl," *and* "The Gentleman From New Orleans" *from* The Complete Works of Kate Chopin *edited by Per Seyersted. Copyright © 1969 by Louisiana State University Press. Reprinted by permission.*

"On the Verandah," *by Irving Ramsey Wiles. Courtesy of Terra Museum of American Art, part of the Daniel Terra Collection, Chicago, 5. 1985.*

ISBN 0-553-21405-5

Published simultaneously in the United States and Canada

Bantam Books are published by Bantam Books, a division of Bantam Doubleday Dell Publishing Group, Inc. Its trademark, consisting of the words "Bantam Books" and the portrayal of a rooster, is Registered in U.S. Patent and Trademark Office and in other countries. Marca Registrada. Bantam Books, 666 Fifth Avenue, New York, New York 10103.

PRINTED IN THE UNITED STATES OF AMERICA

OPM   0 9 8 7 6 5 4 3 2 1

Contents

Introduction

> The brute instinct that drives men at each other's throat was awake and stirring in these two. Each saw in the other a thing to be wiped out of his way—out of existence if need be. Passion and blind rage directed the blows which they dealt, and steeled the tension of muscles and clutch of fingers.
>
> > "A Night in Acadie"

 Here are two Cajun men struggling before the fire in a cabin at midnight, and here is the vision of Kate Chopin: an exaltation of passion set in the dark heart of a wilderness.

This vision derives from the Creole south of Louisiana, the place where Chopin spent her own most passionate years, the place that gave her vision form and validation. It was there that Chopin found her own emotional homeland, it was this landscape that bodied forth her most profound feelings, it was those people with whom she felt the deepest sympathy. It was in response to the Creole south that Chopin produced her most intense and dreamlike work. At its best this is so deeply felt, so powerfully experienced, that we feel it rush through us like one of the great rivers of the Louisiana countryside.

Kate Chopin did not grow up in the Creole South. She was born in 1850 in the industrial midwestern city of St. Louis, where she lived until she was twenty years old. Born Catherine O'Flaherty to an Irish father and a half-Irish mother she was one-quarter Creole—a "Quadreole," if French blood, not black, were quantified. The Creole quarter was the dominant one, however, for living with the O'Flaherty family was Kate's maternal great-grandmother, Madame Victoire Verdon Charleville. Madame Charleville was purest Creole, and, according to Chopin's biographer, Emily Toth, a puissant influence. Madame Charleville came from a distinguished and venerable Creole family, and she taught her great-granddaughter the language, manners, and mores of the ancient and arcane Creole world.

The word *Creole* has become increasingly imprecise since its inception. Originally the word denoted a child born in New World colonies to French- or Spanish-born parents; it came from *criollo*, the term for a New World child born to Spanish parents. Its meaning grew to include all the New World offspring of European forebears, though now it is often used to refer to a polyglot of origins and races. *Webster's New World Dictionary* starts off brisk and specific with "native-born," but finally throws up its hands with "loosely, anyone from Louisiana." The word's first function was to denote racial purity, distinguishing between the offspring of European or "white" colonists and the mixed-blood offspring of Europeans and indigenous Indians—*mestizos*—or Europeans and African slaves—mulattoes.

The issue of racial purity was critical to the whole of the eighteenth-century American South, with its slave-based economy, but the concept was treated very differently by the Creoles than by their eastern counterparts. The eastern South was settled by Anglo-Saxon Protestant men and women. Although mixed-blood children, the offspring of white men and black women, were common during the era of slavery, they were usually the result of brief encounters, and the children were generally unacknowledged by their fathers. Mixed-blood children shared their mothers' racial designation and their mothers' destiny, which was slavery. An attitude as rigid as it was simplistic determined that any fraction of "black blood," however small, predominated over any fraction of "white blood," however large, and determined the bearer's race as black. Given the premise that supported slavery—the genetic superiority of whites to blacks—this attitude paradoxically assumed the superior potency of "black" blood over "white."

The settlement and kinship patterns in Louisiana were different from those in the East. The original settlers there, in the first years of the eighteenth century, were French Catholic men unaccompanied by women. They established liaisons with the women they found: indigenous Indians and African slaves. These liaisons were long-term and domestic, and the early priests wrote pragmatically back to France, asking that they either be allowed to recognize mixed-blood liaisons officially or that Frenchwomen be sent over to correct the situation. By the time European women arrived, a pattern had already been established of close and enduring relationships between white men and nonwhite women—a pattern that was officially forbidden but tacitly condoned by the Church. When offspring were produced, a Creole man often freed the black woman and the children she bore, to save his children from slavery. This response acknowledged the racial connection between white father and mixed-blood offspring and asserted the potency of white or European blood. The pattern of racial mingling and the freeing of mixed-blood children resulted in a racially discrete group called "free mulattoes," or *gens du couleur libre*. Free mulattoes could own property and slaves, and they became a significant proportion of the Louisiana population.

Creole technically included all European inhabitants and their descendants, but the word had a strong Gallic bias and, in Chopin's time, an aristocratic one as well. The first French settlers established a cultural supremacy in Louisiana that lasted, despite nearly forty years of Spanish rule, well into the twentieth century. Some of those early settlers were aristocrats, and they modeled their world after the late seventeenth-century French court. Louisiana was under Spanish rule during both the American and French revolutions, which meant that the French colony never revolted against a monarchy and never experienced the strong populist and democratic surge that swept through the eastern American states. The use of French titles continued, and the aristocratic ideal remained powerful in Creole society.

The Creole upper classes were French-speaking, French-oriented, and supremely self-confident. Other ethnic groups—excepting Americans—were absorbed into this society. Newcomers' names were gallicized, they learned to speak French, and they adopted Creole manners and mores. After a generation or two of inter-marriage they assumed the title of Creole.

Kate Chopin's own experience reflected this French supremacism. Kate's substantial Irish heritage seems to have played a minor part in her upbringing, and is barely apparent in her writing. The Creole experience predominates, and the French elitist attitude responsi-ble for such dominance is evident in the title story of this collection. In this, the supremely xenophobic Madame Carambeau "despised Americans, Germans and all people of a different faith from her own. Any-thing not French had, in her opinion, little right to existence." In an exquisite refinement of ethnic dis-crimination she has "an original theory that the Irish voice is distressing to the sick."

Kate Chopin's response to her great-grandmother Charleville's influence could hardly be made clearer than by her choice of husband. This was the handsome Oscar Chopin, a French-speaking, full-blooded Creole. Oscar's father was born in France, hated Americans, and had his son educated in the mother country. Oscar grew up in a purely Creole world, and it was he who took Kate from St. Louis to Louisiana, where she en-tered into this world.

In 1870, when Kate was twenty, she and Oscar moved to New Orleans. Oscar was a cotton factor, and the Chopins were comfortably off, though not rich. The young bride was introduced to the insular and complicated New Orleans society. Some aspects of this exotic life baffled her, some of it she understood very well—thanks to her excellent French and her excellent French great-grandmother. Kate's status, as an outsider with inside information, allowed her the combination of alienation and connection necessary to a writer's sensibility.

The Chopins' five sons were born in New Orleans, where the family lived for the next nine years. In 1879, however, following financial reverses, the Chopins moved to the family property in the community where Oscar had grown up. This was rural Natchitoches (pronounced Nacketosh) Parish, some four hundred miles northwest of New Orleans, on the banks of the Red River. For the next three years, the family lived in tiny single-street, French-speaking Cloutierville (pronounced Cloochyville), where Oscar managed his property and ran a country store. The last Chopin child, a daughter, was born there. Oscar died of malaria in 1882, but Kate stayed on after her husband's death, assuming the management of the store and the property, and becoming romantically involved with another handsome Creole, Albert Sampité. Sampité seems to have been responsible for a passionate interlude in Chopin's life, but he was neither particularly desirable nor available. Hot-tempered, hard-drinking, and already married, he had the unsympathetic habit of taking a leather strap to his wife. In 1884, two years after Oscar's death, Kate returned to St. Louis, at the age of thirty-four. Some four years afterward she began to write, remembering and recreating the years spent in Louisiana.

In her later novel, *The Awakening*, Chopin wrote about the rarefied atmosphere of upper-class Creole life in New Orleans, and it is through that work that she has become best known. Before the novel was published, however, Chopin first produced a collection of short stories, *Bayou Folk*, many of which are included in the present collection. The pieces here are almost entirely set in the Louisiana countryside—the one exception being the title story. Arranged chronologically, the collection charts Chopin's progress as a writer, observer, and thinker, moving from the sentimentality of "A Rude Awakening" of 1891 to the radical vision of female sexuality in "The Storm" of 1898.

The collection provides a remarkable portrait of a place and its people. The place names are real, and the family names and characters recur, creating the sense of a regional chronicle. The place is Natchitoches Parish, and Cloutierville, the village with one street, is the psychological center.

Though she was raised in a city, Chopin's response to the Natchitoches countryside was powerful and immediate. She spent much of her time riding and walking in it, and her descriptions demonstrate her sensuous delight. On one plantation there grew "a dense wood . . . [that] held much mystery, and witchery of sound and shadow, and strange lights when the sun shone." On another, "there was the hedge . . . filling the night with fragrance. . . . The land did not look as if it ever had been plowed for a field. It was a smooth, green meadow, with cattle huddled upon the cool sward, or moving with slow, stately tread as they nibbled the tender shoots." Many of these narratives depend upon crops and weather, planting and harvesting: the land is not only beautiful, but a powerful economic force.

To the south of Natchitoches is Avoyelles Parish, where Chopin's Cajuns lived. The Cajuns were also French emigrants, but a very different sort from the early arrivals from continental France. The Cajuns came from Acadia, Nova Scotia—hence the name "Acadians," which became " 'Cadians" and then "Cajuns." They arrived in Louisiana in the mid-eighteenth century when the English took over Nova Scotia and after the original French settlers were already established in the Territory. The Cajuns were independent farmers accustomed to working their own land; they spoke a rough colonial French, and they had no aristocratic tradition or pretensions. Many arrived penniless and were granted swampy bayou land to the west of New Orleans. In Chopin's stories, however, their territory is nearby Avoyelles. Gregarious and generous, Chopin's Cajuns—especially the women—are wilder than her Creoles; they are more dramatic and less conventional. In "A Night in Acadie" the strong-willed, flamboyant Zaïda "carried herself boldly and stepped out freely and easily, like a negress."

"At the 'Cadian Ball" of 1892, one of the best of these stories, provides a social diagram of the relations between the Cajun and Creole worlds. Alcée Laballière, the handsome young Creole, is managing his family's land in an effort to recover its wealth. Though he "worked like a mule," there is nothing stolid about Alcée. One day without warning he takes his mother's goddaughter, the genteel Clarisse, in his arms "and panted a volley of hot, blistering love-words into her face." Clarisse, however, values manners more than passion: " '*Par exemple!*' she muttered disdainfully, as she turned from him." When a storm destroys Alcée's rice harvest, "his speechlessness was frightful." At midnight—when many of Chopin's most powerful scenes take place—he leaves Clarisse's ordered environs, setting off for the wilder, more permissive Cajun world. " 'Nice conduc' for a Laballière,' " Clarisse says indignantly when she hears.

The Cajun ball is a rollicking affair, with three fiddlers, and chicken gumbo served at midnight. Cajun manners are simple but strict. "Any one who is white may go to a 'Cadian ball, but . . . he must behave himself like a 'Cadian." There has been "but one disturbance, and that was caused by American railroaders, who were not in touch with their surroundings and had no business there. 'Ces maudits gens du raiderode,' " they were called.

Chopin's Cajuns are hard-working, good-hearted, and slow-witted. The men at the ball are "dull-looking and clumsy," and though the women are "very beautiful," their dark eyes are like those of "young heifers." (Clarisse, by contrast, is "dainty as a lily.") The vivacious Calixta escapes the stolid Cajun stereotype because of her Spanish blood, which gives her "Such animation! and abandon! such flashes of wit!" The Spanish strain also elevates her socially, making her more appropriate as Alcée's choice than the other Cajun girls. Alcée's rival for Calixta is "big, brown, good-natured Bobinôt," who yearns for the "Spanish vixen" despite her public mockery of him.

After Alcée leaves, Clarisse admits the strength of her emotions and rides after him. When she finds him with Calixta, instead of perceiving the Cajun girl as an equal and a romantic threat, Clarisse treats her with the exquisite courtesy shown by the ruling class to inferiors. " 'Ah, c'est vous, Calixta? Comment ça va, mon enfant?' " How are things with you, she asks in elegant Creole French with unconscious arrogance as she plucks Calixta's lover from her arms. Though Calixta once slapped the face of another Cajun girl, screaming insults at her, she now responds politely to Clarisse. In her rough Cajun French, she answers according to formula—" 'Tcha va b'en; et vous, mam'zélle?' "

At the end of the dance the musicians fire gunshots into the air, signaling that "_le bal est fini_," and the moment of license and irresponsibility is over. Ultimately, the class structure is reinforced: Calixta is punished for her social temerity and sentenced to a loveless marriage with the Cajun Bobinôt, while the Creole aristocrats pledge themselves to each other. The story is not, however, a celebration of the class structure, but of passion. Clarisse, though the least sympathetic of the three characters, is the most powerful. It is Clarisse's revelation, the recognition of her own emotion, that generates the action. It is Clarisse who saves them all: Alcée from pursuit of an irresponsible and destructive relationship, Calixta from the ruin of her reputation and her future, and herself from a repressed and loveless life. It is Clarisse who takes the greatest risk, setting out on a midnight ride into Cajun territory, her heart on her sleeve. It is Clarisse who undergoes the most profound change by acknowledging the power of emotion—a theme to which Chopin would return.

"The Storm," a sequel to "At the 'Cadian Ball,"

carries still further the notion of the Creole-Cajun relationship. Calixta, now happily married to the good Bobinôt, is mother to his son. She again encounters Alcée,
who shelters in her house during a storm which provides opportunity and metaphor for the sexual passion
that sweeps over them. This story was not published
in Chopin's lifetime—unsurprisingly, since it is both
steamily explicit and radical in its implications. Calixta
is a voluntary and enthusiastic partner in illicit passion,
and, more shockingly, capable of a sexual relationship
without emotional ties. She waves a cheerful good-bye
to Alcée, and serves her son and husband a warm wel-
coming meal when they return. Again and more
overtly, the Creole Alcée must leave the confining
world represented by Clarisse, his social peer, in order
to experience a thunderous sexual encounter. Clarisse
is at the seashore with the children, and in respose to
Alcée's absence she reveals a genteel frigidity. "Devoted as she was to her husband, their intimate conjugal life was something which she was more than willing
to forego for a while."

If Avoyelles, to the south of Natchitouches, represented a sensual world and a certain moral permis-
siveness, Sabine Parish, to the west, represented the
savage badlands of Texas that lay beyond it. In Chopin's
world Texas stands for both a physical and moral wilderness; Americans *ces maudits gens,* were barbarians.
"In Sabine" is set perilously close to Texas and concerns
an American villain, a Cajun victim, and a Creole sav-
ior. Bud Aiken, the alcoholic American husband, is
without redeeming qualities. Chopin writes about Cajun
and Creole men who both drink and lie, but these men
make an emotional connection to their women that is
lacking in Aiken's world. Aiken is "a big good-looking
brute," cold, dishonest, and physically abusive, who
holds his frightened and humiliated Cajun wife a virtual
prisoner. The Creole, Grégoire Santien, by contrast,
"loved women. He liked their nearness, their atmosphere; the tones of their voices and the things they
said; their ways of moving and turning about; the

brushing of their garments when they passed him by."
The dichotomy between the two men demonstrates
Chopin's view of the profound difference between the
American and Creole sensibilities. The former is chill,
self-absorbed, and dishonest; the latter sensual, com-
passionate, and morally courageous. When Santien
tricks the bully out of his prey, this represents a triumph of the Creole code—humanistic and compassion-
ate—over that of the American barbarian.

The Creole code of honor plays a central part in
"A No-Account Creole," one of the most fully realized
of these stories. Another Santien, Placide, is caught in
the post-Civil War decline of the plantation economy.
The family acres taken over by the bank and the wealth
dissipated, Placide has become an itinerant handyman,
known contemptuously as "a no-account creole." But
despite his poverty, Placide is "a Santien always, with
the best blood in the country running in his veins."
The idea of Santien blood, and its attendant responsibilities, lies at the heart of this story. Based on a romantic
triangle, its verticies are Placide, who represents the
waning power of the Creole landowners; Wallace Offdean, an Anglo Saxon, who represents the waxing
power of the urban financiers; and Euphrasie, an odd
and contradictory heroine. Beautiful and good, she represents moral purity, but she is also a symbol of the social
flexibility of the Creole world. Though it is Euphrasie's
radical ideas that set the plot in motion, she is strangely
passive concerning her own destiny, trapped by a code
of behavior that prohibits acknowledgment of her feelings. It is Placide who takes command, responding to
the challenge made to his Creole honor. In the romantic tradition of noblesse oblige he sacrifices his own
happiness for that of the woman he loves. His act has
a redemptive power that saves the physical life of Offdean and the spiritual lives of both Euphrasie and Placide himself.

On one level the story concerns the old order giving way to the new, but on another it explores the
internal subtleties of Creole society. Euphrasie, though

lovely and pure as convention requires a heroine to be, is base-born. Engaged to "the best blood in the country," she is herself only the daughter of a Cajun plantation manager, "and a problematic mother a good deal less than nobody." This dramatic social inequality throws into sharp relief the reality behind the Creole social structure. This appeared to be fixed and hierarchical, but there were ways for a beautiful young woman to move from one social level to another.

Euphrasie was not raised by her problematic mother, but by a rich and aristocratic Creole, Madame Duplan. "Euphrasie went to the convent . . . and was taught all gentle things, the pretty arts of manner and speech." Though she first appears as an unpretentious rustic, in New Orleans Euphrasie reveals herself as an intimate member of the innermost Creole circles, which were exclusive and French-speaking, governed by kinship and social connections.

Euphrasie's social mobility is radical, since it implies the crossing of the racial barrier. Someone socially inferior to a Cajun, someone "a good deal less than nobody," suggests a free mulatto, and black blood. The crossing of the racial line was not condoned, but it was not unknown in Creole society, even in the upper classes. One of the eighteenth-century Spanish governor Ulloa's first acts in office was to grant permission for a marriage between a Frenchman and a black woman, and in another Chopin story, "Desirée's Baby" (not in this collection), an arrogant and aristocratic Creole discovers that his mother was descended from "the race cursed with the brand of slavery." The line between the races was not always clear, as Kate Chopin's own family history attests. Two of her Charleville great-uncles had mixed-blood offspring, and one of these audaciously took his father's name and became a successful horse trader. A grand eighteenth-century Creole, one M. de Volsay, left most of his property to his illegitimate mixed-blood daughter.

In fact, young mulatto women played a significant part in Louisiana society. By 1788 there were fifteen hundred free unmarried "women of color" in New Orleans. These women were French-speaking demi-mondaines, elegant enough to threaten their Creole counterparts: a decree forbade them to wear silks, plumes or jewels in public. As young women they made their debuts at the infamous "Quadroon Balls," a New Orleans tradition that lasted well into the nineteenth century. The girls were chaperoned by their mothers, and only Creole men could attend. A wealthy Creole "protector" would set a girl up with a house and provide for their children. When he married another Creole, it was not uncommon for him to give the house to the mulatto and her children. The daughters, lighter-skinned with each generation, would make their own debuts at the Quadroon Balls.

Chopin's countryside contains no glamorous quadroon maidens in jewels, but there are plenty of free mulattoes, and an island set aside for them, *l'Isle des Mulâtres*. In "Regret" a mulatto neighbor is a white woman's social equal, though in "In and Out of Old Natchitoches" the mulattoes' inferior social status is central to the plot. Ambiguity about racial distinction comes into sharp focus in "Mamouche," when a black servant suspiciously questions a bedraggled young waif.

" 'Is you w'ite o' is you black?' he asked. 'Dat w'at I wants ter know 'fo' I kiar' victuals to yo in de settin'-room.'

" 'I'm w'ite, me,' the boy responded, promptly.

" 'I ain't disputin'; go ahead. All right fer dem w'at wants ter take yo' wud fer it,' " grumbles the servant.

The fact that this question was both necessary and possible demonstrates the flexibility and subtlety of the racial barrier. The blurring of the line was due partly to the fact that the French and Spanish were themselves dark-haired and often dark-complected, and the growing light-skinned mulatto poulation would increasingly and inevitably resemble that of the Europeans.

Chopin lived in Cloutierville twenty years after the Civil War, at a time when slavery was still a powerful presence. Though there are references made to brutal-

ity—such as the offhand mentions of "giving twenty"
(lashes)—relations between the two races are shown as
generally sympathetic. Though Chopin's work often re-
flects the sentimentality of her era, these stories are
not sentimental fantasies. There were many post-War
stories of enduring affection and support between ex-
slaves and masters, written of and remarked on by con-
temporaries. Chopin's stories portray a powerful net-
work of continuing friendship between blacks and whites.
"Regret," "Odalie Misses Mass," and "Ozème's Holiday" all concern whites who sacrifice their own pleasures in order to benefit blacks. "Loka," "A Dresden
Lady in Dixie," and "Tante Cat'rinette" show the ob-
verse of this dynamic: two black protagonists and a Indian one selflessly relinquish their own interests in
order to benefit whites.

"Tante Cat'rinette" is interesting linguistically as
well as socially, for Cat'rinette moves in and out of a
variety of languages. In public she speaks a mixture of
English and French; a deed is "All wrote down en règle
befo' de cote!" Alone, she lapses into the French Creole
patois, for which Chopin herself felt great affection.
Cat'rinette calls to a mockingbird, "asking why it cried
out so, and threatening to secure it and put it into a
cage. 'Ca to pé crié comme ça, ti céléra? Arete, mo
trapé zozos la, mo mété li dan ain bon lacage.' "

Cat'rinette was not unusual. African slaves who
were sent to Louisiana were taught to speak French,
not English, and at auctions a French-speaking slave
was identified as a "Negro Creole." White children,
growing up among the black servants, learned their
patois, as the blacks had learned the whites' French.
English, Spanish, European Creole French, rough
Cajun French and French patois (also confusingly called
"Creole"), all contribute to the rich linguistic mix of
this world.

Chopin's 1899 novel, *The Awakening*, deals with a
young woman struggling against the constraints of upper-class Creole society in New Orleans, and has attracted much contemporary attention because of its

sexually liberåted and intellectually independent heroine. The novel's advanced point of view is not reflected in most of these stories, however, all but two of which were written prior to *The Awakening*. In this collection, social status is inversely related to female power: Chopin's black women are more powerful than the whites, and Cajun women more powerful than Creoles. Though the aristocratic Clarisse wins a genteel victory over Calixta in "At the 'Cadian Ball," she hardly seems to deserve it. Moreover, the vivid Calixta ultimately triumphs over her pallid Creole rival in the later story, "The Storm." Zaïda, in "A Night in Acadie," fails in her bold venture only because of an editor's timidity: Chopin rewrote the ending to ensure its publication. Originally, Zaïda had faced the battered but victorious Telèsphore and demanded, in a brilliant tactical move, that Telèsphore himself marry her, insistently controlling her own destiny and producing her own triumph.

According to her biographer, Emily Toth, Chopin seldom edited her stories. Some of them demonstrate this to their detriment; some seem unfinished, unshaped, and meandering. But formal perfection is not Chopin's forte, and we look in this collection for other virtues, just as we look for other subjects beside language, race, and social distinctions. These stories are about kinship and family, about love and responsibility, about a rich countryside suddenly impoverished. They are about language and its pleasures, about race and its complications, about the intimate shifts of a community in flux.

Beyond these subjects, however, there is a rich emotional content that enlarges these stories, that elevates and ennobles them. They are informed by that swift upswelling of feeling that starts people out on midnight rides, that hurls men at each others' throats, that sets women shouting insults and slapping faces. Underlying them is passion of all sorts: for beloved children, beloved servants, beloved masters, personal codes, and, of course, for tempestuous lovers. It is this turbulent undercurrent that gives the best of these sto-

ries their depth, energy, and resonance. It is this that
lies at the core of the Creole world, a world to which
Chopin has laid successful claim and which, in so doing,
she has so powerfully revealed.

ROXANA ROBINSON

A Matter of Prejudice and Other Stories

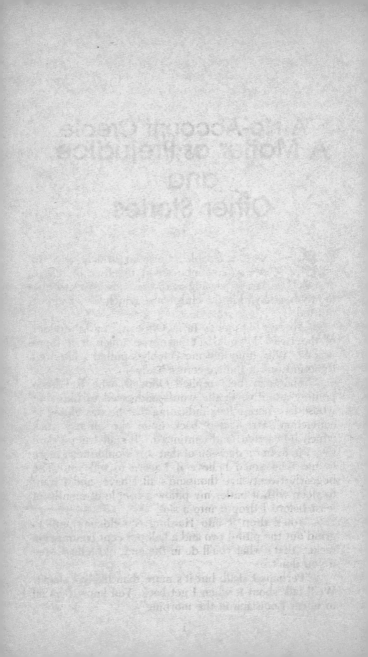

A No-Account Creole
1891

I

One agreeable afternoon in late autumn two young men stood together on Canal Street, closing a conversation that had evidently begun within the club-house which they had just quitted.

"There's big money in it, Offdean," said the elder of the two. "I would n't have you touch it if there was n't. Why, they tell me Patchly's pulled a hundred thousand out of the concern a'ready."

"That may be," replied Offdean, who had been politely attentive to the words addressed to him, but whose face bore a look indicating that he was closed to conviction. He leaned back upon the clumsy stick which he carried, and continued: "It's all true, I dare say, Fitch; but a decision of that sort would mean more to me than you'd believe if I were to tell you. The beggarly twenty-five thousand's all I have, and I want to sleep with it under my pillow a couple of months at least before I drop it into a slot."

"You'll drop it into Harding & Offdean's mill to grind out the pitiful two and a half per cent commission racket; that's what you'll do in the end, old fellow—see if you don't."

"Perhaps I shall; but it's more than likely I shan't. We'll talk about it when I get back. You know I 'm off to north Louisiana in the morning"—

1

"No! What the deuce"—

"Oh, business of the firm."

"Write me from Shreveport, then; or wherever it is."

"Not so far as that. But don't expect to hear from me till you see me. I can't say when that will be."

Then they shook hands and parted. The rather portly Fitch boarded a Prytania Street car, and Mr. Wallace Offdean hurried to the bank in order to replenish his portemonnaie, which had been materially lightened at the club through the medium of unpropitious jack-pots and bobtail flushes.

He was a sure-footed fellow, this young Offdean, despite an occasional fall in slippery places. What he wanted, now that he had reached his twenty-sixth year and his inheritance, was to get his feet well planted on solid ground, and to keep his head cool and clear.

With his early youth he had had certain shadowy intentions of shaping his life on intellectual lines. That is, he wanted to; and he meant to use his faculties intelligently, which means more than is at once apparent. Above all, he would keep clear of the maelstroms of sordid work and senseless pleasure in which the average American business man may be said alternately to exist, and which reduce him, naturally, to a rather ragged condition of soul.

Offdean had done, in a temperate way, the usual things which young men do who happen to belong to good society, and are possessed of moderate means and healthy instincts. He had gone to college, had traveled a little at home and abroad, had frequented society and the clubs, and had worked in his uncle's commission-house; in all of which employments he had expended much time and a modicum of energy.

But he felt all through that he was simply in a preliminary stage of being, one that would develop later into something tangible and intelligent, as he liked to tell himself. With his patrimony of twenty-five thousand dollars came what he felt to be the turning-point in his life,—the time when it behooved him to choose a course, and to get himself into proper trim to follow it manfully and consistently.

When Messrs. Harding & Offdean determined to have some one look after what they called "a troublesome piece of land on Red River," Wallace Offdean requested to be intrusted with that special commission of land-inspector.

A shadowy, ill-defined piece of land in an unfamiliar part of his native State, might, he hoped, prove a sort of closet into which he could retire and take counsel with his inner and better self.

II

What Harding & Offdean had called a piece of land on Red River was better known to the people of Natchitoches* parish as "the old Santien place."

In the days of Lucien Santien and his hundred slaves, it had been very splendid in the wealth of its thousand acres. But the war did its work, of course. Then Jules Santien was not the man to mend such damage as the war had left. His three sons were even less able than he had been to bear the weighty inheritance of debt that came to them with the dismantled plantation; so it was a deliverance to all when Harding & Offdean, the New Orleans creditors, relieved them of the place with the responsibility and indebtedness which its ownership had entailed.

Hector, the eldest, and Grégoire, the youngest of these Santien boys, had gone each his way. Placide alone tried to keep a desultory foothold upon the land which had been his and his forefathers'. But he too was given to wandering—within a radius, however, which rarely took him so far that he could not reach the old place in an afternoon of travel, when he felt so inclined.

There were acres of open land cultivated in a slovenly fashion, but so rich that cotton and corn and weed

*Pronounced Nack-e-tosh.

and "cocoa-grass" grew rampant if they had only the semblance of a chance. The negro quarters were at the far end of this open stretch, and consisted of a long row of old and very crippled cabins. Directly back of these a dense wood grew, and held much mystery, and witchery of sound and shadow, and strange lights when the sun shone. Of a gin-house there was left scarcely a trace; only so much as could serve as inadequate shelter to the miserable dozen cattle that huddled within it in winter-time.

A dozen rods or more from the Red River bank stood the dwelling-house, and nowhere upon the plantation had time touched so sadly as here. The steep, black, moss-covered roof sat like an extinguisher above the eight large rooms that it covered, and had come to do its office so poorly that not more than half of these were habitable when the rain fell. Perhaps the live-oaks made too thick and close a shelter about it. The verandas were long and broad and inviting; but it was well to know that the brick pillar was crumbling away under one corner, that the railing was insecure at another, and that still another had long ago been condemned as unsafe. But that, of course, was not the corner in which Wallace Offdean sat the day following his arrival at the Santien place. This one was comparatively secure. A gloire-de-Dijon, thick-leaved and charged with huge creamy blossoms, grew and spread here like a hardy vine upon the wires that stretched from post to post. The scent of the blossoms was delicious; and the stillness that surrounded Offdean agreeably fitted his humor that asked for rest. His old host, Pierre Manton, the manager of the place, sat talking to him in a soft, rhythmic monotone; but his speech was hardly more of an interruption than the hum of the bees among the roses. He was saying:—

"If it would been me myse'f, I would nevair grumb'. W'en a chimbly breck, I take one, two de boys; we patch 'im up bes' we know how. We keep on men' de fence', firs' one place, anudder; an' if it would n' be fer dem mule' of Lacroix—*tonnerre!* I don' wan' to talk 'bout dem mule'. But me, I would n' grumb'. It's

Euphrasie, hair. She say dat's all fool nonsense fer rich man lack Hardin'-Offde'n to let a piece o' lan' goin' lack dat."

"Euphrasie?" questioned Offdean, in some surprise; for he had not yet heard of any such person.

"Euphrasie, my li'le chile. Escuse me one minute," Pierre added, remembering that he was in his shirt-sleeves, and rising to reach for his coat, which hung upon a peg near by. He was a small, square man, with mild, kindly face, brown and roughened from healthy exposure. His hair hung gray and long beneath the soft felt hat that he wore. When he had seated himself, Offdean asked:—

"Where is your little child? I have n't seen her," inwardly marveling that a little child should have uttered such words of wisdom as those recorded of her.

"She yonder to Mme. Duplan on Cane River. I been kine espectin' hair sence yistiday—hair an' Placide," casting an unconscious glance down the long plantation road. "But Mme. Duplan she nevair want to let Euphrasie go. You know it's hair raise' Euphrasie sence hair po' ma die', Mr. Offde'n. She teck dat li'le chile, an' raise it, sem lack she raisin' Ninette. But it 's mo' 'an a year now Euphrasie say dat 's all fool nonsense to leave me livin' 'lone lack dat, wid nuttin' 'cep' dem nigger'—an' Placide once a w'ile. An' she came yair bossin'! My goodness!" The old man chuckled, "Dat 's hair been writin' all dem letter' to Hardin'-Offde'n. If it would been me myse'f"—

III

Placide seemed to have a foreboding of ill from the start when he found that Euphrasie began to interest herself in the condition of the plantation. This ill feeling voiced itself partly when he told her it was none of her lookout if the place went to the dogs. "It 's good enough for Joe Duplan to run things *en grand seigneur*, Euphrasie; that 's w'at 's spoiled you."

Placide might have done much single-handed to

keep the old place in better trim, if he had wished.
For there was no one more clever than he to do a
hand's turn at any and every thing. He could mend
a saddle or bridle while he stood whistling a tune. If a
wagon required a brace or a bolt, it was nothing for
him to step into a shop and turn out one as deftly as
the most skilled blacksmith. Any one seeing him at
work with plane and rule and chisel would have declared him a born carpenter. And as for mixing paints,
and giving a fine and lasting coat to the side of a house
or barn, he had not his equal in the country.

This last talent he exercised little in his native parish. It was in a neighboring one, where he spent the
greater part of his time, that his fame as a painter was
established. There, in the village of Orville, he owned
a little shell of a house, and during odd times it was
Placide's great delight to tinker at this small home,
inventing daily new beauties and conveniences to add
to it. Lately it had become a precious possession to
him, for in the spring he was to bring Euphrasie there
as his wife.

Maybe it was because of his talent, and his indifference in turning it to good, that he was often called "a
no-account creole" by thriftier souls than himself. But
no-account creole or not, painter, carpenter, blacksmith, and whatever else he might be at times, he was
a Santien always, with the best blood in the country
running in his veins. And many thought his choice had
fallen in very low places when he engaged himself to
marry little Euphrasie, the daughter of old Pierre Manton and a problematic mother a good deal less than
nobody.

Placide might have married almost any one, too;
for it was the easiest thing in the world for a girl to fall
in love with him,—sometimes the hardest thing in the
world not to, he was such a splendid fellow, such a
careless, happy, handsome fellow. And he did not seem
to mind in the least that young men who had grown
up with him were lawyers now, and planters, and members of Shakespeare clubs in town. No one ever expected anything quite so humdrum as that of the

Santien boys. As youngsters, all three had been the despair of the country schoolmaster; then of the private tutor who had come to shackle them, and had failed in his design. And the state of mutiny and revolt that they had brought about at the college of Grand Coteau when their father, in a moment of weak concession to prejudice, had sent them there, is a thing yet remembered in Natchitoches.

And now Placide was going to marry Euphrasie. He could not recall the time when he had not loved her. Somehow he felt that it began the day when he was six years old, and Pierre, his father's overseer, had called him from play to come and make her acquaintance. He was permitted to hold her in his arms a moment, and it was with silent awe that he did so. She was the first whitefaced baby he remembered having seen, and he straightway believed she had been sent to him as a birthday gift to be his little playmate and friend. If he loved her, there was no great wonder; every one did, from the time she took her first dainty step, which was a brave one, too.

She was the gentlest little lady ever born in old Natchitoches parish, and the happiest and merriest. She never cried or whimpered for a hurt. Placide never did, why should she? When she wept, it was when she did what was wrong, or when he did; for that was to be a coward, she felt. When she was ten, and her mother was dead, Mme. Duplan, the Lady Bountiful of the parish, had driven across from her plantation, Les Chêniers, to old Pierre's very door, and there had gathered up this precious little maid, and carried her away, to do with as she would.

And she did with the child much as she herself had been done by. Euphrasie went to the convent soon, and was taught all gentle things, the pretty arts of manner and speech that the ladies of the "Sacred Heart" can teach so well. When she quitted them, she left a trail of love behind her; she always did.

Placide continued to see her at intervals, and to love her always. One day he told her so; he could not help it. She stood under one of the big oaks at Les

Chêniers. It was midsummer time, and the tangled
sunbeams had enmeshed her in a golden fretwork.
When he saw her standing there in the sun's glamour,
which was like a glory upon her, he trembled. He
seemed to see her for the first time. He could only
look at her, and wonder why her hair gleamed so, as
it fell in those thick chestnut waves about her ears and
neck. He had looked a thousand times into her eyes
before; was it only to-day they held that sleepy, wistful
light in them that invites love? How had he not seen
it before? Why had he not known before that her lips
were red, and cut in fine, strong curves? that her flesh
was like cream? How had he not seen that she was
beautiful? "Euphrasie," he said, taking her hands,—
"Euphrasie, I love you!"

She looked at him with a little astonishment. "Yes;
I know, Placide." She spoke with the soft intonation of
the creole.

"No, you don't, Euphrasie. I did n' know myse'f
how much tell jus' now."

Perhaps he did only what was natural when he
asked her next if she loved him. He still held her hands.
She looked thoughtfully away, unready to answer.

"Do you love anybody better?" he asked jealously.
"Any one jus' as well as me?"

"You know I love papa better, Placide, an' Maman
Duplan jus' as well."

Yet she saw no reason why she should not be his
wife when he asked her to.

Only a few months before this, Euphrasie had returned to live with her father. The step had cut her off
from everything that girls of eighteen call pleasure. If
it cost her one regret, no one could have guessed it.
She went often to visit the Duplans, however; and Placide had gone to bring her home from Les Chêniers
the very day of Offdean's arrival at the plantation.

They had traveled by rail to Natchitoches, where
they found Pierre's no-top buggy awaiting them, for
there was a drive of five miles to be made through the
pine woods before the plantation was reached. When
they were at their journey's end, and had driven some

distance up the long plantation road that led to the house in the rear, Euphrasie exclaimed:—

"W'y, there's some one on the gall'ry with papa, Placide!"

"Yes; I see."

"It looks like some one f'om town. It mus' be Mr. Gus Adams; but I don' see his horse."

" 'T ain't no one f'om town that I know. It's boun' to be some one f'om the city."

"Oh, Placide, I should n' wonder if Harding & Offdean have sent some one to look after the place at las'," she exclaimed a little excitedly.

They were near enough to see that the stranger was a young man of very pleasing appearance. Without apparent reason, a chilly depression took hold of Placide.

"I tole you it was n' yo' lookout f'om the firs', Euphrasie," he said to her.

IV

Wallace Offdean remembered Euphrasie at once as a young person whom he had assisted to a very high perch on his clubhouse balcony the previous Mardi Gras night. He had thought her pretty and attractive then, and for the space of a day or two wondered who she might be. But he had not made even so fleeting an impression upon her; seeing which, he did not refer to any former meeting when Pierre introduced them.

She took the chair which he offered her, and asked him very simply when he had come, if his journey had been pleasant, and if he had not found the road from Natchitoches in very good condition.

"Mr. Offde'n only come sence yistiday, Euphrasie," interposed Pierre. "We been talk' plenty 'bout de place, him an' me. I been tole 'im all 'bout it—*va!* An' if Mr. Offde'n want to escuse me now, I b'lieve I go he'p Placide wid dat hoss an' buggy;" and he descended the steps slowly, and walked lazily with his bent figure in the direction of the shed beneath which Placide had driven, after depositing Euphrasie at the door.

"I dare say you find it strange," began Offdean, "that the owners of this place have neglected it so long and shamefully. But you see," he added, smiling, "the management of a plantation does n't enter into the routine of a commission merchant's business. The place has already cost them more than they hope to get from it, and naturally they have n't the wish to sink further money in it." He did not know why he was saying these things to a mere girl, but he went on: "I'm authorized to sell the plantation if I can get anything like a reasonable price for it." Euphrasie laughed in a way that made him uncomfortable, and he thought he would say no more at present,—not till he knew her better, anyhow.

"Well," she said in a very decided fashion, "I know you 'll fin' one or two persons in town who 'll begin by running down the lan' till you would n' want it as a gif', Mr. Offdean; and who will en' by offering to take it off yo' han's for the promise of a song, with the lan' as security again."

They both laughed, and Placide, who was approaching, scowled. But before he reached the steps his instinctive sense of the courtesy due to a stranger had banished the look of ill humor. His bearing was so frank and graceful, and his face such a marvel of beauty, with its dark, rich coloring and soft lines, that the well-clipped and groomed Offdean felt his astonishment to be more than half admiration when they shook hands. He knew that the Santiens had been the former owners of this plantation which he had come to look after, and naturally he expected some sort of cooperation or direct assistance from Placide in his efforts at reconstruction. But Placide proved non-committal, and exhibited an indifference and ignorance concerning the condition of affairs that savored surprisingly of affectation.

He had positively nothing to say so long as the talk touched upon matters concerning Offdean's business there. He was only a little less taciturn when more general topics were approached, and directly after supper he saddled his horse and went away. He would not wait until morning, for the moon would be rising about midnight, and he knew the road as well by night as by day. He knew just where the best fords were across the bayous, and the safest paths across the hills. He knew for a certainty whose plantations he might traverse, and whose fences he might derail. But, for that matter, he would derail what he liked, and cross where he pleased.

Euphrasie walked with him to the shed when he went for his horse. She was bewildered at his sudden determination, and wanted it explained.

"I don' like that man," he admitted frankly; "I can't stan' him. Sen' me word w'en he 's gone, Euphrasie."

She was patting and rubbing the pony, which knew her well. Only their dim outlines were discernible in the thick darkness.

"You are foolish, Placide," she replied in French. "You would do better to stay and help him. No one knows the place so well as you"—

"The place is n't mine, and it 's nothing to me," he answered bitterly. He took her hands and kissed them passionately, but stooping, she pressed her lips upon his forehead.

"Oh!" he exclaimed rapturously, "you do love me, Euphrasie?" His arms were holding her, and his lips brushing her hair and cheeks as they eagerly but ineffectually sought hers.

"Of co'se I love you, Placide. Ain't I going to marry you nex' spring? You foolish boy!" she replied, disengaging herself from his clasp.

When he was mounted, he stooped to say, "See yere, Euphrasie, don't have too much to do with that d——Yankee."

"But, Placide, he is n't a—a—'d——Yankee;' he 's a Southerner, like you,—a New Orleans man."

"Oh, well, he looks like a Yankee." But Placide laughed, for he was happy since Euphrasie had kissed him, and he whistled softly as he urged his horse to a canter and disappeared in the darkness.

The girl stood awhile with clasped hands, trying to understand a little sigh that rose in her throat, and that was not one of regret. When she regained the house, she went directly to her room, and left her father talking to Offdean in the quiet and perfumed night.

V

When two weeks had passed, Offdean felt very much at home with old Pierre and his daughter, and found the business that had called him to the country so engrossing that he had given no thought to those personal questions he had hoped to solve in going there.

The old man had driven him around in the no-top buggy to show him how dismantled the fences and barns were. He could see for himself that the house was a constant menace to human life. In the evenings the three would sit out on the gallery and talk of the land and its strong points and its weak ones, till he came to know it as if it had been his own.

Of the rickety condition of the cabins he got a fair notion, for he and Euphrasie passed them almost daily on horseback, on their way to the woods. It was seldom that their appearance together did not rouse comment among the darkies who happened to be loitering about.

La Chatte, a broad black woman with ends of white wool sticking out from under her *tignon*, stood with arms akimbo watching them as they disappeared one day. Then she turned and said to a young woman who sat in the cabin door:—

"Dat young man, ef he want to listen to me, he gwine quit dat ar caperin' roun' Miss 'Phrasie."

The young woman in the doorway laughed, and showed her white teeth, and tossed her head, and fingered the blue beads at her throat, in a way to indicate that she was in hearty sympathy with any question that touched upon gallantry.

"Law! La Chatte, you ain' gwine hinder a gemman

f'om payin' intentions to a young lady w'en he a mine to."

"Dat all I got to say," returned La Chatte, seating herself lazily and heavily on the doorstep. "Nobody don' know dem Sanchun boys bettah 'an I does. Did n' I done part raise 'em? W'at you reckon my ha'r all tu'n plumb w'ite dat-a-way ef it warn't dat Placide w'at done it?"

"How come he make yo' ha'r tu'n w'ite, La Chatte?"

"Dev'ment, pu' dev'ment, Rose. Did n' he come in dat same cabin one day, w'en he warn't no bigga 'an dat Pres'dent Hayes w'at you sees gwine 'long de road wid dat cotton sack 'crost 'im? He come an' sets down by de do', on dat same t'ree-laigged stool w'at you's a-settin' on now, wid his gun in his han', an' he say: 'La Chatte, I wants some croquignoles, an' I wants 'em quick, too.' I 'low: 'G' 'way f'om dah, boy. Don' you see I's flutin' yo' ma's petticoat?' He say: 'La Chatte, put 'side dat ar flutin'-i'on an' dat ar petticoat;' an' he cock dat gun an' p'int it to my head. 'Dar de ba'el,' he say: 'git out dat flour, git out dat butta an' dat aigs; step roun' dah, ole 'oman. Dis heah gun don' quit yo' head tell dem croquignoles is on de table, wid a w'ite tableclof an' a cup o' coffee.' Ef I goes to de ba'el, de gun's a-p'intin'. Ef I goes to de fiah, de gun's a-p'intin'. W'en I rolls out de dough, de gun 's a-p'intin'; an' him neva say nuttin', an' me a-trim'lin' like ole Uncle Noah w'en de mis'ry strike 'im."

"Lordy! w'at you reckon he do ef he tu'n roun' an' git mad wid dat young gemman f'om de city?"

"I don' reckon nuttin'; I knows w'at he gwine do,—same w'at his pa done."

"W'at his pa done, La Chatte?"

"G' 'long 'bout yo' business; you 's axin' too many questions." And La Chatte arose slowly and went to gather her party-colored wash that hung drying on the jagged and irregular points of a dilapidated picket-fence.

But the darkies were mistaken in supposing that Offdean was paying attention to Euphrasie. Those little jaunts in the wood were purely of a business character. Offdean had made a contract with a neighboring mill for fencing, in exchange for a certain amount of uncut timber. He had made it his work—with the assistance of Euphrasie—to decide upon what trees he wanted felled, and to mark such for the woodman's axe.

If they sometimes forgot what they had gone into the woods for, it was because there was so much to talk about and to laugh about. Often, when Offdean had blazed a tree with the sharp hatchet which he carried at his pommel, and had further discharged his duty by calling it "a fine piece of timber," they would sit upon some fallen and decaying trunk, maybe to listen to a chorus of mocking-birds above their heads, or to exchange confidences, as young people will.

Euphrasie thought she had never heard any one talk quite so pleasantly as Offdean did. She could not decide whether it was his manner or the tone of his voice, or the earnest glance of his dark and deep-set blue eyes, that gave such meaning to everything he said; for she found herself afterward thinking of his every word.

One afternoon it rained in torrents, and Rose was forced to drag buckets and tubs into Offdean's room to catch the streams that threatened to flood it. Euphrasie said she was glad of it; now he could see for himself.

And when he had seen for himself, he went to join her out on a corner of the gallery, where she stood with a cloak around her, close up against the house. He leaned against the house, too, and they stood thus together, gazing upon as desolate a scene as it is easy to imagine.

The whole landscape was gray, seen through the driving rain. Far away the dreary cabins seemed to sink and sink to earth in abject misery. Above their heads the live-oak branches were beating with sad monotony against the blackened roof. Great pools of water had formed in the yard, which was deserted by every living thing; for the little darkies had scampered away to their cabins, the dogs had run to their kennels, and the hens were puffing big with wretchedness under the scanty shelter of a fallen wagon-body.

Certainly a situation to make a young man groan with ennui, if he is used to his daily stroll on Canal Street, and pleasant afternoons at the club. But Offdean thought it delightful. He only wondered that he had never known, or some one .had never told him, how charming a place an old, dismantled plantation can be—when it rains. But as well as he liked it, he could not linger there forever. Business called him back to New Orleans, and after a few days he went away.

The interest which he felt in the improvement of this plantation was of so deep a nature, however, that he found himself thinking of it constantly. He wondered if the timber had all been felled, and how the fencing was coming on. So great was his desire to know such things that much correspondence was required between himself and Euphrasie, and he watched eagerly for those letters that told him of her trials and vexations with carpenters, bricklayers, and shingle-bearers. But in the midst of it, Offdean suddenly lost interest in the progress of work on the plantation. Singularly enough, it happened simultaneously with the arrival of a letter from Euphrasie which announced in a modest postscript that she was going down to the city with the Duplans for Mardi Gras.

VI

When Offdean learned that Euphrasie was coming to New Orleans, he was delighted to think he would have an opportunity to make some return for the hospitality which he had received from her father. He decided at once that she must see everything: day processions and night parades, balls and tableaux, operas and plays. He would arrange for it all, and he went to the length of begging to be relieved of certain duties that had been assigned him at the club, in order that he might feel himself perfectly free to do so.

The evening following Euphrasie's arrival, Offdean hastened to call upon her, away down on Esplanade Street. She and the Duplans were staying there with old Mme. Carantelle, Mrs. Duplan's mother, a delightfully conservative old lady who had not "crossed Canal Street" for many years.

He found a number of people gathered in the long high-ceiled drawing-room,—young people and old people, all talking French, and some talking louder than they would have done if Madame Carantelle had not been so very deaf.

When Offdean entered, the old lady was greeting some one who had come in just before him. It was Placide, and she was calling him Grégoire, and wanting to know how the crops were up on Red River. She met every one from the country with this stereotyped inquiry, which placed her at once on the agreeable and easy footing she liked.

Somehow Offdean had not counted on finding Euphrasie so well provided with entertainment, and he spent much of the evening in trying to persuade himself that the fact was a pleasing one in itself. But he wondered why Placide was with her, and sat so persistently beside her, and danced so repeatedly with her when Mrs. Duplan played upon the piano. Then he could not see by what right these young creoles had already arranged for the Proteus ball, and every other entertainment that he had meant to provide for her.

He went away without having had a word alone with the girl whom he had gone to see. The evening had proved a failure. He did not go to the club as usual, but went to his rooms in a mood which inclined him to read a few pages from a stoic philosopher whom he sometimes affected. But the words of wisdom that had often before helped him over disagreeable places left no impress tonight. They were powerless to banish from his thoughts the look of a pair of brown eyes, or to drown the tones of a girl's voice that kept singing in his soul.

Placide was not very well acquainted with the city; but that made no difference to him so long as he was at Euphrasie's side. His brother Hector, who lived in some obscure corner of the town, would willingly have made his knowledge a more intimate one; but Placide did not choose to learn the lessons that Hector was ready to teach. He asked nothing better than to walk with Euphrasie along the streets, holding her parasol at an agreeable angle over her pretty head, or to sit beside her in the evening at the play, sharing her frank delight.

When the night of the Mardi Gras ball came, he felt like a lost spirit during the hours he was forced to remain away from her. He stood in the dense crowd on the street gazing up at her, where she sat on the clubhouse balcony amid a bevy of gayly dressed women. It was not easy to distinguish her, but he could think of no more agreeable occupation than to stand down there on the street trying to do so.

She seemed during all this pleasant time to be entirely his own, too. It made him very fierce to think of the possibility of her not being entirely his own. But he had no cause whatever to think this. She had grown conscious and thoughtful of late about him and their relationship. She often communed with herself, and as a result tried to act toward him as an engaged girl would toward her *fiancé.* Yet a wistful look came sometimes into the brown eyes when she walked the streets with Placide, and eagerly scanned the faces of passersby.

Offdean had written her a note, very studied, very formal, asking to see her a certain day and hour, to consult about matters on the plantation, saying he had found it so difficult to obtain a word with her, that he was forced to adopt this means, which he trusted would not be offensive.

This seemed perfectly right to Euphrasie. She agreed to see him one afternoon—the day before leaving town—in the long, stately drawing-room, quite alone.

It was a sleepy day, too warm for the season. Gusts of moist air were sweeping lazily through the long corridors, rattling the slats of the half-closed green shutters, and bringing a delicious perfume from the courtyard where old Charlot was watering the spreading palms and brilliant parterres. A group of little children had stood awhile quarreling noisily under the windows, but had moved on down the street and left quietness reigning.

Offdean had not long to wait before Euphrasie came to him. She had lost some of that ease which had marked her manner during their first acquaintance. Now, when she seated herself before him, she showed a disposition to plunge at once into the subject that had brought him there. He was willing enough that it should play some rôle, since it had been his pretext for coming; but he soon dismissed it, and with it much restraint that had held him till now. He simply looked into her eyes, with a gaze that made her shiver a little, and began to complain because she was going away next day and he had seen nothing of her; because he had wanted to do so many things when she came—why had she not let him?

"You fo'get I 'm no stranger here," she told him. "I know many people. I've been coming so often with Mme. Duplan. I wanted to see mo' of you, Mr. Offdean"—

"Then you ought to have managed it; you could have done so. It 's—it 's aggravating," he said, far more bitterly than the subject warranted, "when a man has so set his heart upon something."

"But it was n' anything ver' important," she interposed; and they both laughed, and got safely over a situation that would soon have been strained, if not critical.

Waves of happiness were sweeping through the soul and body of the girl as she sat there in the drowsy afternoon near the man whom she loved. It mattered not what they talked about, or whether they talked at all. They were both scintillant with feeling. If Offdean had taken Euphrasie's hands in his and leaned forward and kissed her lips, it would have seemed to both only the rational outcome of things that stirred them.

But he did not do this. He knew now that overwhelming passion was taking possession of him. He had not to heap more coals upon the fire; on the contrary, it was a moment to put on the brakes, and he was a young gentleman able to do this when circumstances required.

However, he held her hand longer than he needed to when he bade her good-by. For he got entangled in explaining why he should have to go back to the plantation to see how matters stood there, and he dropped her hand only when the rambling speech was ended.

He left her sitting by the window in a big brocaded armchair. She drew the lace curtain aside to watch him pass in the street. He lifted his hat and smiled when he saw her. Any other man she knew would have done the same thing, but this simple act caused the blood to surge to her cheeks. She let the curtain drop, and sat there like one dreaming. Her eyes, intense with the unnatural light that glowed in them, looked steadily into vacancy, and her lips stayed parted in the half-smile that did not want to leave them.

Placide found her thus, a good while afterward, when he came in, full of bustle, with theatre tickets in his pocket for the last night. She started up, and went eagerly to meet him.

"W'ere have you been, Placide?" she asked with unsteady voice, placing her hands on his shoulders with a freedom that was new and strange to him.

He appeared to her suddenly as a refuge from something, she did not know what, and she rested her hot cheek against his breast. This made him mad, and he lifted her face and kissed her passionately upon the lips.

She crept from his arms after that, and went away to her room, and locked herself in. Her poor little inexperienced soul was torn and sore. She knelt down beside her bed, and sobbed a little and prayed a little. She felt that she had sinned, she did not know exactly in what; but a fine nature warned her that it was in Placide's kiss.

VII

The spring came early in Orville, and so subtly that no one could tell exactly when it began. But one morning the roses were so luscious in Placide's sunny parterres, the peas and bean-vines and borders of strawberries so rank in his trim vegetable patches, that he called out lustily, "No mo' winta, Judge!" to the staid Judge Blount, who went ambling by on his gray pony.

"There 's right smart o' folks don't know it, Santien," responded the judge, with occult meaning that might be applied to certain indebted clients back on the bayou who had not broken land yet. Ten minutes later the judge observed sententiously, and apropos of nothing, to a group that stood waiting for the post-office to open:—

"I see Santien 's got that noo fence o' his painted. And a pretty piece o' work it is," he added reflectively.

"Look lack Placide goin' pent mo' 'an de fence," sagaciously snickered 'Tit-Edouard, a strolling *maigre-échine* of indefinite occupation. "I seen 'im, me, pesterin' wid all kine o' pent on a piece o' bo'd yistiday."

"I knows he gwine paint mo' 'an de fence," emphatically announced Uncle Abner, in a tone that carried conviction. "He gwine paint de house; dat what he gwine do. Did n' Marse Luke Williams orda de paints? An' did n' I done kyar' 'em up dah myse'f?"

Seeing the deference with which this positive piece of knowledge was received, the judge coolly changed the subject by announcing that Luke Williams's Durham bull had broken a leg the night before in Luke's new pasture ditch,—a piece of news that fell among his hearers with telling, if paralytic effect.

But most people wanted to see for themselves these astonishing things that Placide was doing. And the young ladies of the village strolled slowly by of afternoons in couples and arm in arm. If Placide happened to see them, he would leave his work to hand them a fine rose or a bunch of geraniums over the dazzling white fence. But if it chanced to be 'Tit-Edouard or Luke Williams, or any of the young men of Orville, he pretended not to see them, or to hear the ingratiating cough that accompanied their lingering footsteps.

In his eagerness to have his home sweet and attractive for Euphrasie's coming, Placide had gone less frequently than ever before up to Natchitoches. He worked and whistled and sang until the yearning for the girl's presence became a driving need; then he would put away his tools and mount his horse as the day was closing, and away he would go across bayous and hills and fields until he was with her again. She had never seemed to Placide so lovable as she was then. She had grown more womanly and thoughtful. Her cheek had lost much of its color, and the light in her eyes flashed less often. But her manner had gained a something of pathetic tenderness toward her lover that moved him with an intoxicating happiness. He could hardly wait with patience for that day in early April which would see the fulfillment of his lifelong hopes.

After Euphrasie's departure from New Orleans, Offdean told himself honestly that he loved the girl. But being yet unsettled in life, he felt it was no time to think of marrying, and, like the worldly-wise young gentleman that he was, resolved to forget the little Natchitoches girl. He knew it would be an affair of some difficulty, but not an impossible thing, so he set about forgetting her.

The effort made him singularly irascible. At the office he was gloomy and taciturn; at the club he was a bear. A few young ladies whom he called upon were astonished and distressed at the cynical views of life which he had so suddenly adopted.

When he had endured a week or more of such humor, and inflicted it upon others, he abruptly changed his tactics. He decided not to fight against his love for Euphrasie. He would not marry her,—certainly

not; but he would let himself love her to his heart's
bent, until that love should die a natural death, and
not a violent one as he had designed. He abandoned
himself completely to his passion, and dreamed of the
girl by day and thought of her by night. How delicious
had been the scent of her hair, the warmth of her
breath, the nearness of her body, that rainy day when
they stood close together upon the veranda! He recalled the glance of her honest, beautiful eyes, that told
him things which made his heart beat fast now when
he thought of them. And then her voice! Was there
another like it when she laughed or when she talked!
Was there another woman in the world possessed of so
alluring a charm as this one he loved!

He was not bearish now, with these sweet
thoughts crowding his brain and thrilling his blood; but
he sighed deeply, and worked languidly, and enjoyed
himself listlessly.

One day he sat in his room puffing the air thick
with sighs and smoke, when a thought came suddenly
to him—an inspiration, a very message from heaven,
to judge from the cry of joy with which he greeted it.
He sent his cigar whirling through the window, over
the stone paving of the street, and he let his head fall
down upon his arms, folded upon the table.

It had happened to him, as it does to many, that
the solution of a vexed question flashed upon him when
he was hoping least for it. He positively laughed aloud,
and somewhat hysterically. In the space of a moment
he saw the whole delicious future which a kind fate had
mapped out for him: those rich acres upon the Red
River his own, bought and embellished with his inheritance; and Euphrasie, whom he loved, his wife and
companion throughout a life such as he knew now he
had craved for,—a life that, imposing bodily activity,
admits the intellectual repose in which thought unfolds.

Wallace Offdean was like one to whom a divinity
had revealed his vocation in life,—no less a divinity
because it was love. If doubts assailed him of Euphrasie's consent, they were soon stilled. For had they not
spoken over and over to each other the mute and sub-

tile language of reciprocal love—out under the forest trees, and in the quiet night-time on the plantation when the stars shone? And never so plainly as in the stately old drawing-room down on Esplanade Street. Surely no other speech was needed then, save such as their eyes told. Oh, he knew that she loved him; he was sure of it! The knowledge made him all the more eager now to hasten to her, to tell her that he wanted her for his very own.

VIII

If Offdean had stopped in Natchitoches on his way to the plantation, he would have heard something there to astonish him, to say the very least; for the whole town was talking of Euphrasie's wedding, which was to take place in a few days. But he did not linger. After securing a horse at the stable, he pushed on with all the speed of which the animal was capable, and only in such company as his eager thoughts afforded him.

The plantation was very quiet, with that stillness which broods over broad, clean acres that furnish no refuge for so much as a bird that sings. The negroes were scattered about the fields at work, with hoe and plow, under the sun, and old Pierre, on his horse, was far off in the midst of them.

Placide had arrived in the morning, after traveling all night, and had gone to his room for an hour or two of rest. He had drawn the lounge close up to the window to get what air he might through the closed shutters. He was just beginning to doze when he heard Euphrasie's light footsteps approaching. She stopped and seated herself so near that he could have touched her if he had but reached out his hand. Her nearness banished all desire to sleep, and he lay there content to rest his limbs and think of her.

The portion of the gallery on which Euphrasie sat was facing the river, and away from the road by which Offdean had reached the house. After fastening his horse, he mounted the steps, and traversed the broad hall that intersected the house from end to end, and that was open wide. He found Euphrasie engaged upon a piece of sewing. She was hardly aware of his presence before he had seated himself beside her.

She could not speak. She only looked at him with frightened eyes, as if his presence were that of some disembodied spirit.

"Are you not glad that I have come?" he asked her. "Have I made a mistake in coming?" He was gazing into her eyes, seeking to read the meaning of their new and strange expression.

"Am I glad?" she faltered. "I don' know. W'at has that to do? You've come to see the work, of co'se. It 's—it 's only half done, Mr. Offdean. They would n' listen to me or to papa, an' you did n' seem to care."

"I have n't come to see the work," he said, with a smile of love and confidence. "I am here only to see you,—to say how much I want you, and need you—to tell you how I love you."

She rose, half choking with words she could not utter. But he seized her hands and held her there.

"The plantation is mine, Euphrasie,—or it will be when you say that you will be my wife," he went on excitedly. "I know that you love me"—

"I do not!" she exclaimed wildly. "W'at do you mean? How do you dare," she gasped, "to say such things w'en you know that in two days I shall be married to Placide?" The last was said in a whisper; it was like a wail.

"Married to Placide!" he echoed, as if striving to understand,—to grasp some part of his own stupendous folly and blindness. "I knew nothing of it," he said hoarsely. "Married to Placide! I would never have spoken to you as I did, if I had known. You believe me, I hope? Please say that you forgive me."

He spoke with long silences between his utterances.

"Oh, there is n' anything to fo'give. You've only made a mistake. Please leave me, Mr. Offdean. Papa is out in the fiel', I think, if you would like to speak with him. Placide is somew'ere on the place."

"I shall mount my horse and go see what work has

been done," said Offdean, rising. An unusual pallor had overspread his face, and his mouth was drawn with suppressed pain. "I must turn my fool's errand to some practical good," he added, with a sad attempt at playfulness; and with no further word he walked quickly away.

She listened to his going. Then all the wretchedness of the past months, together with the sharp distress of the moment, voiced itself in a sob: "O God— O my God, he'p me!"

But she could not stay out there in the broad day for any chance comer to look upon her uncovered sorrow.

Placide heard her rise and go to her room. When he had heard the key turn in the lock, he got up, and with quiet deliberation prepared to go out. He drew on his boots, then his coat. He took his pistol from the dressing-bureau, where he had placed it a while before, and after examining its chambers carefully, thrust it into his pocket. He had certain work to do with the weapon before night. But for Euphrasie's presence he might have accomplished it very surely a moment ago, when the hound—as he called him—stood outside his window. He did not wish her to know anything of his movements, and he left his room as quietly as possible, and mounted his horse, as Offdean had done.

"La Chatte," called Placide to the old woman, who stood in her yard at the washtub, "w'ich way did that man go?"

"W'at man dat? I is n' studyin' 'bout no mans; I got 'nough to do wid dis heah washin'. 'Fo' God, I don' know w'at man you 's talkin' 'bout"—

"La Chatte, w'ich way did that man go? Quick, now!" with the deliberate tone and glance that had always quelled her.

"Ef you 's talkin' 'bout dat Noo Orleans man, I could 'a' tole you dat. He done tuck de road to de cocoa-patch," plunging her black arms into the tub with unnecessary energy and disturbance.

"That's enough. I know now he 's gone into the woods. You always was a liar, La Chatte."

"Dat his own lookout, de smoove-tongue' raskil,"

soliloquized the woman a moment later. "I done said he did n' have no call to come heah, caperin' roun' Miss 'Phrasie."

Placide was possessed by only one thought, which was a want as well,—to put an end to this man who had come between him and his love. It was the same brute passion that drives the beast to slay when he sees the object of his own desire laid hold of by another.

He had heard Euphrasie tell the man she did not love him, but what of that? Had he not heard her sobs, and guessed what her distress was? It needed no very flexible mind to guess as much, when a hundred signs besides, unheeded before, came surging to his memory. Jealousy held him, and rage and despair.

Offdean, as he rode along under the trees in apathetic despondency, heard some one approaching him on horseback, and turned aside to make room in the narrow pathway.

It was not a moment for punctilious scruples, and Placide had not been hindered by such from sending a bullet into the back of his rival. The only thing that stayed him was that Offdean must know why he had to die.

"Mr. Offdean," Placide said, reining his horse with one hand, while he held his pistol openly in the other, "I was in my room 'w'ile ago, and yeared w'at you said to Euphrasie. I would 'a' killed you then if she had n' been 'longside o' you. I could 'a' killed you jus' now w'en I come up behine you."

"Well, why did n't you?" asked Offdean, meanwhile gathering his faculties to think how he had best deal with this madman.

"Because I wanted you to know who done it, an' w'at he done it for."

"Mr. Santien, I suppose to a person in your frame of mind it will make no difference to know that I'm unarmed. But if you make any attempt upon my life, I shall certainly defend myself as best I can."

"Defen' yo'se'f, then."

"You must be mad," said Offdean, quickly, and looking straight into Placide's eyes, "to want to soil your happiness with murder. I thought a creole knew better than that how to love a woman."

"By——! are you goin' to learn me how to love a woman?"

"No, Placide," said Offdean eagerly, as they rode slowly along; "your own honor is going to tell you that. The way to love a woman is to think first of her happiness. If you love Euphrasie, you must go to her clean. I love her myself enough to want you to do that. I shall leave this place tomorrow; you will never see me again if I can help it. Is n't that enough for you? I 'm going to turn here and leave you. Shoot me in the back if you like; but I know you won't." And Offdean held out his hand.

"I don' want to shake han's with you," said Placide sulkily. "Go 'way f'om me."

He stayed motionless watching Offdean ride away. He looked at the pistol in his hands, and replaced it slowly in his pocket; then he removed the broad felt hat which he wore, and wiped away the moisture that had gathered upon his forehead.

Offdean's words had touched some chord within him and made it vibrant; but they made him hate the man no less.

"The way to love a woman is to think firs' of her happiness," he muttered reflectively. "He thought a creole knew how to love. Does he reckon he 's goin' to learn a creole how to love?"

His face was white and set with despair now. The rage had all left it as he rode deeper on into the wood.

IX

Offdean rose early, wishing to take the morning train to the city. But he was not before Euphrasie, whom he found in the large hall arranging the breakfast-table. Old Pierre was there too, walking slowly about with hands folded behind him, and with bowed head.

A restraint hung upon all of them, and the girl

turned to her father and asked him if Placide were up,
seemingly for want of something to say. The old man
fell heavily into a chair, and gazed upon her in the
deepest distress.

"Oh, my po' li'le Euphrasie! my po' li'le chile! Mr.
Offde'n, you ain't no stranger."

"*Bon Dieu!* Papa!" cried the girl sharply, seized
with a vague terror. She quitted her occupation at the
table, and stood in nervous apprehension of what might
follow.

"I yaired people say Placide was one no-'count creole. I nevair want to believe dat, me. Now I know dat
's true. Mr. Offde'n, you ain't no stranger, you."

Offdean was gazing upon the old man in amazement.

"In de night," Pierre continued, "I yaired some
noise on de winder. I go open, an' dere Placide,
standin' wid his big boot' on, an' his w'ip w'at he
knocked wid on de winder, an' his hoss all saddle'. Oh,
my po' li'le chile! He say, 'Pierre, I yaired say Mr.
Luke William' want his house pent down in Orville. I
reckon I go git de job befo' somebody else teck it. I
say, 'You come straight back, Placide?' He say, 'Don'
look fer me.' An w'en I ax 'im w'at I goin' tell to my
li'le chile, he say, 'Tell Euphrasie Placide know better
'an anybody livin' w'at goin' make her happy.' An' he
start 'way; den he come back an' say, 'Tell dat man'—
I don' know who he was talk' 'bout—'tell 'im he ain't
goin' learn nuttin' to a creole.' *Mon Dieu! Mon Dieu!*
I don' know w'at all dat mean."

He was holding the half-fainting Euphrasie in his
arms, and stroking her hair.

"I always yaired say he was one no-'count creole.
I nevair want to believe dat."

"Don't—don't say that again, papa," she whisper-
ingly entreated, speaking in French. "Placide has saved
me!"

"He has save' you f'om w'at, Euphrasie?" asked
her father, in dazed astonishment.

"From sin," she replied to him under her breath.

"I don' know w'at all dat mean," the old man muttered, bewildered, as he arose and walked out on the gallery.

Offdean had taken coffee in his room, and would not wait for breakfast. When he went to bid Euphrasie good-by, she sat beside the table with her head bowed upon her arm.

He took her hand and said good-by to her, but she did not look up.

"Euphrasie," he asked eagerly, "I may come back? Say that I may—after a while."

She gave him no answer, and he leaned down and pressed his cheek caressingly and entreatingly against her soft thick hair.

"May I, Euphrasie?" he begged. "So long as you do not tell me no, I shall come back, dearest one."

She still made him no reply, but she did not tell him no.

So he kissed her hand and her cheek,—what he could touch of it, that peeped out from her folded arm,—and went away.

An hour later, when Offdean passed through Natchitoches, the old town was already ringing with the startling news that Placide had been dismissed by his *fiancée*, and the wedding was off, information which the young creole was taking the trouble to scatter broadcast as he went.

A Rude Awakening
1891

"Take de do' an' go! You year me? Take de do'!"

Lolotte's brown eyes flamed. Her small frame quivered. She stood with her back turned to a meagre supper-table, as if to guard it from the man who had just entered the cabin. She pointed toward the door, to order him from the house.

"You mighty cross to-night, Lolotte. You mus' got up wid de wrong foot to 's mo'nin'. *Hein*, Veveste? *hein*, Jacques, w'at you say?"

The two small urchins who sat at table giggled in sympathy with their father's evident good humor.

"I'm wo' out, me!" the girl exclaimed, desperately, as she let her arms fall limp at her side. "Work, work! Fu w'at? Fu feed de lazies' man in Natchitoches pa'ish."

"Now, Lolotte, you think w'at you sayin'," expostulated her father. "Sylveste Bordon don' ax nobody to feed 'im."

"W'en you brought a poun' of suga in de house?" his daughter retorted hotly, "or a poun' of coffee? W'en did you brought a piece o' meat home, you? An' Nonomme all de time sick. Co'n bread an' po'k, dat's good fu Veveste an' me an' Jacques; but Nonomme? no!"

She turned as if choking, and cut into the round, soggy "pone" of corn bread which was the main feature of the scanty supper.

"Po' li'le Nonomme; we mus' fine some'in' to break

30

dat fevah. You want to kill a chicken once a w'ile fu Nonomme, Lolotte." He calmly seated himself at the table.

"Did n' I done put de las' roostah in de pot?" she cried with exasperation. "Now you come axen me fu kill de hen'! W'ere I goen to fine aigg' to trade wid, w'en de hen' be gone? Is I got one picayune in de house fu trade wid, me?"

"Papa," piped the young Jacques, "w'at dat I yeard you drive in de yard, w'ile go?"

"Dat 's it! W'en Lolotte would n' been talken' so fas', I could tole you 'bout dat job I got fu to-morrow. Dat was Joe Duplan's team of mule' an' wagon, wid t'ree bale' of cotton, w'at you yaird. I got to go soon in de mo'nin' wid dat load to de landin'. An' a man mus' eat w'at got to work; dat's sho."

Lolotte's bare brown feet made no sound upon the rough boards as she entered the room where Nonomme lay sick and sleeping. She lifted the coarse mosquito net from about him, sat down in the clumsy chair by the bedside, and began gently to fan the slumbering child.

Dusk was falling rapidly, as it does in the South. Lolotte's eyes grew round and big, as she watched the moon creep up from branch to branch of the moss-draped live-oak just outside her window. Presently the weary girl slept as profoundly as Nonomme. A little dog sneaked into the room, and socially licked her bare feet. The touch, moist and warm, awakened Lolotte.

The cabin was dark and quiet. Nonomme was crying softly, because the mosquitoes were biting him. In the room beyond, old Sylveste and the others slept. When Lolotte had quieted the child, she went outside to get a pail of cool, fresh water at the cistern. Then she crept into bed beside Nonomme, who slept again.

Lolotte's dreams that night pictured her father returning from work, and bringing luscious oranges home in his pocket for the sick child.

When at the very break of day she heard him astir in his room, a certain comfort stole into her heart. She lay and listened to the faint noises of his preparations to go out. When he had quitted the house, she waited to hear him drive the wagon from the yard.

She waited long, but heard no sound of horse's tread or wagon-wheel. Anxious, she went to the cabin door and looked out. The big mules were still where they had been fastened the night before. The wagon was there, too.

Her heart sank. She looked quickly along the low rafters supporting the roof of the narrow porch to where her father's fishing pole and pail always hung. Both were gone.

" 'T ain' no use, 't ain' no use," she said, as she turned into the house with a look of something like anguish in her eyes.

When the spare breakfast was eaten and the dishes cleared away, Lolotte turned with resolute mien to the two little brothers.

"Veveste," she said to the older, "go see if dey got co'n in dat wagon fu feed dem mule'."

"Yes, dey got co'n. Papa done feed 'em, fur I see de co'n-cob in de trough, me."

"Den you goen he'p me hitch dem mule, to de wagon. Jacques, go down de lane an' ax Aunt Minty if she come set wid Nonomme w'ile I go drive dem mule' to de landin'.' "

Lolotte had evidently determined to undertake her father's work. Nothing could dissuade her; neither the children's astonishment nor Aunt Minty's scathing disapproval. The fat black negress came laboring into the yard just as Lolotte mounted upon the wagon.

"Git down f'om dah, chile! Is you plumb crazy?" she exclaimed.

"No, I ain't crazy; I'm hungry, Aunt Minty. We all hungry. Somebody got fur work in dis fam'ly."

"Dat ain't no work fur a gal w'at ain't bar' seventeen year ole; drivin' Marse Duplan's mules! W'at I gwine tell yo' pa?"

"Fu me, you kin tell 'im w'at you want. But you watch Nonomme. I done cook his rice an' set it 'side."

"Don't you bodda," replied Aunt Minty; "I got somepin heah fur my boy. I gwine 'ten' to him."

Lolotte had seen Aunt Minty put something out of sight when she came up, and made her produce it. It was a heavy fowl.

"Sence w'en you start raisin' Brahma chicken', you?" Lolotte asked mistrustfully.

"My, but you is a cu'ious somebody! Ev'ything w'at got fedders on its laigs is Brahma chicken wid you. Dis heah ole hen"—

"All de same, you don't got fur give dat chicken to eat to Nonomme. You don't got fur cook 'im in my house."

Aunt Minty, unheeding, turned to the house with blustering inquiry for her boy, while Lolotte drove away with great clatter.

She knew, notwithstanding her injunction, that the chicken would be cooked and eaten. Maybe she herself would partake of it when she came back, if hunger drove her too sharply.

"Nax' thing I'm goen be one rogue," she muttered; and the tears gathered and fell one by one upon her cheeks.

"It *do* look like one Brahma, Aunt Mint," remarked the small and weazened Jacques, as he watched the woman picking the lusty fowl.

"How ole is you?" was her quiet retort.

"I don' know, me."

"Den if you don't know dat much, you betta keep yo' mouf shet, boy."

Then silence fell, but for a monotonous chant which the woman droned as she worked. Jacques opened his lips once more.

"It *do* look like one o' Ma'me Duplan' Brahma, Aunt Mint."

"Yonda, whar I come f'om, befo' de wah"—

"Ole Kaintuck, Aunt Mint?"

"Ole Kaintuck."

"Dat ain't one country like dis yere, Aunt Mint?"

"You mighty right, chile, dat ain't no sech kentry

as dis heah. Yonda, in Kaintuck, w'en boys says de word 'Brahma chicken,' we takes an' gags em, an' ties dar han's behines 'em, an' fo'ces 'em ter stan' up watchin' folks settin' down eatin' chicken soup."

Jacques passed the back of his hand across his mouth; but lest the act should not place sufficient seal upon it, he prudently stole away to go and sit beside Nonomme, and wait there as patiently as he could the coming feast.

And what a treat it was! The luscious soup,—a great pot of it,—golden yellow, thickened with the flaky rice that Lolotte had set carefully on the shelf. Each mouthful of it seemed to carry fresh blood into the veins and a new brightness into the eyes of the hungry children who ate of it.

And that was not all. The day brought abundance with it. Their father came home with glistening perch and trout that Aunt Minty broiled deliciously over glowing embers, and basted with the rich chicken fat.

"You see," explained old Sylveste, "w'en I git up to 's mo'nin' an' see it was cloudy, I say to me, 'Sylveste, w'en you go wid dat cotton, rememba you got no tarpaulin. Maybe it rain, an' de cotton was spoil. Betta you go yonda to Lafirme Lake, w'ere de trout was bitin' fas'er 'an mosquito, an' so you git a good mess fur de chil'en.' Lolotte—w'at she goen do yonda? You ought stop Lolotte, Aunt Minty, w'en you see w'at she was want to do."

"Did n' I try to stop 'er? Did n' I ax 'er, 'W'at I gwine tell yo' pa?' An' she 'low, 'Tell 'im to go hang hisse'f, de triflind ole rapscallion! I 's de one w'at 's runnin' dis heah fambly!' "

"Dat don' soun' like Lolotte, Aunt Minty; you mus' yaird 'er crooked; *hein*, Nonomme?"

The quizzical look in his good-natured features was irresistible. Nonomme fairly shook with merriment.

"My head feel so good," he declared. "I wish Lolotte would come, so I could tole 'er." And he turned in his bed to look down the long, dusty lane, with the hope of seeing her appear as he had watched her go, sitting on one of the cotton bales and guiding the mules.

But no one came all through the hot morning. Only at noon a broad-shouldered young negro appeared in view riding through the dust. When he had dismounted at the cabin door, he stood leaning a shoulder lazily against the jamb.

"Well, heah you is," he grumbled, addressing Sylveste with no mark of respect. "Heah you is, settin' down like comp'ny, an' Marse Joe yonda sont me see if you was dead."

"Joe Duplan boun' to have his joke, him," said Sylveste, smiling uneasily.

"Maybe it look like a joke to you, but 't aint no joke to him, man, to have one o' his wagons smoshed to kindlin', an' his bes' team tearin' t'rough de country. You don't want to let 'im lay han's on you, joke o' no joke."

"*Malédiction!*" howled Sylveste, as he staggered to his feet. He stood for one instant irresolute; then he lurched past the man and ran wildly down the lane. He might have taken the horse that was there, but he went tottering on afoot, a frightened look in his eyes, as if his soul gazed upon an inward picture that was horrible.

The road to the landing was little used. As Sylveste went he could readily trace the marks of Lolotte's wagon-wheels. For some distance they went straight along the road. Then they made a track as if a madman had directed their course, over stump and hillock, tearing the bushes and barking the trees on either side.

At each new turn Sylveste expected to find Lolotte stretched senseless upon the ground, but there was never a sign of her.

At last he reached the landing, which was a dreary spot, slanting down to the river and partly cleared to afford room for what desultory freight might be left there from time to time. There were the wagon-tracks, clean down to the river's edge and partly in the water, where they made a sharp and senseless turn. But Sylveste found no trace of his girl.

"Lolotte!" the old man cried out into the stillness. "Lolotte, *ma fille*, Lolotte!" But no answer came; no sound but the echo of his own voice, and the soft splash of the red water that lapped his feet.

He looked down at it, sick with anguish and apprehension.

Lolotte had disappeared as completely as if the earth had opened and swallowed her. After a few days it became the common belief that the girl had been drowned. It was thought that she must have been hurled from the wagon into the water during the sharp turn that the wheel-tracks indicated, and carried away by the rapid current.

During the days of search, old Sylveste's excitement kept him up. When it was over, an apathetic despair seemed to settle upon him.

Madame Duplan, moved by sympathy, had taken the little four-year-old Nonomme to the plantation Les Chêniers, where the child was awed by the beauty and comfort of things that surrounded him there. He thought always that Lolotte would come back, and watched for her every day; for they did not tell him the sad tidings of her loss.

The other two boys were placed in the temporary care of Aunt Minty; and old Sylveste roamed like a persecuted being through the country. He who had been a type of indolent content and repose had changed to a restless spirit.

When he thought to eat, it was in some humble negro cabin that he stopped to ask for food, which was never denied him. His grief had clothed him with a dignity that imposed respect.

One morning very early he appeared before the planter with a disheveled and hunted look.

"M'sieur Duplan," he said, holding his hat in his hand and looking away into vacancy, "I been try ev'-thing. I been try settin' down still on de sto' gall'ry. I been walk, I been run; 't ain' no use. Dey got al'ays some'in' w'at push me. I go fishin', an' it's some'in' w'at push me worser 'an ever. By gracious! M'sieur Duplan, gi' me some work!"

The planter gave him at once a plow in hand, and no plow on the whole plantation dug so deep as that one, nor so fast. Sylveste was the first in the field, as he was the last one there. From dawn to nightfall he worked, and after, till his limbs refused to do his bidding.

People came to wonder, and the negroes began to whisper hints of demoniacal possession.

When Mr. Duplan gave careful thought to the subject of Lolotte's mysterious disappearance, an idea came to him. But so fearful was he to arouse false hopes in the breasts of those who grieved for the girl that to no one did he impart his suspicions save to his wife. It was on the eve of a business trip to New Orleans that he told her what he thought, or what he hoped rather.

Upon his return, which happened not many days later, he went out to where old Sylveste was toiling in the field with frenzied energy.

"Sylveste," said the planter, quietly, when he had stood a moment watching the man at work, "have you given up all hope of hearing from your daughter?"

"I don' know, me; I don' know. Le' me work, M'sieur Duplan."

"For my part, I believe the child is alive."

"You b'lieve dat, you?" His rugged face was pitiful in its imploring lines.

"I know it," Mr. Duplan muttered, as calmly as he could. "Hold up! Steady yourself, man! Come; come with me to the house. There is some one there who knows it, too; some one who has seen her."

The room into which the planter led the old man was big, cool, beautiful, and sweet with the delicate odor of flowers. It was shady, too, for the shutters were half closed; but not so darkened but Sylveste could at once see Lolotte, seated in a big wicker chair.

She was almost as white as the gown she wore. Her neatly shod feet rested upon a cushion, and her black hair, that had been closely cut, was beginning to make little rings about her temples.

"Aie!" he cried sharply, at sight of her, grasping his seamed throat as he did so. Then he laughed like a madman, and then he sobbed.

He only sobbed, kneeling upon the floor beside her, kissing her knees and her hands, that sought his. Little Nonomme was close to her, with a health flush creeping into his cheek. Veveste and Jacques were there, and rather awed by the mystery and grandeur of everything.

"W'ere'bouts you find her, M'sieur Duplan?" Sylveste asked, when the first flush of his joy had spent itself, and he was wiping his eyes with his rough cotton shirt sleeve.

"M'sieur Duplan find me 'way yonda to de city, papa, in de hospital," spoke Lolotte, before the planter could steady his voice to reply. "I did n' know who ev'ybody was, me. I did n' know me, myse'f, tell I tu'n roun' one day an' see M'sieur Duplan, w'at stan'en dere."

"You was boun' to know M'sieur Duplan, Lolotte," laughed Sylveste, like a child.

"Yes, an' I know right 'way how dem mule was git frighten' w'en de boat w'istle fu stop, an' pitch me plumb on de groun'. An' I rememba it was one *mulâtresse* w'at call herse'f one chembamed, all de time aside me."

"You must not talk too much, Lolotte," interposed Madame Duplan, coming to place her hand with gentle solicitude upon the girl's forehead, and to feel how her pulse beat.

Then to save the child further effort of speech, she herself related how the boat had stopped at this lonely landing to take on a load of cottonseed. Lolotte had been found stretched insensible by the river, fallen apparently from the clouds, and had been taken on board.

The boat had changed its course into other waters after that trip, and had not returned to Duplan's Landing. Those who had tended Lolotte and left her at the hospital supposed, no doubt, that she would make known her identity in time, and they had troubled themselves no further about her.

"An' dah you is!" almost shouted Aunt Minty, whose black face gleamed in the doorway; "dah you is, settin' down, lookin' jis' like w'ite folks!"

"Ain't I always was w'ite folks, Aunt Mint?" smiled Lolotte, feebly.

"G'long, chile. You knows me. I don' mean no harm."

"And now, Sylveste," said Mr. Duplan, as he rose and started to walk the floor, with hands in his pockets, "listen to me. It will be a long time before Lolotte is strong again. Aunt Minty is going to look after things for you till the child is fully recovered. But what I want to say is this: I shall trust these children into your hands once more, and I want you never to forget again that you are their father—do you hear?—that you are a man!"

Old Sylveste stood with his hand in Lolotte's, who rubbed it lovingly against her cheek.

"By gracious! M'sieur Duplan," he answered, "w'en God want to he'p me, I'm goen try my bes'!"

Love on the Bon-Dieu
1891

Upon the pleasant veranda of Père Antoine's cottage, that adjoined the church, a young girl had long been seated, awaiting his return. It was the eve of Easter Sunday, and since early afternoon the priest had been engaged in hearing the confessions of those who wished to make their Easters the following day. The girl did not seem impatient at his delay; on the contrary, it was very restful to her to lie back in the big chair she had found there, and peep through the thick curtain of vines at the people who occasionally passed along the village street.

She was slender, with a frailness that indicated lack of wholesome and plentiful nourishment. A pathetic, uneasy look was in her gray eyes, and even faintly stamped her features, which were fine and delicate. In lieu of a hat, a barège veil covered her light brown and abundant hair. She wore a coarse white cotton "josie," and a blue calico skirt that only half concealed her tattered shoes.

As she sat there, she held carefully in her lap a parcel of eggs securely fastened in a red bandana handkerchief.

Twice already a handsome, stalwart young man in quest of the priest had entered the yard, and penetrated to where she sat. At first they had exchanged the uncompromising "howdy" of strangers, and nothing more. The second time, finding the priest still absent, he hesitated to go at once. Instead, he stood upon the step, and narrowing his brown eyes, gazed beyond the river, off towards the west, where a murky streak of mist was spreading across the sun.

"It look like mo' rain," he remarked, slowly and carelessly.

"We done had 'bout 'nough," she replied, in much the same tone.

"It's no chance to thin out the cotton," he went on.

"An' the Bon-Dieu," she resumed, "it 's on'y to-day you can cross him on foot."

"You live yonda on the Bon-Dieu, *donc?*" he asked, looking at her for the first time since he had spoken.

"Yas, by Nid d'Hibout, m'sieur."

Instinctive courtesy held him from questioning her further. But he seated himself on the step, evidently determined to wait there for the priest. He said no more, but sat scanning critically the steps, the porch, and pillar beside him, from which he occasionally tore away little pieces of detached wood, where it was beginning to rot at its base.

A click at the side gate that communicated with the churchyard soon announced Père Antoine's return. He came hurriedly across the garden-path, between the tall, lusty rosebushes that lined either side of it, which were now fragrant with blossoms. His long, flapping cassock added something of height to his undersized, middle-aged figure, as did the skullcap which rested securely back on his head. He saw only the young man at first, who rose at his approach.

"Well, Azenor," he called cheerily in French, extending his hand. "How is this? I expected you all the week."

"Yes, monsieur; but I knew well what you wanted with me, and I was finishing the doors for Gros-Léon's new house;" saying which, he drew back, and indicated by a motion and look that some one was present who had a prior claim upon Père Antoine's attention.

"Ah, Lalie!" the priest exclaimed, when he had

mounted to the porch, and saw her there behind the vines. "Have you been waiting here since you confessed? Surely an hour ago!"

"Yes, monsieur."

"You should rather have made some visits in the village, child."

"I am not acquainted with any one in the village," she returned.

The priest, as he spoke, had drawn a chair, and seated himself beside her, with his hands comfortably clasping his knees. He wanted to know how things were out on the bayou.

"And how is the grandmother?" he asked. "As cross and crabbed as ever? And with that"—he added reflectively—"good for ten years yet! I said only yesterday to Butrand—you know Butrand, he works on Le Blôt's Bon-Dieu place—'And that Madame Zidore: how is it with her, Butrand? I believe God has forgotten her here on earth.' 'It is n't that, your reverence,' said Butrand, 'but it's neither God nor the Devil that wants her!'" And Père Antoine laughed with a jovial frankness that took all sting of ill-nature from his very pointed remarks.

Lalie did not reply when he spoke of her grandmother; she only pressed her lips firmly together, and picked nervously at the red bandana.

"I have come to ask, Monsieur Antoine," she began, lower than she needed to speak—for Azenor had withdrawn at once to the far end of the porch— "to ask if you will give me a little scrap of paper—a piece of writing for Monsieur Chartrand at the store over there. I want new shoes and stockings for Easter, and I have brought eggs to trade for them. He says he is willing, yes, if he was sure I would bring more every week till the shoes are paid for."

With good-natured indifference, Père Antoine wrote the order that the girl desired. He was too familiar with distress to feel keenly for a girl who was able to buy Easter shoes and pay for them with eggs.

She went immediately away then, after shaking hands with the priest, and sending a quick glance of her

pathetic eyes towards Azenor, who had turned when he
heard her rise, and nodded when he caught the look.
Through the vines he watched her cross the village
street.

"How is it that you do not know Lalie, Azenor?
You surely must have seen her pass your house often.
It lies on her way to the Bon-Dieu."

"No, I don't know her; I have never seen her,"
the young man replied, as he seated himself—after the
priest—and kept his eyes absently fixed on the store
across the road, where he had seen her enter.

"She is the granddaughter of that Madame Izidore"—

"What! Ma'ame Zidore whom they drove off the
island last winter?"

"Yes, yes. Well, you know, they say the old
woman stole wood and things,—I don't know how true
it is,—and destroyed people's property out of pure
malice."

"And she lives now on the Bon-Dieu?"

"Yes, on Le Blôt's place, in a perfect wreck of a
cabin. You see, she gets it for nothing; not a negro on
the place but has refused to live in it."

"Surely, it can't be that old abandoned hovel near
the swamp, that Michon occupied ages ago?"

"That is the one, the very one."

"And the girl lives there with that old wretch?"
the young man marveled.

"Old wretch to be sure, Azenor. But what can you
expect from a woman who never crosses the threshold
of God's house—who even tried to hinder the child
doing so as well? But I went to her. I said: 'See here,
Madame Zidore,'—you know it 's my way to handle
such people without gloves,—'you may damn your soul
if you choose,' I told her, 'that is a privilege which we
all have; but none of us has a right to imperil the salva-
tion of another. I want to see Lalie at mass hereafter
on Sundays, or you will hear from me;' and I shook my
stick under her nose. Since then the child has never
missed a Sunday. But she is half starved, you can see
that. You saw how shabby she is—how broken her
shoes are? She is at Chartrand's now, trading for new

ones with those eggs she brought, poor thing! There is no doubt of her being ill-treated. Butrand says he thinks Madame Zidore even beats the child. I don't know how true it is, for no power can make her utter a word against her grandmother."

Azenor, whose face was a kind and sensitive one, had paled with distress as the priest spoke; and now at these final words he quivered as though he felt the sting of a cruel blow upon his own flesh.

But no more was said of Lalie, for Père Antoine drew the young man's attention to the carpenter-work which he wished to intrust to him. When they had talked the matter over in all its lengthy details, Azenor mounted his horse and rode away.

A moment's gallop carried him outside the village. Then came a half-mile strip along the river to cover. Then the lane to enter, in which stood his dwelling midway, upon a low, pleasant knoll.

As Azenor turned into the lane, he saw the figure of Lalie far ahead of him. Somehow he had expected to find her there, and he watched her again as he had done through Père Antoine's vines. When she passed his house, he wondered if she would turn to look at it. But she did not. How could she know it was his? Upon reaching it himself, he did not enter the yard, but stood there motionless, his eyes always fastened upon the girl's figure. He could not see, away off there, how coarse her garments were. She seemed, through the distance that divided them, as slim and delicate as a flower-stalk. He stayed till she reached the turn of the lane and disappeared into the woods.

Mass had not yet begun when Azenor tiptoed into church on Easter morning. He did not take his place with the congregation, but stood close to the holy-water font, and watched the people who entered.

Almost every girl who passed him wore a white mull, a dotted swiss, or a fresh-starched muslin at least. They were bright with ribbons that hung from their persons, and flowers that bedecked their hats. Some carried fans and cambric handkerchiefs. Most of them wore gloves, and were odorant of *poudre de riz* and nice toilet-waters; while all carried gay little baskets filled with Easter-eggs.

But there was one who came empty-handed, save for the worn prayer-book which she bore. It was Lalie, the veil upon her head, and wearing the blue print and cotton bodice which she had worn the day before.

He dipped his hand into the holy water when she came, and held it out to her, though he had not thought of doing this for the others. She touched his fingers with the tips of her own, making a slight inclination as she did so; and after a deep genuflection before the Blessed Sacrament, passed on to the side. He was not sure if she had known him. He knew she had not looked into his eyes, for he would have felt it.

He was angered against other young women who passed him, because of their flowers and ribbons, when she wore none. He himself did not care, but he feared she might, and watched her narrowly to see if she did.

But it was plain that Lalie did not care. Her face, as she seated herself, settled into the same restful lines it had worn yesterday, when she sat in Père Antoine's big chair. It seemed good to her to be there. Sometimes she looked up at the little colored panes through which the Easter sun was streaming; then at the flaming candles, like stars; or at the embowered figures of Joseph and Mary, flanking the central tabernacle which shrouded the risen Christ. Yet she liked just as well to watch the young girls in their spring freshness, or to sensuously inhale the mingled odor of flowers and incense that filled the temple.

Lalie was among the last to quit the church. When she walked down the clean pathway that led from it to the road, she looked with pleased curiosity towards the groups of men and maidens who were gayly matching their Easter-eggs under the shade of the China-berry trees.

Azenor was among them, and when he saw her coming solitary down the path, he approached her and, with a smile, extended his hat, whose crown was quite lined with the pretty colored eggs.

"You mus' of forgot to bring aiggs," he said. "Take some o' mine."

"Non, merci," she replied, flushing and drawing back.

But he urged them anew upon her. Much pleased, then, she bent her pretty head over the hat, and was evidently puzzled to make a selection among so many that were beautiful.

He picked out one for her,—a pink one, dotted with white clover-leaves.

"Yere," he said, handing it to her, "I think this is the pretties'; an' it look' strong too. I'm sho' it will break all of the res'." And he playfully held out another, half-hidden in his fist, for her to try its strength upon. But she refused to. She would not risk the ruin of her pretty egg. Then she walked away, without once having noticed that the girls, whom Azenor had left, were looking curiously at her.

When he rejoined them, he was hardly prepared for their greeting; it startled him.

"How come you talk to that girl? She 's real canaille, her," was what one of them said to him.

"Who say' so? Who say she 's canaille? If it's a man, I 'll smash 'is head!" he exclaimed, livid. They all laughed merrily at this.

"An' if it 's a lady, Azenor? W'at you goin' to do 'bout it?" asked another, quizzingly.

" 'T ain' no lady. No lady would say that 'bout a po' girl, w'at she don't even know."

He turned away, and emptying all his eggs into the hat of a little urchin who stood near, walked out of the churchyard. He did not stop to exchange another word with any one; neither with the men who stood all *endimanchés* before the stores, nor the women who were mounting upon horses and into vehicles, or walking in groups to their homes.

He took a short cut across the cotton-field that extended back of the town, and walking rapidly, soon reached his home. It was a pleasant house of few rooms and many windows, with fresh air blowing through from every side; his workshop was beside it. A broad strip of greensward, studded here and there with trees, sloped down to the road.

Azenor entered the kitchen, where an amiable old black woman was chopping onion and sage at a table.

"Tranquiline," he said abruptly, "they 's a young girl goin' to pass yere afta a w'ile. She 's got a blue dress an' w'ite josie on, an' a veil on her head. W'en you see her, I want you to go to the road an' make her res' there on the bench, an' ask her if she don't want a cup o' coffee. I saw her go to communion, me; so she did n't eat any breakfas'. Eve'ybody else f'om out o' town, that went to communion, got invited somew'ere another. It's enough to make a person sick to see such meanness."

"An' you want me ter go down to de gate, jis' so, an' ax 'er pineblank ef she wants some coffee?" asked the bewildered Tranquiline.

"I don't care if you ask her poin' blank o' not; but you do like I say." Tranquiline was leaning over the gate when Lalie came along.

"Howdy," offered the woman.

"Howdy," the girl returned.

"Did you see a yalla calf wid black spots a t'arin' down de lane, missy?"

"Non; not yalla, an' not with black spot'. *Mais* I see one li'le w'ite calf tie by a rope, yonda 'roun' the ben'."

"Dat warn't hit. Dis heah one was yalla. I hope he done flung hisse'f down de bank an' broke his nake. Sarve 'im right! But whar you come f'om, chile? You look plum wo' out. Set down dah on dat bench, an' le' me fotch you a cup o' coffee."

Azenor had already in his eagerness arranged a tray, upon which was a smoking cup of *café au lait*. He had buttered and jellied generous slices of bread, and was searching wildly for something when Tranquiline re-entered.

"W'at become o' that half of chicken-pie, Tranquiline, that was yere in the *garde manger* yesterday?"

"W'at chicken-pie? W'at *garde manger*?" blustered the woman.

"Like we got mo' 'en one *garde manger* in the house, Tranquiline!"

"You jis' like ole Ma'ame Azenor use' to be, you is! You 'spec' chicken-pie gwine las' etarnal? W'en some'pin done sp'ilt, I flings it 'way. Dat's me—dat 's Tranquiline!"

So Azenor resigned himself,—what else could he do?—and sent the tray, incomplete, as he fancied it, out to Lalie.

He trembled at the thought of what he did; he, whose nerves were usually as steady as some piece of steel mechanism.

Would it anger her if she suspected? Would it please her if she knew? Would she say this or that to Tranquiline? And would Tranquiline tell him truly what she said—how she looked?

As it was Sunday, Azenor did not work that afternoon. Instead, he took a book out under the trees, as he often did, and sat reading it, from the first sound of the Vesper bell, that came faintly across the fields, till the Angelus. All that time! He turned many a page, yet in the end did not know what he had read. With his pencil he had traced "Lalie" upon every margin, and was saying it softly to himself.

Another Sunday Azenor saw Lalie at mass—and again. Once he walked with her and showed her the short cut across the cotton-field. She was very glad that day, and told him she was going to work—her grandmother said she might. She was going to hoe, up in the fields with Monsieur Le Blôt's hands. He entreated her not to; and when she asked his reason, he could not tell her, but turned and tore shyly and savagely at the elder-blossoms that grew along the fence.

Then they stopped where she was going to cross the fence from the field into the lane. He wanted to tell her that was his house which they could see not far away; but he did not dare to, since he had fed her there on the morning she was hungry.

"An' you say yo' gran'ma 's goin' to let you work? She keeps you f'om workin', *donc?*" He wanted to question her about her grandmother, and could think of no other way to begin.

"Po' ole grand'mère!" she answered. "I don' b'lieve she know mos' time w'at she 's doin'. Sometime she say' I ain't no betta an' one nigga, an' she fo'ce me to work. Then she say she know I 'm goin' be one canaille like maman, an' she make me set down still, like she would want to kill me if I would move. Her, she on'y want' to be out in the wood', day an' night, day an' night. She ain' got her right head, po' grand'mère. I know she ain't."

Lalie had spoken low and in jerks, as if every word gave her pain. Azenor could feel her distress as plainly as he saw it. He wanted to say something to her—to do something for her. But her mere presence paralyzed him into inactivity—except his pulses, that beat like hammers when he was with her. Such a poor, shabby little thing as she was, too!

"I 'm goin' to wait yere nex' Sunday fo' you, Lalie," he said, when the fence was between them. And he thought he had said something very daring.

But the next Sunday she did not come. She was neither at the appointed place of meeting in the lane, nor was she at mass. Her absence—so unexpected—affected Azenor like a calamity. Late in the afternoon, when he could stand the trouble and bewilderment of it no longer, he went and leaned over Père Antoine's fence. The priest was picking the slugs from his roses on the other side.

"That young girl from the Bon-Dieu," said Azenor—"she was not at mass to-day. I suppose her grandmother has forgotten your warning."

"No," answered the priest. "The child is ill, I hear. Butrand tells me she has been ill for several days from overwork in the fields. I shall go out to-morrow to see about her. I would go to-day, if I could."

"The child is ill," was all Azenor heard or understood of Père Antoine's words. He turned and walked resolutely away, like one who determines suddenly upon action after meaningless hesitation.

He walked towards his home and past it, as if it

were a spot that did not concern him. He went on down the lane and into the wood where he had seen Lalie disappear that day.

Here all was shadow, for the sun had dipped too low in the west to send a single ray through the dense foliage of the forest.

Now that he found himself on the way to Lalie's home, he strove to understand why he had not gone there before. He often visited other girls in the village and neighborhood,—why not have gone to her, as well? The answer lay too deep in his heart for him to be more than half-conscious of it. Fear had kept him,— dread to see her desolate life face to face. He did not know how he could bear it.

But now he was going to her at last. She was ill. He would stand upon that dismantled porch that he could just remember. Doubtless Ma'ame Zidore would come out to know his will, and he would tell her that Père Antoine had sent to inquire how Mamzelle Lalie was. No! Why drag in Père Antoine? He would simply stand boldly and say, "Ma'ame Zidore, I learn that Lalie is ill. I have come to know if it is true, and to see her, if I may."

When Azenor reached the cabin where Lalie dwelt, all sign of day had vanished. Dusk had fallen swiftly after the sunset. The moss that hung heavy from great live oak branches was making fantastic silhouettes against the eastern sky that the big, round moon was beginning to light. Off in the swamp beyond the bayou, hundreds of dismal voices were droning a lullaby. Upon the hovel itself, a stillness like death rested.

Oftener than once Azenor tapped upon the door, which was closed as well as it could be, without obtaining a reply. He finally approached one of the small unglazed windows, in which coarse mosquito-netting had been fastened, and looked into the room.

By the moonlight slanting in he could see Lalie stretched upon a bed; but of Ma'ame Zidore there was no sign. "Lalie!" he called softly. "Lalie!"

The girl slightly moved her head upon the pillow. Then he boldly opened the door and entered.

Upon a wretched bed, over which was spread a cover of patched calico, Lalie lay, her frail body only half concealed by the single garment that was upon it. One hand was plunged beneath her pillow; the other, which was free, he touched. It was as hot as flame; so was her head. He knelt sobbing upon the floor beside her, and called her his love and his soul. He begged her to speak a word to him,—to look at him. But she only muttered disjointedly that the cotton was all turning to ashes in the fields, and the blades of the corn were in flames.

If he was choked with love and grief to see her so, he was moved by anger as well; rage against himself, against Père Antoine, against the people upon the plantation and in the village, who had so abandoned a helpless creature to misery and maybe death. Because she had been silent—had not lifted her voice in complaint—they believed she suffered no more than she could bear.

But surely the people could not be utterly without heart. There must be one somewhere with the spirit of Christ. Père Antoine would tell him of such a one, and he would carry Lalie to her,—out of this atmosphere of death. He was in haste to be gone with her. He fancied every moment of delay was a fresh danger threatening her life.

He folded the rude bed-cover over Lalie's naked limbs, and lifted her in his arms. She made no resistance. She seemed only loath to withdraw her hand from beneath the pillow. When she did, he saw that she held lightly but firmly clasped in her encircling fingers the pretty Easter-egg he had given her! He uttered a low cry of exultation as the full significance of this came over him. If she had hung for hours upon his neck telling him that she loved him, he could not have known it more surely than by this sign. Azenor felt as if some mysterious bond had all at once drawn them heart to heart and made them one.

No need now to go from door to door begging admittance for her. She was his. She belonged to him. He knew now where her place was, whose roof must shelter her, and whose arms protect her.

So Azenor, with his loved one in his arms, walked through the forest, surefooted as a panther. Once, as he walked, he could hear in the distance the weird chant which Ma'ame Zidore was crooning—to the moon, maybe—as she gathered her wood.

Once, where the water was trickling cool through rocks, he stopped to lave Lalie's hot cheeks and hands and forehead. He had not once touched his lips to her. But now, when a sudden great fear came upon him because she did not know him, instinctively he pressed his lips upon hers that were parched and burning. He held them there till hers were soft and pliant from the healthy moisture of his own.

Then she knew him. She did not tell him so, but her stiffened fingers relaxed their tense hold upon the Easter bauble. It fell to the ground as she twined her arm around his neck; and he understood.

"Stay close by her, Tranquiline," said Azenor, when he had laid Lalie upon his own couch at home. "I'm goin' for the doctor en' for Père Antoine. Not because she is goin' to die," he added hastily, seeing the awe that crept into the woman's face at mention of the priest. "She is goin' to live! Do you think I would let my wife die, Tranquiline?"

After the Winter
1891

I

Trézinie, the blacksmith's daughter, stepped out upon the gallery just as M'sieur Michel passed by. He did not notice the girl but walked straight on down the village street.

His seven hounds skulked, as usual, about him. At his side hung his powder-horn, and on his shoulder a gunny-bag slackly filled with game that he carried to the store. A broad felt hat shaded his bearded face and in his hand he carelessly swung his old-fashioned rifle. It was doubtless the same with which he had slain so many people, Trézinie shudderingly reflected. For Cami, the cobbler's son—who must have known—had often related to her how this man had killed two Choctaws, as many Texans, a free mulatto and numberless blacks, in that vague locality known as "the hills."

Older people who knew better took little trouble to correct this ghastly record that a younger generation had scored against him. They themselves had come to half-believe that M'sieur Michel might be capable of anything, living as he had, for so many years, apart from humanity, alone with his hounds in a kennel of a cabin on the hill. The time seemed to most of them fainter than a memory when, a lusty young fellow of twenty-five, he had cultivated his strip of land across the lane from Les Chêniers; when home and toil and

53

wife and child were so many benedictions that he humbly thanked heaven for having given him.

But in the early '60's he went with his friend Duplan and the rest of the "Louisiana Tigers." He came back with some of them. He came to find—well, death may lurk in a peaceful valley lying in wait to ensnare the toddling feet of little ones. Then, there are women—there are wives with thoughts that roam and grow wanton with roaming; women whose pulses are stirred by strange voices and eyes that woo; women who forget the claims of yesterday, the hopes of to-morrow, in the impetuous clutch of to-day.

But that was no reason, some people thought, why he should have cursed men who found their blessings where they had left them—cursed God, who had abandoned him.

Persons who met him upon the road had long ago stopped greeting him. What was the use? He never answered them; he spoke to no one; he never so much as looked into men's faces. When he bartered his game and fish at the village store for powder and shot and such scant food as he needed, he did so with few words and less courtesy. Yet feeble as it was, this was the only link that held him to his fellow-beings.

Strange to say, the sight of M'sieur Michel, though more forbidding than ever that delightful spring afternoon, was so suggestive to Trézinie as to be almost an inspiration.

It was Easter eve and the early part of April. The whole earth seemed teeming with new, green, vigorous life everywhere—except the arid spot that immediately surrounded Trézinie. It was no use; she had tried. Nothing would grow among those cinders that filled the yard; in that atmosphere of smoke and flame that was constantly belching from the forge where her father worked at his trade. There were wagon wheels, bolts and bars of iron, plowshares and all manner of unpleasant-looking things littering the bleak, black yard; nothing green anywhere except a few weeds that would force themselves into fence corners. And Trézi-

nie knew that flowers belong to Easter time, just as
dyed eggs do. She had plenty of eggs; no one had more
or prettier ones; she was not going to grumble about
that. But she did feel distressed because she had not a
flower to help deck the altar on Easter morning. And
every one else seemed to have them in such abundance! There was 'Dame Suzanne among her roses
across the way. She must have clipped a hundred since
noon. An hour ago Trézinie had seen the carriage from
Les Chêniers pass by on its way to church with Mamzelle Euphrasie's pretty head looking like a picture en-
framed with the Easter lilies that filled the vehicle.

For the twentieth time Trézinie walked out upon
the gallery. She saw M'sieur Michel and thought of the
pine hill. When she thought of the hill she thought of
the flowers that grew there—free as sunshine. The girl
gave a joyous spring that changed to a farandole as
her feet twinkled across the rough, loose boards of the
gallery.

"Hé, Cami!" she cried, clapping her hands together.

Cami rose from the bench where he sat pegging
away at the clumsy sole of a shoe, and came lazily to
the fence that divided his abode from Trézinie's.

"Well, w'at?" he inquired with heavy amiability.
She leaned far over the railing to better communicate
with him.

"You'll go with me yonda on the hill to pick flowers
fo' Easter, Cami? I'm goin' to take La Fringante along,
too, to he'p with the baskets. W'at you say?"

"No!" was the solid reply. "I'm boun' to finish
them shoe', if it is fo' a nigga."

"Not now," she returned impatiently; "to-morrow
mo'nin' at sun-up. An' I tell you, Cami, my flowers'll
beat all! Look yonda at 'Dame Suzanne pickin' her roses
a'ready. An' Mamzelle Euphrasie she's car'ied her lilies
an' gone, her. You tell me all that's goin' be fresh to-
moro'!"

"Jus' like you say," agreed the boy, turning to resume his work. "But you want to mine out fo' the ole
possum up in the wood. Let M'sieur Michel set eyes

on you!" and he raised his arms as if aiming with a gun. "Pim, pam, poum! No mo' Trézinie, no mo' Cami, no mo' La Fringante—all stretch'!"

The possible risk which Cami so vividly foreshadowed but added a zest to Trézinie's projected excursion.

II

It was hardly sun-up on the following morning when the three children—Trézinie, Cami and the little negress, La Fringante—were filling big, flat Indian baskets from the abundance of brilliant flowers that studded the hill.

In their eagerness they had ascended the slope and penetrated deep into the forest without thought of M'sieur Michel or of his abode. Suddenly, in the dense wood, they came upon his hut—low, forbidding, seeming to scowl rebuke upon them for their intrusion.

La Fringante dropped her basket, and, with a cry, fled. Cami looked as if he wanted to do the same. But Trézinie, after the first tremor, saw that the ogre himself was away. The wooden shutter of the one window was closed. The door, so low that even a small man must have stooped to enter it, was secured with a chain. Absolute silence reigned, except for the whirr of wings in the air, the fitful notes of a bird in the treetop.

"Can't you see it's nobody there!" cried Trézinie impatiently.

La Fringante, distracted between curiosity and terror, had crept cautiously back again. Then they all peeped through the wide chinks between the logs of which the cabin was built.

M'sieur Michel had evidently begun the construction of his house by felling a huge tree, whose remaining stump stood in the centre of the hut, and served him as a table. This primitive table was worn smooth by twenty-five years of use. Upon it were such humble utensils as the man required. Everything within the hovel, the sleeping bunk, the one seat, were as rude as a savage would have fashioned them.

The stolid Cami could have stayed for hours with his eyes fastened to the aperture, morbidly seeking some dead, mute sign of that awful pastime with which he believed M'sieur Michel was accustomed to beguile his solitude. But Trézinie was wholly possessed by the thought of her Easter offerings. She wanted flowers and flowers, fresh with the earth and crisp with dew.

When the three youngsters scampered down the hill again there was not a purple verbena left about M'sieur Michel's hut; not a May apple blossom, not a stalk of crimson phlox—hardly a violet.

He was something of a savage, feeling that the solitude belonged to him. Of late there had been forming within his soul a sentiment toward man, keener than indifference, bitter as hate. He was coming to dread even that brief intercourse with others into which his traffic forced him.

So when M'sieur Michel returned to his hut, and with his quick, accustomed eye saw that his woods had been despoiled, rage seized him. It was not that he loved the flowers that were gone more than he loved the stars, or the wind that trailed across the hill, but they belonged to and were a part of that life which he had made for himself, and which he wanted to live alone and unmolested.

Did not those flowers help him to keep his record of time that was passing? They had no right to vanish until the hot May days were upon him. How else should he know? Why had these people, with whom he had nothing in common, intruded upon his privacy and violated it? What would they not rob him of next?

He knew well enough it was Easter; he had heard and seen signs yesterday in the store that told him so. And he guessed that his woods had been rifled to add to the mummery of the day.

M'sieur Michel sat himself moodily down beside his table—centuries old—and brooded. He did not even notice his hounds that were pleading to be fed. As he revolved in his mind the event of the morning—innocent as it was in itself—it grew in importance and assumed a significance not at first apparent. He could not remain passive under pressure of its disturbance. He rose to his feet, every impulse aggressive, urging him to activity. He would go down among those people all gathered together, blacks and whites, and face them for once and all. He did not know what he would say to them, but it would be defiance—something to voice the hate that oppressed him.

The way down the hill, then across a piece of flat, swampy woodland and through the lane to the village was so familiar that it required no attention from him to follow it. His thoughts were left free to revel in the humor that had driven him from his kennel.

As he walked down the village street he saw plainly that the place was deserted save for the appearance of an occasional negress, who seemed occupied with preparing the midday meal. But about the church scores of horses were fastened; and M'sieur Michel could see that the edifice was thronged to the very threshold.

He did not once hesitate, but obeying the force that impelled him to face the people wherever they might be, he was soon standing with the crowd within the entrance of the church. His broad, robust shoulders had forced space for himself, and his leonine head stood higher than any there.

"Take off yo' hat!"

It was an indignant mulatto who addressed him. M'sieur Michel instinctively did as he was bidden. He saw confusedly that there was a mass of humanity close to him, whose contact and atmosphere affected him strangely. He saw his wild-flowers, too. He saw them plainly, in bunches and festoons, among the Easter lilies and roses and geraniums. He was going to speak out, now; he had the right to and he would, just as soon as that clamor overhead would cease.

"Bonté divine! M'sieur Michel!" whispered 'Dame Suzanne tragically to her neighbor. Trézinie heard. Cami saw. They exchanged an electric glance, and tremblingly bowed their heads low.

M'sieur Michel looked wrathfully down at the puny mulatto who had ordered him to remove his hat.

Why had he obeyed? That initial act of compliance had somehow weakened his will, his resolution. But he would regain firmness just as soon as that clamor above gave him chance to speak.

It was the organ filling the small edifice with volumes of sound. It was the voices of men and women mingling in the "Gloria in excelsis Deo!"

The words bore no meaning for him apart from the old familiar strain which he had known as a child and chanted himself in that same organ-loft years ago. How it went on and on! Would it never cease! It was like a menace; like a voice reaching out from the dead past to taunt him.

"Gloria in excelsis Deo!" over and over! How the deep basso rolled it out! How the tenor and alto caught it up and passed it on to be lifted by the high, flute-like ring of the soprano, till all mingled again in the wild pæan, "Gloria in excelsis!"

How insistent was the refrain! and where, what, was that mysterious, hidden quality in it; the power which was overcoming M'sieur Michel, stirring within him a turmoil that bewildered him?

There was no use in trying to speak, or in wanting to. His throat could not have uttered a sound. He wanted to escape, that was all. "Bonæ voluntatis,"—he bent his head as if before a beating storm. "Gloria! Gloria! Gloria!" He must fly; he must save himself, regain his hill where sights and odors and sounds and saints or devils would cease to molest him. "In excelsis Deo!" He retreated, forcing his way backward to the door. He dragged his hat down over his eyes and staggered away down the road. But the refrain pursued him—"Pax! pax! pax!"—fretting him like a lash. He did not slacken his pace till the tones grew fainter than an echo, floating, dying away in an "in excelsis!" When he could hear it no longer he stopped and breathed a sigh of rest and relief.

III

All day long M'sieur Michel stayed about his hut engaged in some familiar employment that he hoped might efface the unaccountable impressions of the morning. But his restlessness was unbounded. A longing had sprung up within him as sharp as pain and not to be appeased. At once, on this bright, warm Easter morning the voices that till now had filled his solitude became meaningless. He stayed mute and uncomprehending before them. Their significance had vanished before the driving want for human sympathy and companionship that had reawakened in his soul.

When night came on he walked through the woods down the slant of the hill again.

"It mus' be all fill' up with weeds," muttered M'sieur Michel to himself as he went. "Ah, Bon Dieu! with trees, Michel, with trees—in twenty-five years, man."

He had not taken the road to the village, but was pursuing a different one in which his feet had not walked for many days. It led him along the river bank for a distance. The narrow stream, stirred by the restless breeze, gleamed in the moonlight that was flooding the land.

As he went on and on, the scent of the newplowed earth that had been from the first keenly perceptible, began to intoxicate him. He wanted to kneel and bury his face in it. He wanted to dig into it; turn it over. He wanted to scatter the seed again as he had done long ago, and watch the new, green life spring up as if at his bidding.

When he turned away from the river, and had walked a piece down the lane that divided Joe Duplan's plantation from that bit of land that had once been his, he wiped his eyes to drive away the mist that was making him see things as they surely could not be.

He had wanted to plant a hedge that time before he went away, but he had not done so. Yet there was the hedge before him, just as he had meant it to be, and filling the night with fragrance. A broad, low gate divided its length, and over this he leaned and looked before him in amazement. There were no weeds as he had fancied; no trees except the scattered live oaks that he remembered.

Could that row of hardy fig trees, old, squat and gnarled, be the twigs that he himself had set one day into the ground? One raw December day when there was a fine, cold mist falling. The chill of it breathed again upon him; the memory was so real. The land did not look as if it ever had been plowed for a field. It was a smooth, green meadow, with cattle huddled upon the cool sward, or moving with slow, stately tread as they nibbled the tender shoots.

There was the house unchanged, gleaming white in the moon, seeming to invite him beneath its calm shelter. He wondered who dwelt within it now. Whoever it was he would not have them find him, like a prowler, there at the gate. But he would come again and again like this at night-time, to gaze and refresh his spirit.

A hand had been laid upon M'sieur Michel's shoulder and some one called his name. Startled, he turned to see who accosted him.

"Duplan!"

The two men who had not exchanged speech for so many years stood facing each other for a long moment in silence.

"I knew you would come back some day, Michel. It was a long time to wait, but you have come home at last."

M'sieur Michel cowered instinctively and lifted his hands with expressive deprecatory gesture. "No, no; it's no place for me, Joe; no place!"

"Isn't a man's home a place for him, Michel?" It seemed less a question than an assertion, charged with gentle authority.

"Twenty-five years, Duplan; twenty-five years! It's no use; it's too late."

"You see, I have used it," went on the planter,

quietly, ignoring M'sieur Michel's protestations. "Those
are my cattle grazing off there. The house has served
me many a time to lodge guests or workmen, for whom
I had no room at Les Chêniers. I have not exhausted
the soil with any crops. I had not the right to do that.
Yet am I in your debt, Michel, and ready to settle en
bon ami."

The planter had opened the gate and entered the
enclosure, leading M'sieur Michel with him. Together
they walked toward the house.

Language did not come readily to either—one so
unaccustomed to hold intercourse with men; both so
stirred with memories that would have rendered any
speech painful. When they had stayed long in a silence
which was eloquent of tenderness, Joe Duplan spoke:

"You know how I tried to see you, Michel, to
speak with you, and you never would."

M'sieur Michel answered with but a gesture that
seemed a supplication.

"Let the past all go, Michel. Begin your new life
as if the twenty-five years that are gone had been a
long night, from which you have only awakened. Come
to me in the morning," he added with quick resolution,
"for a horse and a plow." He had taken the key of the
house from his pocket and placed it in M'sieur Michel's
hand.

"A horse?" M'sieur Michel repeated uncertainly;
"a plow! Oh, it's too late, Duplan; too late."

"It isn't too late. The land has rested all these
years, man; it's fresh, I tell you; and rich as gold. Your
crop will be the finest in the land." He held out his
hand and M'sieur Michel pressed it without a word in
reply, save a muttered "Mon ami."

Then he stood there watching the planter disappear behind the high, clipped hedge.

He held out his arms. He could not have told if it
was toward the retreating figure, or in welcome to an
infinite peace that seemed to descend upon him and
envelop him.

All the land was radiant except the hill far off that
was in black shadow against the sky.

Old Aunt Peggy
1892

When the war was over, old Aunt Peggy went to Monsieur, and said:—

"Massa, I ain't never gwine to quit yer. I'm gittin' ole an' feeble, an' my days is few in dis heah lan' o' sorrow an' sin. All I axes is a li'le co'ner whar I kin set down an' wait peaceful fu de en'."

Monsieur and Madame were very much touched at this mark of affection and fidelity from Aunt Peggy. So, in the general reconstruction of the plantation which immediately followed the surrender, a nice cabin, pleasantly appointed, was set apart for the old woman. Madame did not even forget the very comfortable rocking-chair in which Aunt Peggy might "set down," as she herself feelingly expressed it, "an' wait fu de en'."

She has been rocking ever since.

At intervals of about two years Aunt Peggy hobbles up to the house, and delivers the stereotyped address which has become more than familiar:—

"Mist'ess, I 's come to take a las' look at you all. Le' me look at you good. Le' me look at de chillun,— de big chillun an' de li'le chillun. Le' me look at de picters an' de photygraphts an' de pianny, an' eve'ything 'fo' it 's too late. One eye is done gone, an' de udder 's a-gwine fas'. Any mo'nin' yo' po' ole Aunt Peggy gwine wake up an' fin' herse'f stone-bline."

After such a visit Aunt Peggy invariably returns to her cabin with a generously filled apron.

63

The scruple which Monsieur one time felt in supporting a woman for so many years in idleness has entirely disappeared. Of late his attitude towards Aunt Peggy is simply one of profound astonishment,—wonder at the surprising age which an old black woman may attain when she sets her mind to it, for Aunt Peggy is a hundred and twenty-five, so she says.

It may not be true, however. Possibly she is older.

The Lilies
1892

That little vagabond Mamouche amused himself one afternoon by letting down the fence rails that protected Mr. Billy's young crop of cotton and corn. He had first looked carefully about him to make sure there was no witness to this piece of rascality. Then he crossed the lane and did the same with the Widow Angèle's fence, thereby liberating Toto, the white calf who stood disconsolately penned up on the other side.

It was not ten seconds before Toto was frolicking madly in Mr. Billy's crop, and Mamouche—the young scamp—was running swiftly down the lane, laughing fiendishly to himself as he went.

He could not at first decide whether there could be more fun in letting Toto demolish things at his pleasure, or in warning Mr. Billy of the calf's presence in the field. But the latter course commended itself as possessing a certain refinement of perfidy.

"Ho, the'a, you!" called out Mamouche to one of Mr. Billy's hands, when he got around to where the men were at work; "you betta go yon'a an' see 'bout that calf o' Ma'me Angèle; he done broke in the fiel' an' 'bout to finish the crop, him." Then Mamouche went and sat behind a big tree, where, unobserved, he could laugh to his heart's content.

Mr. Billy's fury was unbounded when he learned that Madame Angèle's calf was eating up and trampling down his corn. At once he sent a detachment of men

65

and boys to expel the animal from the field. Others
were required to repair the damaged fence; while he
himself, boiling with wrath, rode up the lane on his
wicked black charger.

But merely to look upon the devastation was not
enough for Mr. Billy. He dismounted from his horse,
and strode belligerently up to Madame Angèle's door,
upon which he gave, with his riding-whip, a couple of
sharp raps that plainly indicated the condition of his
mind.

Mr. Billy looked taller and broader than ever as
he squared himself on the gallery of Madame Angèle's
small and modest house. She herself half-opened the
door, a pale, sweet-looking woman, somewhat bewildered, and holding a piece of sewing in her hands.
Little Marie Louise was beside her, with big, inquiring,
frightened eyes.

"Well, Madam!" blustered Mr. Billy, "this is a
pretty piece of work! That young beast of yours is a
fence-breaker, Madam, and ought to be shot."

"Oh, non, non, M'sieur. Toto's too li'le; I'm sho
he can't break any fence, him."

"Don't contradict me, Madam. I say he's a fence-
breaker. There's the proof before your eyes. He ought
to be shot, I say, and—don't let it occur again,
Madam." And Mr. Billy turned and stamped down the
steps with a great clatter of spurs as he went.

Madame Angèle was at the time in desperate haste
to finish a young lady's Easter dress, and she could not
afford to let Toto's escapade occupy her to any extent,
much as she regretted it. But little Marie Louise was
greatly impressed by the affair. She went out in the
yard to Toto, who was under the fig-tree, looking not
half so shamefaced as he ought. The child, with arms
clasped around the little fellow's white shaggy neck,
scolded him soundly.

"Ain't you shame', Toto, to go eat up Mr. Billy's
cotton an' co'n? W'at Mr. Billy ev'a done to you, to go
do him that way? If you been hungry, Toto, w'y you
did'n' come like always an' put yo' head in the winda?

I'm goin' tell yo' maman w'en she come back f'om the woods to 's'evenin', M'sieur."

Marie Louise only ceased her mild rebuke when she fancied she saw a penitential look in Toto's big soft eyes.

She had a keen instinct of right and justice for so young a little maid. And all the afternoon, and long into the night, she was disturbed by the thought of the unfortunate accident. Of course, there could be no question of repaying Mr. Billy with money; she and her mother had none. Neither had they cotton and corn with which to make good the loss he had sustained through them.

But had they not something far more beautiful and precious than cotton and corn? Marie Louise thought with delight of that row of Easter lilies on their tall green stems, ranged thick along the sunny side of the house.

The assurance that she would, after all, be able to satisfy Mr. Billy's just anger, was a very sweet one. And soothed by it, Marie Louise soon fell asleep and dreamt a grotesque dream: that the lilies were having a stately dance on the green in the moonlight, and were inviting Mr. Billy to join them.

The following day, when it was nearing noon, Marie Louise said to her mamma: "Maman, can I have some of the Easter lily, to do with like I want?"

Madame Angèle was just then testing the heat of an iron with which to press out the seams in the young lady's Easter dress, and she answered a shade impatiently:

"Yes, yes; va t'en, chérie," thinking that her little girl wanted to pluck a lily or two.

So the child took a pair of old shears from her mother's basket, and out she went to where the tall, perfumed lilies were nodding, and shaking off from their glistening petals the rain-drops with which a passing cloud had just laughingly pelted them.

Snip, snap, went the shears here and there, and never did Marie Louise stop plying them till scores of those long-stemmed lilies lay upon the ground. There were far more than she could hold in her small hands, so she literally clasped the great bunch in her arms, and staggered to her feet with it.

Marie Louise was intent upon her purpose, and lost no time in its accomplishment. She was soon trudging earnestly down the lane with her sweet burden, never stopping, and only once glancing aside to cast a reproachful look at Toto, whom she had not wholly forgiven.

She did not in the least mind that the dogs barked, or that the darkies laughed at her. She went straight on to Mr. Billy's big house, and right into the dining-room, where Mr. Billy sat eating his dinner all alone.

It was a finely-furnished room, but disorderly—very disorderly, as an old bachelor's personal surroundings sometimes are. A black boy stood waiting upon the table. When little Marie Louise suddenly appeared, with that armful of lilies, Mr. Billy seemed for a moment transfixed at the sight.

"Well—bless—my soul! what's all this? What's all this?" he questioned, with staring eyes.

Marie Louise had already made a little curtsy. Her sunbonnet had fallen back, leaving exposed her pretty round head; and her sweet brown eyes were full of confidence as they looked into Mr. Billy's.

"I'm bring some lilies to pay back fo' yo' cotton an' co'n w'at Toto eat all up, M'sieur."

Mr. Billy turned savagely upon Pompey. "What are you laughing at, you black rascal? Leave the room!"

Pompey, who out of mistaken zeal had doubled himself with merriment, was too accustomed to the admonition to heed it literally, and he only made a pretense of withdrawing from Mr. Billy's elbow.

"Lilies! well, upon my—isn't it the little one from across the lane?"

"Dat's who," affirmed Pompey, cautiously insinuating himself again into favor.

"Lilies! who ever heard the like? Why, the baby's buried under 'em. Set 'em down somewhere, little one; anywhere." And Marie Louise, glad to be relieved from the weight of the great cluster, dumped them all on the table close to Mr. Billy.

The perfume that came from the damp, massed flowers was heavy and almost sickening in its pungency. Mr. Billy quivered a little, and drew involuntarily back, as if from an unexpected assailant, when the odor reached him. He had been making cotton and corn for so many years, he had forgotten there were such things as lilies in the world.

"Kiar 'em out? fling 'em 'way?" questioned Pompey, who had observed his master cunningly.

"Let 'em alone! Keep your hands off them! Leave the room, you outlandish black scamp! Whar are you standing there for? Can't you set the Mamzelle a place at table, and draw up a chair?"

So Marie Louise—perched upon a fine old-fashioned chair, supplemented by a Webster's Unabridged—sat down to dine with Mr. Billy.

She had never eaten in company with so peculiar a gentlemen before; so irascible toward the inoffensive Pompey, and so courteous to herself. But she was not ill at ease, and conducted herself properly as her mamma had taught her how.

Mr. Billy was anxious that she should enjoy her dinner, and began by helping her generously to Jambalaya. When she had tasted it she made no remark, only laid down her fork, and looked composedly before her.

"Why, bless me! what ails the little one? You don't eat your rice."

"It ain't cook', M'sieur," replied Marie Louise politely.

Pompey nearly strangled in his attempt to smother an explosion.

"Of course it isn't cooked," echoed Mr. Billy, excitedly, pushing away his plate. "What do you mean, setting a mess of that sort before human beings? Do you take us for a couple of—of rice-birds? What are you standing there for; can't you look up some jam or something to keep the young one from starving? Where's all that jam I saw stewing a while back, here?"

Pompey withdrew, and soon returned with a platter of black-looking jam. Mr. Billy ordered cream for it. Pompey reported there was none.

"No cream, with twenty-five cows on the plantation if there's one!" cried Mr. Billy, almost springing from his chair with indignation.

"Aunt Printy 'low she sot de pan o' cream on de winda-sell, suh, an' Unc' Jonah come 'long an' tu'n it cl'ar ova; neva lef' a drap in de pan."

But evidently the jam, with or without cream, was as distasteful to Marie Louise as the rice was; for after tasting it gingerly she laid away her spoon as she had done before.

"O, no! little one; you don't tell me it isn't cooked this time," laughed Mr. Billy. "I saw the thing boiling a day and a half. Wasn't it a day and a half, Pompey? if you know how to tell the truth."

"Aunt Printy alluz do cooks her p'esarves tell dey plumb done, sho," agreed Pompey.

"It's burn', M'sieur," said Marie Louise, politely, but decidedly, to the utter confusion of Mr. Billy, who was as mortified as could be at the failure of his dinner to please his fastidious little visitor.

Well, Mr. Billy thought of Marie Louise a good deal after that; as long as the lilies lasted. And they lasted long, for he had the whole household employed in taking care of them. Often he would chuckle to himself: "The little rogue, with her black eyes and her lilies! And the rice wasn't cooked, if you please; and the jam was burnt. And the best of it is, she was right."

But when the lilies withered finally, and had to be thrown away, Mr. Billy donned his best suit, a starched shirt and fine silk necktie. Thus attired, he crossed the lane to carry his somewhat tardy apologies to Madame Angèle and Mamzelle Marie Louise, and to pay them a first visit.

Loka
1892

She was a half-breed Indian girl, with hardly a rag to her back. To the ladies of the Band of United Endeavor who questioned her, she said her name was Loka, and she did not know where she belonged, unless it was on Bayou Choctaw.

She had appeared one day at the side door of Frobissaint's "oyster saloon" in Natchitoches, asking for food. Frobissaint, a practical philanthropist, engaged her on the spot as tumbler-washer.

She was not successful at that; she broke too many tumblers. But, as Frobissaint charged her with the broken glasses, he did not mind, until she began to break them over the heads of his customers. Then he seized her by the wrist and dragged her before the Band of United Endeavor, then in session around the corner. This was considerate on Frobissaint's part, for he could have dragged her just as well to the police station.

Loka was not beautiful, as she stood in her red calico rags before the scrutinizing band. Her coarse, black, unkempt hair framed a broad, swarthy face without a redeeming feature, except eyes that were not bad; slow in their movements, but frank eyes enough. She was big-boned and clumsy.

She did not know how old she was. The minister's wife reckoned she might be sixteen. The judge's wife thought that it made no difference. The doctor's wife suggested that the girl have a bath and change before

71

she be handled, even in discussion. The motion was not seconded. Loka's ultimate disposal was an urgent and difficult consideration.

Some one mentioned a reformatory. Every one else objected.

Madame Laballière, the planter's wife, knew a respectable family of 'Cadians living some miles below, who, she thought, would give the girl a home, with benefit to all concerned. The 'Cadian woman was a deserving one, with a large family of small children, who had all her own work to do. The husband cropped in a modest way. Loka would not only be taught to work at the Padues', but would receive a good moral training beside.

That settled it. Every one agreed with the planter's wife that it was a chance in a thousand; and Loka was sent to sit on the steps outside, while the band proceeded to the business next in order.

Loka was afraid of treading upon the little Padues when she first got amongst them,—there were so many of them,—and her feet were like leaden weights, encased in the strong brogans with which the band had equipped her.

Madame Padue, a small, black-eyed, aggressive woman, questioned her in a sharp, direct fashion peculiar to herself.

"How come you don't talk French, you?" Loka shrugged her shoulders.

"I kin talk English good 's anybody; an' lit' bit Choctaw, too," she offered, apologetically.

"*Ma foi,* you kin fo'git yo' Choctaw. Soona the betta for me. Now if you willin', an' ent too lazy an' sassy, we'll git 'long somehow. *Vrai sauvage ça,*" she muttered under her breath, as she turned to initiate Loka into some of her new duties.

She herself was a worker. A good deal more fussy one than her easy-going husband and children thought necessary or agreeable. Loka's slow ways and heavy motions aggravated her. It was in vain Monsieur Padue expostulated:—

"She 's on'y a chile, rememba, Tontine."

"She 's *vrai sauvage*, that 's w'at. It 's got to be work out of her," was Tontine's only reply to such remonstrance.

The girl was indeed so deliberate about her tasks that she had to be urged constantly to accomplish the amount of labor that Tontine required of her. Moreover, she carried to her work a stolid indifference that was exasperating. Whether at the wash-tub, scrubbing the floors, weeding the garden, or learning her lessons and catechism with the children on Sundays, it was the same.

It was only when intrusted with the care of little Bibine, the baby, that Loka crept somewhat out of her apathy. She grew very fond of him. No wonder; such a baby as he was! So good, so fat, and complaisant! He had such a way of clasping Loka's broad face between his pudgy fists and savagely biting her chin with his hard, toothless gums! Such a way of bouncing in her arms as if he were mounted upon springs! At his antics the girl would laugh a wholesome, ringing laugh that was good to hear.

She was left alone to watch and nurse him one day. An accommodating neighbor who had become the possessor of a fine new spring wagon passed by just after the noon-hour meal, and offered to take the whole family on a jaunt to town. The offer was all the more tempting as Tontine had some long-delayed shopping to do; and the opportunity to equip the children with shoes and summer hats could not be slighted. So away they all went. All but Bibine, who was left swinging in his branle with only Loka for company.

This branle consisted of a strong circular piece of cotton cloth, securely but slackly fastened to a large, stout hoop suspended by three light cords to a hook in a rafter of the gallery. The baby who has not swung in a branle does not know the quintessence of baby luxury. In each of the four rooms of the house was a hook from which to hang this swing.

Often it was taken out under the trees. But to-day

it swung in the shade of the open gallery; and Loka sat beside it, giving it now and then a slight impetus that sent it circling in slow, sleep-inspiring undulations.

Bibine kicked and cooed as long as he was able. But Loka was humming a monotonous lullaby; the branle was swaying to and fro, the warm air fanning him deliciously; and Bibine was soon fast asleep.

Seeing this, Loka quietly let down the mosquito net, to protect the child's slumber from the intrusion of the many insects that were swarming in the summer air.

Singularly enough, there was no work for her to do; and Tontine, in her hurried departure, had failed to provide for the emergency. The washing and ironing were over; the floors had been scrubbed, and the rooms righted; the yard swept; the chickens fed; vegetables picked and washed. There was absolutely nothing to do, and Loka gave herself up to the dreams of idleness.

As she sat comfortably back in the roomy rocker, she let her eyes sweep lazily across the country. Away off to the right peeped up, from amid densely clustered trees, the pointed roofs and long pipe of the steam-gin of Laballière's. No other habitation was visible except a few low, flat dwellings far over the river, that could hardly be seen.

The immense plantation took up all the land in sight. The few acres that Baptiste Padue cultivated were his own, that Laballière, out of friendly consideration, had sold to him. Baptiste's fine crop of cotton and corn was "laid by" just now, waiting for rain; and Baptiste had gone with the rest of the family to town. Beyond the river and the field and everywhere about were dense woods.

Loka's gaze, that had been slowly traveling along the edge of the horizon, finally fastened upon the woods, and stayed there. Into her eyes came the absent look of one whose thought is projected into the future or the past, leaving the present blank. She was seeing a vision. It had come with a whiff that the strong south breeze had blown to her from the woods.

She was seeing old Marot, the squaw who drank

whiskey and plaited baskets and beat her. There was something, after all, in being beaten, if only to scream out and fight back, as at that time in Natchitoches, when she broke a glass on the head of a man who laughed at her and pulled her hair, and called her "fool names."

Old Marot wanted her to steal and cheat, to beg and lie, when they went out with the baskets to sell. Loka did not want to. She did not like to. That was why she had run away—and because she was beaten. But—but ah! the scent of the sassafras leaves hanging to dry in the shade! The pungent camomile! The sound of the bayou tumbling over that old slimy log! Only to lie there for hours and watch the glistening lizards glide in and out was worth a beating.

She knew the birds must be singing in chorus out there in the woods where the gray moss was hanging, and the trumpetvine trailing from the trees, spangled with blossoms. In spirit she heard the songsters.

She wondered if Choctaw Joe and Sambite played dice every night by the campfire, as they used to do; and if they still fought and slashed each other when wild with drink. How good it felt to walk with mocca-sined feet over the springy turf, under the trees! What fun to trap the squirrels, to skin the otter; to take those swift flights on the pony that Choctaw Joe had stolen from the Texans!

Loka sat motionless; only her breast heaved tumul-tuously. Her heart was aching with savage homesick-ness. She could not feel just then that the sin and pain of that life were anything beside the joy of its freedom.

Loka was sick for the woods. She felt she must die if she could not get back to them, and to her vagabond life. Was there anything to hinder her? She stooped and unlaced the brogans that were chafing her feet, removed them and her stockings, and threw the things away from her. She stood up all a-quiver, panting, ready for flight.

But there was a sound that stopped her. It was little Bibine, cooing, sputtering, battling hands and feet with the mosquito net that he had dragged over his

face. The girl uttered a sob as she reached down for
the baby she had grown to love so, and clasped him in
her arms. She could not go and leave Bibine behind.

Tontine began to grumble at once when she discovered that Loka was not at hand to receive them on
their return.

"*Bon!*" she exclaimed. "Now w'ere is that Loka?
Ah, that girl, she aggravates me too much. Firs' thing
she knows I 'm goin' sen' her straight back to them
ban' of lady w'ere she come frum."

"Loka!" she called, in short, sharp tones, as she
traversed the house and peered into each room. "Lo—
ka!" She cried loudly enough to be heard half a mile
away when she got out upon the back gallery. Again
and again she called.

Baptiste was exchanging the discomfort of his Sunday coat for the accustomed ease of shirt sleeves.

"*Mais* don't git so excite, Tontine," he implored.
"I 'm sho she 's yonda to the crib shellin' co'n, or some-
w'ere like that."

"Run, François, you, an' see to the crib," the
mother commanded. "Bibine mus' be starve! Run to
the hen-house an' look, Juliette. Maybe she 's fall
asleep in some corna. That 'll learn me 'notha time to
go trus' *une pareille sauvage* with my baby, *va!*"

When it was discovered that Loka was nowhere in
the immediate vicinity, Tontine was furious.

"*Pas possible* she 's walk to Laballière, with Bibine!" she exclaimed.

"I 'll saddle the hoss an' go see, Tontine," interposed Baptiste, who was beginning to share his wife's
uneasiness.

"Go, go, Baptiste," she urged. "An' you, boys, run
yonda down the road to ole Aunt Judy's cabin an' see."

It was found that Loka had not been seen at Laballière's, nor at Aunt Judy's cabin; that she had not taken
the boat, that was still fastened to its moorings down
the bank. Then Tontine's excitement left her. She
turned pale and sat quietly down in her room, with an
unnatural calm that frightened the children.

Some of them began to cry. Baptiste walked rest-
lessly about, anxiously scanning the country in all directions. A wretched hour dragged by. The sun had set,
leaving hardly an afterglow, and in a little while the
twilight that falls so swiftly would be there.

Baptiste was preparing to mount his horse, to start
out again on the round he had already been over. Tontine sat in the same state of intense abstraction when
François, who had perched himself among the lofty
branches of a chinaberry-tree, called out: "Ent that
Loka 'way yon'a, jis' come out de wood? climbin' de
fence down by de melon patch?"

It was difficult to distinguish in the gathering dusk
if the figure were that of man or beast. But the family
was not left long in suspense. Baptiste sped his horse
away in the direction indicated by François, and in a
little while he was galloping back with Bibine in his
arms; as fretful, sleepy and hungry a baby as ever was.

Loka came trudging on behind Baptiste. He did
not wait for explanations; he was too eager to place the
child in the arms of its mother. The suspense over,
Tontine began to cry; that followed naturally, of course.
Through her tears she managed to address Loka, who
stood all tattered and disheveled in the doorway;
"W'ere you been? Tell me that."

"Bibine an' me," answered Loka, slowly and awkwardly, "we was lonesome—we been take lit' 'broad in
de wood."

"You did n' know no betta 'an to take 'way Bibine
like that? W'at Ma'ame Laballière mean, anyhow, to
sen' me such a objec' like you, I want to know?"

"You go'n' sen' me 'way?" asked Loka, passing her
hand in a hopeless fashion over her frowzy hair.

"*Par exemple!* straight you march back to that ban'
w'ere you come from. To give me such a fright like
that! *pas possible.*"

"Go slow, Tontine; go slow," interposed Baptiste.

"Don' sen' me 'way frum Bibine," entreated the
girl, with a note in her voice like a lament.

"To-day," she went on, in her dragging manner,
"I want to run 'way bad, an' take to de wood; an' go

yonda back to Bayou Choctaw to steal an' lie agin. It's on'y Bibine w'at hole me back. I could n' lef' 'im. I could n' do dat. An' we jis' go take lit' 'broad in de wood, das all, him an' me. Don' sen' me 'way like dat!"

Baptiste led the girl gently away to the far end of the gallery, and spoke soothingly to her. He told her to be good and brave, and he would right the trouble for her. He left her standing there and went back to his wife.

"Tontine," he began, with unusual energy, "you got to listen to the truth—once fo' all." He had evidently determined to profit by his wife's lachrymose and wilted condition to assert his authority.

"I want to say who 's masta in this house—it 's me," he went on. Tontine did not protest; only clasped the baby a little closer, which encouraged him to proceed.

"You been grind that girl too much. She ent a bad girl—I been watch her close, 'count of the chil'ren; she ent bad. All she want, it 's li'le mo' rope. You can't drive a ox with the same gearin' you drive a mule. You got to learn that, Tontine."

He approached his wife's chair and stood beside her.

"That girl, she done tole us how she was temp' to-day to turn *canaille*—like we all temp' sometime'. W'at was it save her? That li'le chile w'at you hole in yo' arm. An' now you want to take her guarjun angel 'way f'om her? *Non, non, ma femme*," he said, resting his hand gently upon his wife's head. "We got to rememba she ent like you an' me, po' thing; she 's one Injun, her."

At the 'Cadian Ball
1892

Bobinôt, that big, brown, good-natured Bobinôt, had no intention of going to the ball, even though he knew Calixta would be there. For what came of those balls but heartache, and a sickening disinclination for work the whole week through, till Saturday night came again and his tortures began afresh? Why could he not love Ozéina, who would marry him tomorrow; or Fronie, or any one of a dozen others, rather than that little Spanish vixen? Calixta's slender foot had never touched Cuban soil; but her mother's had, and the Spanish was in her blood all the same. For that reason the prairie people forgave her much that they would not have overlooked in their own daughters or sisters.

Her eyes,—Bobinôt thought of her eyes, and weakened,—the bluest, the drowsiest, most tantalizing that ever looked into a man's; he thought of her flaxen hair that kinked worse than a mulatto's close to her head; that broad, smiling mouth and tiptilted nose, that full figure; that voice like a rich contralto song, with cadences in it that must have been taught by Satan, for there was no one else to teach her tricks on that 'Cadian prairie. Bibinôt thought of them all as he plowed his rows of cane.

There had even been a breath of scandal whispered about her a year ago, when she went to Assumption,—but why talk of it? No one did now. "C'est Espagnol, ça," most of them said with lenient shoulder-

79

shrugs. "Bon chien tient de race," the old men mumbled over their pipes, stirred by recollections. Nothing was made of it, except that Fronie threw it up to Calixta when the two quarreled and fought on the church steps after mass one Sunday, about a lover. Calixta swore roundly in fine 'Cadian French and with true Spanish spirit, and slapped Fronie's face. Fronie had slapped her back; "Tiens, cocotte, va!" "Espèce de lionèse; prends ça, et ça!" till the curé himself was obliged to hasten and make peace between them. Bobinôt thought of it all, and would not go to the ball.

But in the afternoon, over at Friedheimer's store, where he was buying a trace-chain, he heard some one say that Alcée Laballière would be there. Then wild horses could not have kept him away. He knew how it would be—or rather he did not know how it would be—if the handsome young planter came over to the ball as he sometimes did. If Alcée happened to be in a serious mood, he might only go to the card-room and play a round or two; or he might stand out on the galleries talking crops and politics with the old people. But there was no telling. A drink or two could put the devil in his head,—that was what Bobinôt said to himself, as he wiped the sweat from his brow with his red bandanna; a gleam from Calixta's eyes, a flash of her ankle, a twirl of her skirts could do the same. Yes, Bobinôt would go to the ball.

That was the year Alcée Laballière put nine hundred acres in rice. It was putting a good deal of money into the ground, but the returns promised to be glorious. Old Madame Laballière, sailing about the spacious galleries in her white *volante*, figured it all out in her head. Clarisse, her goddaughter, helped her a little, and together they built more air-castles than enough. Alcée worked like a mule that time; and if he did not kill himself, it was because his constitution was an iron one. It was an every-day affair for him to come in from the field well-nigh exhausted, and wet to the waist. He did not mind if there were visitors; he left them to his mother and Clarisse. There were often guests: young

men and women who came up from the city, which
was but a few hours away, to visit his beautiful kins-
woman. She was worth going a good deal farther than
that to see. Dainty as a lily; hardy as a sunflower; slim,
tall, graceful, like one of the reeds that grew in the
marsh. Cold and kind and cruel by turn, and everything that was aggravating to Alcée.

He would have liked to sweep the place of those
visitors, often. Of the men, above all, with their ways
and their manners; their swaying of fans like women,
and dandling about hammocks. He could have pitched
them over the levee into the river, if it had n't meant
murder. That was Alcée. But he must have been crazy
the day he came in from the rice-field, and, toil-stained
as he was, clasped Clarisse by the arms and panted a
volley of hot, blistering love-words into her face. No
man had ever spoken love to her like that.

"Monsieur!" she exclaimed, looking him full in the
eyes, without a quiver. Alcée's hands dropped and his
glance wavered before the chill of her calm, clear eyes.

"Par exemple!" she muttered disdainfully, as she
turned from him, deftly adjusting the careful toilet that
he had so brutally disarranged.

That happened a day or two before the cyclone
came that cut into the rice like fine steel. It was an
awful thing, coming so swiftly, without a moment's
warning in which to light a holy candle or set a piece
of blessed palm burning. Old madame wept openly and
said her beads, just as her son Didier, the New Orleans
one, would have done. If such a thing had happened
to Alphonse, the Laballière planting cotton up in
Natchitoches, he would have raved and stormed like a
second cyclone, and made his surroundings unbearable
for a day or two. But Alcée took the misfortune differently. He looked ill and gray after it, and said nothing.
His speechlessness was frightful. Clarisse's heart
melted with tenderness; but when she offered her soft,
purring words of condolence, he accepted them with
mute indifference. Then she and her nénaine wept
afresh in each other's arms.

A night or two later, when Clarisse went to her

window to kneel there in the moonlight and say her prayers before retiring, she saw that Bruce, Alcée's negro servant, had led his master's saddle-horse noiselessly along the edge of the sward that bordered the gravel-path, and stood holding him near by. Presently, she heard Alcée quit his room, which was beneath her own, and traverse the lower portico. As he emerged from the shadow and crossed the strip of moonlight, she perceived that he carried a pair of well-filled saddle-bags which he at once flung across the animal's back. He then lost no time in mounting, and after a brief exchange of words with Bruce, went cantering away, taking no precaution to avoid the noisy gravel as the negro had done.

Clarisse had never suspected that it might be Alcée's custom to sally forth from the plantation secretly, and at such an hour; for it was nearly midnight. And had it not been for the telltale saddle-bags, she would only have crept to bed, to wonder, to fret and dream unpleasant dreams. But her impatience and anxiety would not be held in check. Hastily unbolting the shutters of her door that opened upon the gallery, she stepped outside and called softly to the old negro.

"Gre't Peter! Miss Clarisse. I was n' sho it was a ghos' o' w'at, stan'in' up dah, plumb in de night, dataway."

He mounted halfway up the long, broad flight of stairs. She was standing at the top.

"Bruce, w'ere has Monsieur Alcée gone?" she asked.

"W'y, he gone 'bout he business, I reckin," replied Bruce, striving to be non-committal at the outset.

"W'ere has Monsieur Alcée gone?" she reiterated, stamping her bare foot. "I won't stan' any nonsense or any lies; mine, Bruce."

"I don' ric'lic ez I eva tole you lie *yit*, Miss Clarisse. Mista Alcée, he all broke up, sho."

"W'ere—has—he gone? Ah, Sainte Vierge! faut de la patience! butor, va!"

"W'en I was in he room, a-breshin' off he clo'es

to-day," the darkey began, settling himself against the
stair-rail, "he look dat speechless an' down, I say, 'You
'pear to me like some pussun w'at gwine have a spell
o' sickness, Mista Alcée.' He say, 'You reckin?' 'I dat
he git up, go look hisse'f stiddy in de glass. Den he go
to de chimbly an' jerk up de quinine bottle an' po' a
gre't hoss-dose on to he han'. An' he swalla dat mess
in a wink, an' wash hit down wid a big dram o' w'iskey
w'at he keep in he room, aginst he come all soppin'
wet outen de fiel'.

"He 'lows, 'No, I ain' gwine be sick, Bruce.' Den
he square off. He say, 'I kin mak out to stan' up an' gi'
an' take wid any man I knows, lessen hit 's John L.
Sulvun. But w'en God A'mighty an' a 'oman jines fo'ces
agin me, dat 's one too many fur me.' I tell 'im, 'Jis
so,' whils' I 'se makin' out to bresh a spot off w'at ain'
dah, on he coat colla. I tell 'im, 'You wants li'le res',
suh.' He say, 'No, I wants li'le fling; dat w'at I wants;
an' I gwine git it. Pitch me a fis'ful o' clo'es in dem 'ar
saddlebags.' Dat w'at he say. Don't you bodda, missy.
He jis' gone a-caperin' yonda to de Cajun ball. Uh—
uh—de skeeters is fair' a-swarmin' like bees roun' yo'
foots!"

The mosquitoes were indeed attacking Clarisse's
white feet savagely. She had unconsciously been alternately rubbing one foot over the other during the darkey's recital.

"The 'Cadian ball," she repeated contemptuously.
"Humph! *Par exemple!* Nice conduc' for a Laballière.
An' he needs a saddle-bag, fill' with clothes, to go to
the 'Cadian ball!"

"Oh, Miss Clarisse; you go on to bed, chile; git yo'
soun' sleep. He 'low he come back in couple weeks o'
so. I kiarn be repeatin' lot o' truck w'at young mans
say, out heah face o' young gal."

Clarisse said no more, but turned and abruptly re-
entered the house.

"You done talk too much wid yo' mouf a'ready,
you ole fool nigga, you," muttered Bruce to himself as
he walked away.

Alcée reached the ball very late, of course—too late for the chicken gumbo which had been served at midnight.

The big, low-ceiled room—they called it a hall—was packed with men and women dancing to the music of three fiddles. There were broad galleries all around it. There was a room at one side where sober-faced men were playing cards. Another, in which babies were sleeping, was called *le parc aux petits*. Any one who is white may go to a 'Cadian ball, but he must pay for his lemonade, his coffee and chicken gumbo. And he must behave himself like a 'Cadian. Grosbœuf was giving this ball. He had been giving them since he was a young man, and he was a middle-aged one, now. In that time he could recall but one disturbance, and that was caused by American railroaders, who were not in touch with their surroundings and had no business there. "Ces maudits gens du raiderode," Grosbœuf called them.

Alcée Laballière's presence at the ball caused a flutter even among the men, who could not but admire his "nerve" after such misfortune befalling him. To be sure, they knew the Laballières were rich—that there were resources East, and more again in the city. But they felt it took a *brave homme* to stand a blow like that philosophically. One old gentleman, who was in the habit of reading a Paris newspaper and knew things, chuckled gleefully to everybody that Alcée's conduct was altogether *chic, mais chic*. That he had more *panache* than Boulanger. Well, perhaps he had.

But what he did not show outwardly was that he was in a mood for ugly things to-night. Poor Bobinôt alone felt it vaguely. He discerned a gleam of it in Alcée's handsome eyes, as the young planter stood in the doorway, looking with rather feverish glance upon the assembly, while he laughed and talked with a 'Cadian farmer who was beside him.

Bobinôt himself was dull-looking and clumsy. Most of the men were. But the young women were very beautiful. The eyes that glanced into Alcée's as they

passed him were big, dark, soft as those of the young
heifers standing out in the cool prairie grass.

But the belle was Calixta. Her white dress was not
nearly so handsome or well made as Fronie's (she and
Fronie had quite forgotten the battle on the church
steps, and were friends again), nor were her slippers
so stylish as those of Ozéina; and she fanned herself
with a handkerchief, since she had broken her red fan
at the last ball, and her aunts and uncles were not
willing to give her another. But all the men agreed she
was at her best to-night. Such animation! and abandon!
such flashes of wit!

"Hé, Bobinôt! *Mais* w'at 's the matta? W'at you
standin' *planté là* like ole Ma'ame Tina's cow in the
bog, you?"

That was good. That was an excellent thrust at
Bobinôt, who had forgotten the figure of the dance with
his mind bent on other things, and it started a clamor
of laughter at his expense. He joined good-naturedly.
It was better to receive even such notice as that from
Calixta than none at all. But Madame Suzonne, sitting in a corner, whispered to her neighbor that if
Ozéina were to conduct herself in a like manner, she
should immediately be taken out to the mule-cart and
driven home. The women did not always approve of
Calixta.

Now and then were short lulls in the dance, when
couples flocked out upon the galleries for a brief respite
and fresh air. The moon had gone down pale in the
west, and in the east was yet no promise of day. After
such an interval, when the dancers again assembled to
resume the interrupted quadrille, Calixta was not
among them.

She was sitting upon a bench out in the shadow,
with Alcée beside her. They were acting like fools. He
had attempted to take a little gold ring from her finger;
just for the fun of it, for there was nothing he could
have done with the ring but replace it again. But she
clinched her hand tight. He pretended that it was a
very difficult matter to open it. Then he kept the hand

in his. They seemed to forget about it. He played with
her earring, a thin crescent of gold hanging from her
small brown ear. He caught a wisp of the kinky hair
that had escaped its fastening, and rubbed the ends of
it against his shaven cheek.

"You know, last year in Assumption, Calixta?"
They belonged to the younger generation, so preferred
to speak English.

"Don't come say Assumption to me, M'sieur Alcée.
I done yeard Assumption till I 'm plumb sick."

"Yes, I know. The idiots! Because you were in
Assumption, and I happened to go to Assumption, they
must have it that we went together. But it was nice—
hein, Calixta?—in Assumption?"

They saw Bobinôt emerge from the hall and stand
a moment outside the lighted doorway, peering uneasily and searchingly into the darkness. He did not see
them, and went slowly back.

"There is Bobinôt looking for you. You are going
to set poor Bobinôt crazy. You'll marry him some day;
hein, Calixta?"

"I don't say no, me," she replied, striving to withdraw her hand, which he held more firmly for the
attempt.

"But come, Calixta; you know you said you would
go back to Assumption, just to spite them."

"No, I neva said that, me. You mus' dreamt that."

"Oh, I thought you did. You know I 'm going down
to the city."

"W'en?"

"To-night."

"Betta make has'e, then; it 's mos' day."

"Well, to-morrow 'll do."

"W'at you goin' do, yonda?"

"I don't know. Drown myself in the lake, maybe;
unless you go down there to visit your uncle."

Calixta's senses were reeling; and they well-nigh
left her when she felt Alcée's lips brush her ear like
the touch of a rose.

"Mista Alcée! Is dat Mista Alcée?" the thick voice

of a negro was asking; he stood on the ground, holding to the banister-rails near which the couple sat.

"W'at do you want now?" cried Alcée impatiently. "Can't I have a moment of peace?"

"I been huntin' you high an' low, suh," answered the man. "Dey—dey some one in de road, onda de mulbare-tree, want see you a minute."

"I would n't go out to the road to see the Angel Gabriel. And if you come back here with any more talk, I'll have to break your neck." The negro turned mumbling away.

Alcée and Calixta laughed softly about it. Her boisterousness was all gone. They talked low, and laughed softly, as lovers do.

"Alcée! Alcée Laballière!"

It was not the negro's voice this time; but one that went through Alcée's body like an electric shock, bringing him to his feet.

Clarisse was standing there in her riding-habit, where the negro had stood. For an instant confusion reigned in Alcée's thoughts, as with one who awakes suddenly from a dream. But he felt that something of serious import had brought his cousin to the ball in the dead of night.

"W'at does this mean, Clarisse?" he asked.

"It means something has happen' at home. You mus' come."

"Happened to maman?" he questioned, in alarm.

"No; nénaine is well, and asleep. It is something else. Not to frighten you. But you mus' come. Come with me, Alcée."

There was no need for the imploring note. He would have followed the voice anywhere.

She had now recognized the girl sitting back on the bench.

"Ah, c'est vous, Calixta? Comment ça va, mon enfant?"

"Teha va b'en; et vous, mam'zélle?"

Alcée swung himself over the low rail and started to follow Clarisse, without a word, without a glance back at the girl. He had forgotten he was leaving her there. But Clarisse whispered something to him, and he turned back to say "Good-night, Calixta," and offer his hand to press through the railing. She pretended not to see it.

"How come that? You settin' yere by yo'se'f, Calixta?" It was Bobinôt who found her there alone. The dancers had not yet come out. She looked ghastly in the faint, gray light struggling out of the east.

"Yes, that's me. Go yonda in the *parc aux petits* an' ask Aunt Olisse fu' my hat. She knows w'ere 't is. I want to go home, me."

"How you came?"

"I come afoot, with the Cateaus. But I 'm goin' now. I ent goin' wait fu' 'em. I 'm plumb wo' out, me."

"Kin I go with you, Calixta?"

"I don' care."

They went together across the open prairie and along the edge of the fields, stumbling in the uncertain light. He told her to lift her dress that was getting wet and bedraggled; for she was pulling at the weeds and grasses with her hands.

"I don' care; it 's got to go in the tub, anyway. You been sayin' all along you want to marry me, Bobinôt. Well, if you want, yet, I don' care, me."

The glow of a sudden and overwhelming happiness shone out in the brown, rugged face of the young Acadian. He could not speak, for very joy. It choked him.

"Oh well, if you don' want," snapped Calixta, flippantly, pretending to be piqued at his silence.

"*Bon Dieu!* You know that makes me crazy, w'at you sayin'. You mean that, Calixta? You ent goin' turn roun' agin?"

"I neva tole you that much *yet*, Bobinôt. I mean that. *Tiens*," and she held out her hand in the business-like manner of a man who clinches a bargain with a hand-clasp. Bobinôt grew bold with happiness and asked Calixta to kiss him. She turned her face, that was almost ugly after the night's dissipation, and looked steadily into his.

"I don' want to kiss you, Bobinôt," she said, turning away again, "not to-day. Some other time. *Bonté divine!* ent you satisfy, *yet!*"

"Oh, I 'm satisfy, Calixta," he said.

Riding through a patch of wood, Clarisse's saddle became ungirted, and she and Alcée dismounted to readjust it.

For the twentieth time he asked her what had happened at home.

"But, Clarisse, w'at is it? Is it a misfortune?"

"Ah Dieu sait! It 's only something that happen' to me."

"To you!"

"I saw you go away las' night, Alcée, with those saddle-bags," she said, haltingly, striving to arrange something about the saddle, "an' I made Bruce tell me. He said you had gone to the ball, an' wouldn' be home for weeks an' weeks. I thought, Alcée—maybe you were going to—to Assumption. I got wild. An' then I knew if you did n't come back, *now*, tonight, I could n't stan' it,—again."

She had her face hidden in her arm that she was resting against the saddle when she said that.

He began to wonder if this meant love. But she had to tell him so, before he believed it. And when she told him, he thought the face of the Universe was changed—just like Bobinôt. Was it last week the cyclone had well-nigh ruined him? The cyclone seemed a huge joke, now. It was he, then, who, an hour ago was kissing little Calixta's ear and whispering nonsense into it. Calixta was like a myth, now. The one, only, great reality in the world was Clarisse standing before him, telling him that she loved him.

In the distance they heard the rapid discharge of pistol-shots; but it did not disturb them. They knew it was only the negro musicians who had gone into the yard to fire their pistols into the air, as the custom is, and to announce *"le bal est fini."*

In and Out of Old Natchitoches
1893

Precisely at eight o'clock every morning except Saturdays and Sundays, Mademoiselle Suzanne St. Denys Godolph would cross the railroad trestle that spanned Bayou Boispourri. She might have crossed in the flat which Mr. Alphonse Laballière kept for his own convenience; but the method was slow and unreliable; so, every morning at eight, Mademoiselle St. Denys Godolph crossed the trestle.

She taught public school in a picturesque little white frame structure that stood upon Mr. Laballière's land, and hung upon the very brink of the bayou.

Laballière himself was comparatively a new-comer in the parish. It was barely six months since he decided one day to leave the sugar and rice to his brother Alcée, who had a talent for their cultivation, and to try his hand at cotton-planting. That was why he was up in Natchitoches parish on a piece of rich, high, Cane River land, knocking into shape a tumbled-down plantation that he had bought for next to nothing.

He had often during his perambulations observed the trim, graceful figure stepping cautiously over the ties, and had sometimes shivered for its safety. He always exchanged a greeting with the girl, and once threw a plank over a muddy pool for her to step upon. He caught but glimpses of her features, for she wore an enormous sun-bonnet to shield her complexion, that seemed marvelously fair; while loosely-fitting leather gloves protected her hands. He knew she was the school-teacher, and also that she was the daughter of that very pig-headed old Madame St. Denys Godolph who was hoarding her barren acres across the bayou as a miser hoards gold. Starving over them, some people said. But that was nonsense; nobody starves on a Louisiana plantation, unless it be with suicidal intent.

These things he knew, but he did not know why Mademoiselle St. Denys Godolph always answered his salutation with an air of chilling hauteur that would easily have paralyzed a less sanguine man.

The reason was that Suzanne, like every one else, had heard the stories that were going the rounds about him. People said he was entirely too much at home with the free mulattoes. It seems a dreadful thing to say, and it would be a shocking thing to think of a Laballière; but it was n't true.

When Laballière took possession of his land, he found the plantation-house occupied by one Giestin and his swarming family. It was past reckoning how long the free mulatto and his people had been there. The house was a six-room, long, shambling affair, shrinking together from decrepitude. There was not an entire pane of glass in the structure; and the Turkey-red curtains flapped in and out of the broken apertures. But there is no need to dwell upon details; it was wholly unfit to serve as a civilized human habitation; and Alphonse Laballière would no sooner have disturbed its contented occupants than he would have scattered a family of partridges nesting in a corner of his field. He established himself with a few belongings in the best cabin he could find on the place, and, without further ado, proceeded to supervise the building of house, of gin, of this, that, and the other, and to look into the hundred details that go to set a neglected plantation in good working order. He took his meals at the free mulatto's, quite apart from the family, of course; and they attended, not too skillfully, to his few domestic wants.

Some loafer whom he had snubbed remarked one day in town that Laballière had more use for a free mulatto than he had for a white man. It was a sort of catching thing to say, and suggestive, and was repeated with the inevitable embellishments.

One morning when Laballière sat eating his solitary breakfast, and being waited upon by the queenly Madame Giestin and a brace of her weazened boys, Giestin himself came into the room. He was about half the size of his wife, puny and timid. He stood beside the table, twirling his felt hat aimlessly and balancing himself insecurely on his high-pointed boot-heels.

"Mr. Laballière," he said, "I reckon I tell you; it 's betta you git shed o' me en' my fambly. Jis like you want, yas."

"What in the name of common sense are you talking about?" asked Laballière, looking up abstractedly from his New Orleans paper. Giestin wriggled uncomfortably.

"It 's heap o' story goin' roun' 'bout you, if you want b'lieve me." And he snickered and looked at his wife, who thrust the end of her shawl into her mouth and walked from the room with a tread like the Empress Eugenie's, in that elegant woman's palmiest days.

"Stories!" echoed Laballière, his face the picture of astonishment. "Who—where—what stories?"

"Yon'a in town en' all about. It 's heap o' tale goin' roun', yas. They say how come you mighty fon' o' mulatta. You done shoshiate wid de mulatta down yon'a on de suga plantation, tell you can't res' lessen it 's mulatta roun' you."

Laballière had a distressingly quick temper. His fist, which was a strong one, came down upon the wobbling table with a crash that sent half of Madame Giestin's crockery bouncing and crashing to the floor. He swore an oath that sent Madame Giestin and her father and grandmother, who were all listening in the next room, into suppressed convulsions of mirth.

"Oh, ho! so I'm not to associate with whom I please in Natchitoches parish. We 'll see about that.

Draw up your chair, Giestin. Call your wife and your grandmother and the rest of the tribe, and we 'll breakfast together. By thunder! if I want to hobnob with mulattoes, or negroes or Choctaw Indians or South Sea savages, whose business is it but my own?"

"I don' know, me. It 's jis like I tell you, Mr. Laballière," and Giestin selected a huge key from an assortment that hung against the wall, and left the room.

A half hour later, Laballière had not yet recovered his senses. He appeared suddenly at the door of the schoolhouse, holding by the shoulder one of Giestin's boys. Mademoiselle St. Denys Godolph stood at the opposite extremity of the room. Her sunbonnet hung upon the wall, now, so Laballière could have seen how charming she was, had he not at the moment been blinded by stupidity. Her blue eyes that were fringed with dark lashes reflected astonishment at seeing him there. Her hair was dark like her lashes, and waved softly about her smooth, white forehead.

"Mademoiselle," began Laballière at once, "I have taken the liberty of bringing a new pupil to you."

Mademoiselle St. Denys Godolph paled suddenly and her voice was unsteady when she replied:—

"You are too considerate, Monsieur. Will you be so kine to give me the name of the scholar whom you desire to int'oduce into this school?" She knew it as well as he.

"What 's your name, youngster? Out with it!" cried Laballière, striving to shake the little free mulatto into speech; but he stayed as dumb as a mummy.

"His name is André Giestin. You know him. He is the son"—

"Then, Monsieur," she interrupted, "permit me to remine you that you have made a se'ious mistake. This is not a school conducted fo' the education of the colored population. You will have to go elsew'ere with yo' protégé."

"I shall leave my protégé right here, Mademoiselle, and I trust you 'll give him the same kind attention you seem to accord to the others;" saying which

Laballière bowed himself out of her presence. The little Giestin, left to his own devices, took only the time to give a quick, wary glance around the room, and the next instant he bounded through the open door, as the nimblest of four-footed creatures might have done.

Mademoiselle St. Denys Godolph conducted school during the hours that remained, with a deliberate calmness that would have seemed ominous to her pupils, had they been better versed in the ways of young women. When the hour for dismissal came, she rapped upon the table to demand attention.

"Chil'ren," she began, assuming a resigned and dignified mien, "you all have been witness to-day of the insult that has been offered to yo' teacher by the person upon whose lan' this schoolhouse stan's. I have nothing further to say on that subjec'. I only shall add that to-morrow yo' teacher shall sen' the key of this schoolhouse, together with her resignation, to the gentlemen who compose the school-boa'd." There followed visible disturbance among the young people.

"I ketch that li'le m'latta, I make 'im see sight', yas," screamed one.

"Nothing of the kine, Mathurin, you mus' take no such step, if only out of consideration fo' my wishes. The person who has offered the affront I consider beneath my notice. André, on the other han', is a chile of good impulse, an' by no means to blame. As you all perceive, he has shown mo' taste and judgment than those above him, f'om whom we might have espected good breeding, at least."

She kissed them all, the little boys and the little girls, and had a kind word for each. *"Et toi, mon petit Numa, j'espère qu'un autre"*—She could not finish the sentence, for little Numa, her favorite, to whom she had never been able to impart the first word of English, was blubbering at a turn of affairs which he had only miserably guessed at.

She locked the schoolhouse door and walked away towards the bridge. By the time she reached it, the little 'Cadians had already disappeared like rabbits, down the road and through and over the fences.

Mademoiselle St. Denys Godolph did not cross the trestle the following day, nor the next nor the next. Laballière watched for her; for his big heart was already sore and filled with shame. But more, it stung him with remorse to realize that he had been the stupid instrument in taking the bread, as it were, from the mouth of Mademoiselle St. Denys Godolph.

He recalled how unflinchingly and haughtily her blue eyes had challenged his own. Her sweetness and charm came back to him and he dwelt upon them and exaggerated them, till no Venus, so far unearthed, could in any way approach Mademoiselle St. Denys Godolph. He would have liked to exterminate the Giestin family, from the great-grandmother down to the babe unborn.

Perhaps Giestin suspected this unfavorable attitude, for one morning he piled his whole family and all his effects into wagons, and went away; over into that part of the parish known as *l'Isle des Mulâtres.*

Laballière's really chivalrous nature told him, beside, that he owed an apology, at least, to the young lady who had taken his whim so seriously. So he crossed the bayou one day and penetrated into the wilds where Madame St. Denys Godolph ruled.

An alluring little romance formed in his mind as he went; he fancied how easily it might follow the apology. He was almost in love with Mademoiselle St. Denys Godolph when he quitted his plantation. By the time he had reached hers, he was wholly so.

He was met by Madame mère, a sweet-eyed, faded woman, upon whom old age had fallen too hurriedly to completely efface all traces of youth. But the house was old beyond question; decay had eaten slowly to the heart of it during the hours, the days, and years that it had been standing.

"I have come to see your daughter, Madame," began Laballière, all too bluntly; for there is no denying he was blunt.

"Mademóiselle St. Denys Godolph is not presently at home, sir," Madame replied. "She is at the time in New Orleans. She fills there a place of high trus' an' employment, Monsieur Laballière."

When Suzanne had ever thought of New Orleans, it was always in connection with Hector Santien, because he was the only soul she knew who dwelt there. He had had no share in obtaining for her the position she had secured with one of the leading dry-goods firms; yet it was to him she addressed herself when her arrangements to leave home were completed.

He did not wait for her train to reach the city, but crossed the river and met her at Gretna. The first thing he did was to kiss her, as he had done eight years before when he left Natchitoches parish. An hour later he would no more have thought of kissing Suzanne than he would have tendered an embrace to the Empress of China. For by that time he had realized that she was no longer twelve nor he twenty-four.

She could hardly believe the man who met her to be the Hector of old. His black hair was dashed with gray on the temples; he wore a short, parted beard and a small moustache that curled. From the crown of his glossy silk hat down to his trimly-gaitered feet, his attire was faultless. Suzanne knew her Natchitoches, and she had been to Shreveport and even penetrated as far as Marshall, Texas, but in all her travels she had never met a man to equal Hector in the elegance of his mien.

They entered a cab, and seemed to drive for an interminable time through the streets, mostly over cobble-stones that rendered conversation difficult. Nevertheless he talked incessantly, while she peered from the windows to catch what glimpses she could, through the night, of that New Orleans of which she had heard so much. The sounds were bewildering; so were the lights, that were uneven, too, serving to make the patches of alternating gloom more mysterious.

She had not thought of asking him where he was taking her. And it was only after they crossed Canal and had penetrated some distance into Royal Street, that he told her. He was taking her to a friend of his, the dearest little woman in town. That was Maman Chavan, who was gong to board and lodge her for a ridiculously small consideration.

Maman Chavan lived within comfortable walking distance of Canal Street, on one of those narrow, intersecting streets between Royal and Chartres. Her house was a tiny, single-story one, with overhanging gable, heavily shuttered door and windows and three wooden steps leading down to the banquette. A small garden flanked it on one side, quite screened from outside view by a high fence, over which appeared the tops of orange trees and other luxuriant shrubbery.

She was waiting for them—a lovable, fresh-looking, white-haired, black-eyed, small, fat little body, dressed all in black. She understood no English; which made no difference. Suzanne and Hector spoke but French to each other.

Hector did not tarry a moment longer than was needed to place his young friend and charge in the older woman's care. He would not even stay to take a bite of supper with them. Maman Chavan watched him as he hurried down the steps and out into the gloom. Then she said to Suzanne: "That man is an angel, Mademoiselle, *un ange du bon Dieu.*"

"Women, my dear Maman Chavan, you know how it is with me in regard to women. I have drawn a circle round my heart, so—at pretty long range, mind you—and there is not one who gets through it, or over it or under it."

"*Blagueur, va!*" laughed Maman Chavan, replenishing her glass from the bottle of sauterne.

It was Sunday morning. They were breakfasting together on the pleasant side gallery that led by a single step down to the garden. Hector came every Sunday morning, an hour or so before noon, to breakfast with them. He always brought a bottle of sauterne, a paté, or a mess of artichokes or some tempting bit of *charcuterie*. Sometimes he had to wait till the two women returned from hearing mass at the cathedral. He did not go to mass himself. They were both making a Novena on that account, and had even gone to the expense of burning a round dozen of candles before the good St. Joseph, for his conversion. When Hector accidentally discovered the fact, he offered to pay for the candles, and was distressed at not being permitted to do so.

Suzanne had been in the city more than a month. It was already the close of February, and the air was flower-scented, moist, and deliciously mild.

"As I said: women, my dear Maman Chavan"—

"Let us hear no more about women!" cried Suzanne, impatiently. *"Cher Maître!* but Hector can be tiresome when he wants. Talk, talk; to say what in the end?"

"Quite right, my cousin; when I might have been saying how charming you are this morning. But don't think that I have n't noticed it," and he looked at her with a deliberation that quite unsettled her. She took a letter from her pocket and handed it to him.

"Here, read all the nice things mamma has to say of you, and the love messages she sends to you." He accepted the several closely written sheets from her and began to look over them.

"Ah, la bonne tante," he laughed, when he came to the tender passages that referred to himself. He had pushed aside the glass of wine that he had only partly filled at the beginning of breakfast and that he had scarcely touched. Maman Chavan again replenished her own. She also lighted a cigarette. So did Suzanne, who was learning to smoke. Hector did not smoke; he did not use tobacco in any form, he always said to those who offered him cigars.

Suzanne rested her elbows on the table, adjusted the ruffles about her wrists, puffed awkwardly at her cigarette that kept going out, and hummed the Kyrie Eleison that she had heard so beautifully rendered an hour before at the Cathedral, while she gazed off into the green depths of the garden. Maman Chavan slipped a little silver medal toward her, accompanying the action with a pantomime that Suzanne readily understood. She, in turn, secretly and adroitly transferred the medal to Hector's coat-pocket. He noticed the action plainly enough, but pretended not to.

"Natchitoches has n't changed," he commented. "The everlasting *can-cans!* when will they have done with them? This is n't little Athénaïse Miché, getting married! *Sapristi!* but it makes one old! And old Papa Jean-Pierre only dead now? I thought he was out of purgatory five years ago. And who is this Laballière? One of the Laballières of St. James?"

"St. James, *mon cher.* Monsieur Alphonse Laballière; an aristocrat from the 'golden coast.' But it is a history, if you will believe me. *Figurez vous,* Maman Chavan,—*pensez donc, mon ami"*—And with much dramatic fire, during which the cigarette went irrevocably out, she proceeded to narrate her experiences with Laballière.

"Impossible!" exclaimed Hector when the climax was reached; but his indignation was not so patent as she would have liked it to be.

"And to think of an affront like that going unpunished!" was Maman Chavan's more sympathetic comment.

"Oh, the scholars were only too ready to offer violence to poor little André, but that, you can understand, I would not permit. And now, here is mamma gone completely over to him; entrapped, God only knows how!"

"Yes," agreed Hector, "I see he has been sending her tamales and *boudin blanc.*"

"*Boudin blanc,* my friend! If it were only that! But I have a stack of letters, so high,—I could show them to you,—singing of Laballière, Laballière, enough to drive one distracted. He visits her constantly. He is a man of attainment, she says, a man of courage, a man of heart; and the best of company. He has sent her a bunch of fat robins as big as a tub"—

"There is something in that—a good deal in that, mignonne," piped Maman Chavan, approvingly.

"And now *boudin blanc!* and she tells me it is the duty of a Christian to forgive. Ah, no; it 's no use; mamma's ways are past finding out."

Suzanne was never in Hector's company elsewhere than at Maman Chavan's. Beside the Sunday visit, he looked in upon them sometimes at dusk, to chat for a moment or two. He often treated them to theatre tickets, and even to the opera, when business was brisk. Business meant a little notebook that he carried in his pocket, in which he sometimes dotted down orders from the country people for wine, that he sold on commission. The women always went together, unaccompanied by any male escort; trotting along, arm in arm, and brimming with enjoyment.

That same Sunday afternoon Hector walked with them a short distance when they were on their way to vespers. The three walking abreast almost occupied the narrow width of the banquette. A gentleman who had just stepped out of the Hotel Royal stood aside to better enable them to pass. He lifted his hat to Suzanne, and cast a quick glance, that pictured stupefaction and wrath, upon Hector.

"It 's he!" exclaimed the girl, melodramatically seizing Maman Chavan's arm.

"Who, he?"

"Laballière!"

"No!"

"Yes!"

"A handsome fellow, all the same," nodded the little lady, approvingly. Hector thought so too. The conversation again turned upon Laballière, and so continued till they reached the side door of the cathedral, where the young man left his two companions.

In the evening Laballière called upon Suzanne. Maman Chavan closed the front door carefully after he entered the small parlor, and opened the side one that looked into the privacy of the garden. Then she lighted the lamp and retired, just as Suzanne entered.

The girl bowed a little stiffly, if it may be said that she did anything stiffly. "Monsieur Laballière." That was all she said.

"Mademoiselle St. Denys Godolph," and that was all he said. But ceremony did not sit easily upon him.

"Mademoiselle," he began, as soon as seated, "I am here as the bearer of a message from your mother. You must understand that otherwise I would not be here."

"I do understan', sir, that you an' maman have become very warm frien's during my absence," she returned, in measured, conventional tones.

"It pleases me immensely to hear that from you," he responded, warmly; "to believe that Madame St. Denys Godolph is my friend."

Suzanne coughed more affectedly than was quite nice, and patted her glossy braids. "The message, if you please, Mr. Laballière."

"To be sure," pulling himself together from the momentary abstraction into which he had fallen in contemplating her. "Well, it 's just this; your mother, you must know, has been good enough to sell me a fine bit of land—a deep strip along the bayou"—

"Impossible! *Mais* w'at sorcery did you use to obtain such a thing of my mother, Mr. Laballière? Lan' that has been in the St. Denys Godolph family since time untole!"

"No sorcery whatever, Mademoiselle, only an appeal to your mother's intelligence and common sense; and she is well supplied with both. She wishes me to say, further, that she desires your presence very urgently and your immediate return home."

"My mother is unduly impatient, surely," replied Suzanne, with chilling politeness.

"May I ask, mademoiselle," he broke in, with an abruptness that was startling, "the name of the man with whom you were walking this afternoon?"

She looked at him with unaffected astonishment, and told him: "I hardly understan' yo' question. That gentleman is Mr. Hector Santien, of one of the firs' families of Natchitoches; a warm ole frien' an' far distant relative of mine."

"Oh, that's his name, is it, Hector Santien? Well,

please don't walk on the New Orleans streets again with Mr. Hector Santien."

"Yo' remarks would be insulting if they were not so highly amusing, Mr. Laballière."

"I beg your pardon if I am insulting; and I have no desire to be amusing," and then Laballière lost his head. "You are at liberty to walk the streets with whom you please, of course," he blurted, with ill-suppressed passion, "but if I encounter Mr. Hector Santien in your company again, in public, I shall wring his neck, then and there, as I would a chicken; I shall break every bone in his body"—Suzanne had arisen.

"You have said enough, sir. I even desire no explanation of yo' words."

"I did n't intend to explain them," he retorted, stung by the insinuation.

"You will excuse me further," she requested icily, motioning to retire.

"Not till—oh, not till you have forgiven me," he cried impulsively, barring her exit; for repentance had come swiftly this time.

But she did not forgive him. "I can wait," she said. Then he stepped aside and she passed by him without a second glance.

She sent word to Hector the following day to come to her. And when he was there, in the late afternoon, they walked together to the end of the vine-sheltered gallery,—where the air was redolent with the odor of spring blossoms.

"Hector," she began, after a while, "some one has told me I should not be seen upon the streets of New Orleans with you."

He was trimming a long rose-stem with his sharp penknife. He did not stop nor start, nor look embarrassed, nor anything of the sort.

"Indeed!" he said.

"But, you know," she went on, "if the saints came down from heaven to tell me there was a reason for it, I could n't believe them."

"You would n't believe them, *ma petite Suzanne?*"

He was getting all the thorns off nicely, and stripping away the heavy lower leaves.

"I want you to look me in the face, Hector, and tell me if there is any reason."

He snapped the knife-blade and replaced the knife in his pocket; then he looked in her eyes, so unflinchingly, that she hoped and believed it presaged a confession of innocence that she would gladly have accepted. But he said indifferently: "Yes, there are reasons."

"Then I say there are not," she exclaimed excitedly; "you are amusing yourself—laughing at me, as you always do. There are no reasons that I will hear or believe. You will walk the streets with me, will you not, Hector?" she entreated, "and go to church with me on Sunday; and, and—oh, it 's nonsense, nonsense for you to say things like that!"

He held the rose by its long, hardy stem, and swept it lightly and caressingly across her forehead, along her cheek, and over her pretty mouth and chin, as a lover might have done with his lips. He noticed how the red rose left a crimson stain behind it.

She had been standing, but now she sank upon the bench that was there, and buried her face in her palms. A slight convulsive movement of the muscles indicated a suppressed sob.

"Ah, Suzanne, Suzanne, you are not going to make yourself unhappy about a *bon à rien* like me. Come, look at me; tell me that you are not." He drew her hands down from her face and held them a while, bidding her good-by. His own face wore the quizzical look it often did, as if he were laughing at her.

"That work at the store is telling on your nerves, *mignonne*. Promise me that you will go back to the country. That will be best."

"Oh, yes; I am going back home, Hector."

"That is right, little cousin," and he patted her hands kindly, and laid them both down gently into her lap.

He did not return; neither during the week nor the following Sunday. Then Suzanne told Maman Cha-

van she was going home. The girl was not too deeply
in love with Hector; but imagination counts for something, and so does youth.

Laballière was on the train with her. She felt,
somehow, that he would be. And yet she did not dream
that he had watched and waited for her each morning
since he parted from her.

He went to her without preliminary of manner or
speech, and held out his hand; she extended her own
unhesitatingly. She could not understand why, and she
was a little too weary to strive to do so. It seemed as
though the sheer force of his will would carry him to
the goal of his wishes.

He did not weary her with attentions during the
time they were together. He sat apart from her, con-
versing for the most time with friends and acquaintances who belonged in the sugar district through
which they traveled in the early part of the day.

She wondered why he had ever left that section to
go up into Natchitoches. Then she wondered if he did
not mean to speak to her at all. As if he had read the
thought, he went and sat down beside her.

He showed her, away off across the country, where
his mother lived, and his brother Alcée, and his cousin
Clarisse.

On Sunday morning, when Maman Chavan strove
to sound the depth of Hector's feeling for Suzanne, he
told her again: "Women, my dear Maman Chavan, you
know how it is with me in regard to women,"—and he
refilled her glass from the bottle of sauterne.

"Farceur va!" and Maman Chavan laughed, and
her fat shoulders quivered under the white *volante* she
wore.

A day or two later, Hector was walking down Canal
Street at four in the afternoon. He might have posed,
as he was, for a fashion-plate. He looked not to the
right nor to the left; not even at the women who passed
by. Some of them turned to look at him.

When he approached the corner of Royal, a young man who stood there nudged his companion.

"You know who that is?" he said, indicating Hector.

"No; who?"

"Well, you are an innocent. Why, that 's Deroustan, the most notorious gambler in New Orleans."

Mamouche
1893

Mamouche stood within the open doorway, which he had just entered. It was night; the rain was falling in torrents, and the water trickled from him as it would have done from an umbrella, if he had carried one.

Old Doctor John-Luis, who was toasting his feet before a blazing hickory-wood fire, turned to gaze at the youngster through his spectacles. Marshall, the old negro who had opened the door at the boy's knock, also looked down at him, and indignantly said:

"G'long back on de gall'ry an' drip yo'se'f! W'at Cynthy gwine say tomorrow w'en she see dat flo' mess' up dat away?"

"Come to the fire and sit down," said Doctor John-Luis.

Doctor John-Luis was a bachelor. He was small and thin; he wore snuff-colored clothes that were a little too large for him, and spectacles. Time had not deprived him of an abundant crop of hair that had once been red, and was not now more than half-bleached.

The boy looked irresolutely from master to man; then went and sat down beside the fire on a split-bottom chair. He sat so close to the blaze that had he been an apple he would have roasted. As he was but a small boy, clothed in wet rags, he only steamed.

Marshall grumbled audibly, and Doctor John-Luis continued to inspect the boy through his glasses.

"Marsh, bring him something to eat," he commanded, tentatively.

Marshall hesitated, and challenged the child with a speculating look.

"Is you w'ite o' is you black?" he asked. "Dat w'at I wants ter know 'fo' I kiar' victuals to yo in de settin'-room."

"I'm w'ite, me," the boy responded, promptly.

"I ain't disputin'; go ahead. All right fer dem w'at wants ter take yo' wud fer it." Doctor John-Luis coughed behind his hand and said nothing.

Marshall brought a platter of cold food to the boy, who rested the dish upon his knees and ate from it with keen appetite.

"Where do you come from?" asked Doctor John-Luis, when his caller stopped for breath. Mamouche turned a pair of big, soft, dark eyes upon his questioner.

"I come from Cloutierville this mo'nin'. I been try to git to the twenty-fo'-mile ferry w'en de rain ketch me."

"What were you going to do at the twenty-four-mile ferry?"

The boy gazed absently into the fire. "I don' know w'at I was goin' to do yonda to the twenty-fo'-mile ferry," he said.

Then you must be a tramp, to be wandering aimlessly about the country in that way!" exclaimed the doctor.

"No; I don' b'lieve I'm a tramp, me." Mamouche was wriggling his toes with enjoyment of the warmth and palatable food.

"Well, what's your name?" continued Doctor John-Luis.

"My name it's Mamouche."

" 'Mamouche.' Fiddlesticks! That's no name."

The boy looked as if he regretted the fact, while not being able to help it.

"But my pa, his name it was Mathurin Peloté," he offered in some palliation.

"Peloté! Peloté!" mused Doctor John-Luis. "Any

kin to Théodule Peloté who lived formerly in Avoyelles parish?"

"W'y, yas!" laughed Mamouche. "Théodule Peloté, it was my gran'pa."

"Your grandfather? Well, upon my word!" He looked again, critically, at the youngster's rags. "Then Stéphanie Galopin must have been your grandmother!"

"Yas," responded Mamouche, complacently; "that was who was my gran'ma. She die two year ago down by Alexandria."

"Marsh," called Doctor John-Luis, turning in his chair, "bring him a mug of milk and another piece of pie!"

When Mamouche had eaten all the good things that were set before him, he found that one side of him was quite dry, and he transferred himself over to the other corner of the fire so as to turn to the blaze the side which was still wet.

The action seemed to amuse Doctor John-Luis, whose old head began to fill with recollections.

"That reminds me of Théodule," he laughed. "Ah, he was a great fellow, your father, Théodule!"

"My gran'pa," corrected Mamouche.

"Yes, yes, your grandfather. He was handsome; I tell you, he was good-looking. And the way he could dance and play the fiddle and sing! Let me see, how did that song go that he used to sing when we went out serenading: 'A ta—à ta—'

> 'A ta fenêtre
> Daignes paraître—tra la la la!' "

Doctor John-Luis' voice, even in his youth, could not have been agreeable; and now it bore no resemblance to any sound that Mamouche had ever heard issue from a human throat. The boy kicked his heels and rolled sideward on his chair with enjoyment. Doctor John-Luis laughed even more heartily, finished the stanza, and sang another one through.

"That's what turned the girls' heads, I tell you, my

boy," said he, when he had recovered his breath; "that fiddling and dancing and tra la la."

During the next hour the old man lived again through his youth; through any number of alluring experiences with his friend Théodule, that merry fellow who had never done a steady week's work in his life; and Stéphanie, the pretty Acadian girl, whom he had never wholly understood, even to this day.

It was quite late when Doctor John-Luis climbed the stairs that led from the sitting-room up to his bedchamber. As he went, followed by the ever attentive Marshall, he was singing:

> "A ta fenêtre
> Daignes paraître,"

but very low, so as not to awaken Mamouche, whom he left sleeping upon a bed that Marshall at his order had prepared for the boy beside the sitting-room fire.

At a very early hour next morning Marshall appeared at his master's bedside with the accustomed morning coffee.

"What is he doing?" asked Doctor John-Luis, as he sugared and stirred the tiny cup of black coffee.

"Who dat, sah?"

"Why, the boy, Mamouche. What is he doing?"

"He gone, sah. He done gone."

"Gone!"

"Yas, sah. He roll his bed up in de corner; he onlock de do'; he gone. But de silver an' ev'thing dah; he ain't kiar' nuttin' off."

"Marshall," snapped Doctor John-Luis, ill-humoredly, "there are times when you don't seem to have sense and penetration enough to talk about! I think I'll take another nap," he grumbled, as he turned his back upon Marshall. "Wake me at seven."

It was no ordinary thing for Doctor John-Luis to be in a bad humor, and perhaps it is not strictly true to say that he was now. He was only in a little less amiable mood than usual when he pulled on his high rubber boots and went splashing out in the wet to see what his people were doing.

He might have owned a large plantation had he wished to own one, for a long life of persistent, intelligent work had left him with a comfortable fortune in his old age; but he preferred the farm on which he lived contentedly and raised an abundance to meet his modest wants.

He went down to the orchard, where a couple of men were busying themselves in setting out a line of young fruit-trees.

"Tut, tut, tut!" They were doing it all wrong; the line was not straight; the holes were not deep. It was strange that he had to come down there and discover such things with his old eyes!

He poked his head into the kitchen to complain to Prudence about the ducks that she had not seasoned properly the day before, and to hope that the accident would never occur again.

He tramped over to where a carpenter was working on a gate; securing it—as he meant to secure all the gates upon his place—with great patent clamps and ingenious hinges, intended to baffle utterly the designs of the evil-disposed persons who had lately been tampering with them. For there had been a malicious spirit abroad, who played tricks, it seemed, for pure wantonness upon the farmers and planters, and caused them infinite annoyance.

As Dr. John-Luis contemplated the carpenter at work, and remembered how his gates had recently all been lifted from their hinges one night and left lying upon the ground, the provoking nature of the offense dawned upon him as it had not done before. He turned swiftly, prompted by a sudden determination, and re-entered the house.

Then he proceeded to write out in immense black characters a half-dozen placards. It was an offer of twenty-five dollars' reward for the capture of the person guilty of the malicious offence already described. These placards were sent abroad with the same eager haste that had conceived and executed them.

After a day or two, Doctor John-Luis' ill humor had resolved itself into a pensive melancholy.

"Marsh," he said, "you know, after all, it's rather dreary to be living alone as I do, without any companion—of my own color, you understand."

"I knows dat, sah. It sho' am lonesome," replied the sympathetic Marshall.

"You see, Marsh, I've been thinking lately," and Doctor John-Luis coughed, for he disliked the inaccuracy of that "lately." "I've been thinking that this property and wealth that I've worked so hard to accumulate, are after all doing no permanent, practical good to any one. Now, if I could find some well-disposed boy whom I might train to work, to study, to lead a decent, honest life—a boy of good heart who would care for me in my old age; for I am still comparatively—hem—not old? hey, Marsh?"

"Dey ain't one in de pa'ish hole yo' own like you does, sah."

"That's it. Now, can you think of such a boy? Try to think."

Marshall slowly scratched his head and looked reflective.

"If you can think of such a boy," said Doctor John-Luis, "you might bring him here to spend an evening with me, you know, without hinting at my intentions, of course. In that way I could sound him; study him up, as it were. For a step of such importance is not to be taken without due consideration, Marsh."

Well, the first whom Marshall brought was one of Baptiste Choupic's boys. He was a very timid child, and sat on the edge of his chair, fearfully. He replied in jerky monosyllables when Doctor John-Luis spoke to him, "Yas, sah—no, sah," as the case might be; with a little nervous bob of the head.

His presence made the doctor quite uncomfortable. He was glad to be rid of the boy at nine o'clock, when he sent him home with some oranges and a few sweetmeats.

Then Marshall had Theodore over; an unfortunate selection that evinced little judgment on Marshall's part. Not to mince matters, the boy was painfully forward. He monopolized the conversation; asked impertinent questions and handled and inspected everything in the room. Dr. John-Luis sent him home with an orange and not a single sweet.

Then there was Hyppolite, who was too ugly to be thought of; and Cami, who was heavy and stupid, and fell asleep in his chair with his mouth wide open. And so it went. If Doctor John-Luis had hoped in the company of any of these boys to repeat the agreeable evening he had passed with Mamouche, he was sadly deceived.

At last he instructed Marshall to discontinue the search of that ideal companion he had dreamed of. He was resigned to spend the remainder of his days without one.

Then, one day when it was raining again, and very muddy and chill, a red-faced man came driving up to Doctor John-Luis' door in a dilapidated buggy. He lifted a boy from the vehicle, whom he held with a vise-like clutch, and whom he straightway dragged into the astonished presence of Doctor John-Luis.

"Here he is, sir," shouted the red-faced man. "We've got him at last! Here he is."

It was Mamouche, covered with mud, the picture of misery. Doctor John-Luis stood with his back to the fire. He was startled, and visibly and painfully moved at the sight of the boy.

"Is it possible!" he exclaimed. "Then it was you, Mamouche, who did this mischievous thing to me? Lifting my gates from their hinges; letting the chickens in among my flowers to ruin them; and the hogs and cattle to trample and uproot my vegetables!"

"Ha! ha!" laughed the red-faced man, "that game's played out, now;" and Doctor John-Luis looked as if he wanted to strike him.

Mamouche seemed unable to reply. His lower lip was quivering.

"Yas, it's me!" he burst out. "It's me w'at take yo' gates off the hinge. It's me w'at turn loose Mr. Morgin's hoss, w'en Mr. Morgin was passing *veillée* wid his sweet-

heart. It's me w'at take down Ma'ame Angèle's fence, an'
lef her calf loose to tramp in Mr. Billy's cotton. It's me
w'at play like a ghos' by the graveyard las' Toussaint to
scare the darkies passin' in the road. It's me w'at—"

The confession had burst out from the depth of
Mamouche's heart like a torrent, and there is no telling
when it would have stopped if Doctor John-Luis had
not enjoined silence.

"And pray tell me," he asked, as severely as he
could, "why you left my house like a criminal, in the
morning, secretly?"

The tears had begun to course down Mamouche's
brown cheeks.

"I was 'shame' of myse'f, that's w'y. If you wouldn'
gave me no suppa, an' no bed, an' no fire, I don' say.
I wouldn' been 'shame' then."

"Well, sir," interrupted the red-faced man, "you've
got a pretty square case against him, I see. Not only
for malicious trespass, but of theft. See this bolt?" producing a piece of iron from his coat pocket. "That's
what gave him away."

"I en't no thief!" blurted Mamouche, indignantly.
"It's one piece o' iron w'at I pick up in the road."

"Sir," said Doctor John-Luis with dignity, "I can
understand how the grandson of Théodule Peloté might
be guilty of such mischievous pranks as this boy has
confessed to. But I know that the grandson of Stéphanie
Galopin could not be a thief."

And he at once wrote out the check for twenty-
five dollars, and handed it to the red-faced man with
the tips of his fingers.

It seemed very good to Doctor John-Luis to have
the boy sitting again at his fireside; and so natural, too.
He seemed to be the incarnation of unspoken hopes;
the realization of vague and fitful memories of the past.

When Mamouche kept on crying, Doctor John-
Luis wiped away the tears with his own brown silk
handkerchief.

"Mamouche," he said, "I want you to stay here; to
live here with me always. To learn how to work; to
learn how to study; to grow up to be an honorable man.

An honorable man, Mamouche, for I want you for my own child."

His voice was pretty low and husky when he said that.

"I shall not take the key from the door tonight," he continued. "If you do not choose to stay and be all this that I say, you may open the door and walk out. I shall use no force to keep you."

"What is he doing, Marsh?" asked Doctor John-Luis the following morning, when he took the coffee that Marshall had brought to him in bed.

"Who dat, sah?"

"Why, the boy Mamouche, of course. What is he doing?"

Marshall laughed.

"He kneelin' down dah on de flo'. He keep on sayin', 'Hail, Mary, full o' grace, de Lord is wid dee. Hail, Mary, full o' grace'—t'ree, fo' times, sah. I tell 'im, 'W'at you sayin' yo' prayer dat away, boy?' He 'low dat w'at his gran'ma larn 'im, ter keep outen mischief. W'en de devil say, 'Take dat gate offen de hinge; do dis; do dat,' he gwine say t'ree Hail Mary, an' de devil gwine tu'n tail an' run."

"Yes, yes," laughed Doctor John-Luis. "That's Sté-phanie all over."

"An' I tell 'im: See heah, boy, you drap a couple o' dem Hail Mary, an' quit studyin' 'bout de devil, an' sot yo'se'f down ter wuk. Dat the oniest way to keep outen mischief."

"What business is it of yours to interfere?" broke in Doctor John-Luis, irritably. "Let the boy do as his grandmother instructed him."

"I ain't desputin', sah," apologized Marshall.

"But you know, Marsh," continued the doctor, re-covering his usual amiability. "I think we'll be able to do something with the boy. I'm pretty sure of it. For, you see, he has his grandmother's eyes; and his grand-mother was a very intelligent woman; a clever woman, Marsh. Her one great mistake was when she married Théodule Peloté."

Madame Célestin's
Divorce
1893

Madame Célestin always wore a neat and snugly fitting calico wrapper when she went out in the morning to sweep her small gallery. Lawyer Paxton thought she looked very pretty in the gray one that was made with a graceful Watteau fold at the back: and with which she invariably wore a bow of pink ribbon at the throat. She was always sweeping her gallery when lawyer Paxton passed by in the morning on his way to his office in St. Denis Street.

Sometimes he stopped and leaned over the fence to say good-morning at his ease; to criticise or admire her rosebushes; or, when he had time enough, to hear what she had to say. Madame Célestin usually had a good deal to say. She would gather up the train of her calico wrapper in one hand, and balancing the broom gracefully in the other, would go tripping down to where the lawyer leaned, as comfortably as he could, over her picket fence.

Of course she had talked to him of her troubles. Every one knew Madame Célestin's troubles.

"Really, madame," he told her once, in his deliberate, calculating, lawyer-tone, "it 's more than human nature—woman's nature—should be called upon to endure. Here you are, working your fingers off"—she glanced down at two rosy finger-tips that showed through the rents in her baggy doeskin gloves—"taking in sewing; giving music lessons; doing God knows what in the way of manual labor to support yourself and those two little ones"—Madame Célestin's pretty face beamed with satisfaction at this enumeration of her trials.

"You right, Judge. Not a picayune, not one, not one, have I lay my eyes on in the pas' fo'months that I can say Célestin give it to me or sen' it to me."

"The scoundrel!" muttered lawyer Paxton in his beard.

"An' *pourtant*," she resumed, "they say he 's making money down roun' Alexandria w'en he wants to work."

"I dare say you have n't seen him for months?" suggested the lawyer.

"It 's good six month' since I seen a sight of Célestin," she admitted.

"That 's it, that 's what I say; he has practically deserted you; fails to support you. It wouldn't surprise me a bit to learn that he has ill treated you."

"Well, you know, Judge," with an evasive cough, "a man that drinks—w'at can you expec'? An' if you would know the promises he has made me! Ah, if I had as many dolla' as I had promise from Célestin, I would n' have to work, *je vous garantis*."

"And in my opinion, Madame, you would be a foolish woman to endure it longer, when the divorce court is there to offer you redress."

"You spoke about that befo', Judge; I 'm goin' think about that divo'ce. I believe you right."

Madame Célestin thought about the divorce and talked about it, too; and lawyer Paxton grew deeply interested in the theme.

"You know, about that divo'ce, Judge," Madame Célestin was waiting for him that morning, "I been talking to my family an' my frien's, an' it 's me that tells you, they all plumb agains' that divo'ce."

"Certainly, to be sure; that 's to be expected, Madame, in this community of Creoles. I warned you that you would meet with opposition, and would have to face it and brave it."

"Oh, don't fear, I'm going to face it! Maman says it's a disgrace like it's neva been in the family. But it's good for Maman to talk, her. W'at trouble she ever had? She says I mus' go by all means consult with Père Duchéron—it's my confessor, you undastan'—Well, I'll go, Judge, to please Maman. But all the confessor' in the worl' ent goin' make me put up with that conduc' of Célestin any longa."

A day or two later, she was there waiting for him again. "You know, Judge, about that divo'ce."

"Yes, yes," responded the lawyer, well pleased to trace a new determination in her brown eyes and in the curves of her pretty mouth. "I suppose you saw Père Duchéron and had to brave it out with him, too."

"Oh, fo' that, a perfec' sermon, I assho you. A talk of giving scandal an' bad example that I thought would neva en'! He says, fo' him, he wash' his hands; I mus' go see the bishop."

"You won't let the bishop dissuade you, I trust," stammered the lawyer more anxiously than he could well understand.

"You don't know me yet, Judge," laughed Madame Célestin with a turn of the head and a flirt of the broom which indicated that the interview was at an end.

"Well, Madame Célestin! And the bishop!" Lawyer Paxton was standing there holding to a couple of the shaky pickets. She had not seen him. "Oh, it's you, Judge?" and she hastened towards him with an *empressement* that could not but have been flattering.

"Yes, I saw Monseigneur," she began. The lawyer had already gathered from her expressive countenance that she had not wavered in her determination. "Ah, he's a eloquent man. It's not a mo' eloquent man in Natchitoches parish. I was fo'ced to cry, the way he talked to me about my troubles; how he undastan's them, an' feels for me. It would move even you, Judge, to hear how he talk' about that step I want to take; its danga, its temptation. How it is the duty of a Catholic

to stan' everything till the las' extreme. An' that life of
retirement an' self-denial I would have to lead,—he
told me all that."

"But he has n't turned you from your resolve, I
see," laughed the lawyer complacently.

"For that, no," she returned emphatically. "The
bishop don't know w'at it is to be married to a man
like Célestin, an' have to endu' that conduc' like I have
to endu' it. The Pope himse'f can't make me stan' that
any longer, if you say I got the right in the law to sen'
Célestin sailing."

A noticeable change had come over lawyer Paxton.
He discarded his work-day coat and began to wear his
Sunday one to the office. He grew solicitous as to the
shine of his boots, his collar, and the set of his tie. He
brushed and trimmed his whiskers with a care that had
not before been apparent. Then he fell into a stupid
habit of dreaming as he walked the streets of the old
town. It would be very good to take unto himself a
wife, he dreamed. And he could dream of no other
than pretty Madame Célestin filling that sweet and sacred office as she filled his thoughts, now. Old Natchitoches would not hold them comfortably, perhaps; but
the world was surely wide enough to live in, outside
of Natchitoches town.

His heart beat in a strangely irregular manner as
he neared Madame Célestin's house one morning, and
discovered her behind the rosebushes, as usual plying
her broom. She had finished the gallery and steps and
was sweeping the little brick walk along the edge of
the violet border.

"Good-morning, Madame Célestin."

"Ah, it 's you, Judge? Good-morning." He waited.
She seemed to be doing the same. Then she ventured, with some hesitancy, "You know, Judge, about
that divo'ce. I been thinking,—I reckon you betta
neva mine about that divo'ce." She was making deep
rings in the palm of her gloved hand with the end of
the broomhandle, and looking at them critically. Her
face seemed to the lawyer to be unusually rosy; but
maybe it was only the reflection of the pink bow at

the throat. "Yes, I reckon you need n' mine. You see, Judge, Célestin came home las' night. An' he 's promise me on his word an' honor he 's going to turn ova a new leaf."

A Matter of Prejudice
1893

Madame Carambeau wanted it strictly understood that she was not to be disturbed by Gustave's birthday party. They carried her big rocking-chair from the back gallery, that looked out upon the garden where the children were going to play, around to the front gallery, which closely faced the green levee bank and the Mississippi coursing almost flush with the top of it.

The house—an old Spanish one, broad, low and completely encircled by a wide gallery—was far down in the French quarter of New Orleans. It stood upon a square of ground that was covered thick with a semitropical growth of plants and flowers. An impenetrable board fence, edged with a formidable row of iron spikes, shielded the garden from the prying glances of the occasional passer-by.

Madame Carambeau's widowed daughter, Madame Cécile Lalonde, lived with her. This annual party, given to her little son, Gustave, was the one defiant act of Madame Lalonde's existence. She persisted in it, to her own astonishment and the wonder of those who knew her and her mother.

For old Madame Carambeau was a woman of many prejudices—so many, in fact, that it would be difficult to name them all. She detested dogs, cats, organgrinders, white servants and children's noises. She despised Americans, Germans and all people of a different faith from her own. Anything not French had, in her opinion, little right to existence.

She had not spoken to her son Henri for ten years because he had married an American girl from Prytania street. She would not permit green tea to be introduced into her house, and those who could not or would not drink coffee might drink tisane of *fleur de Laurier* for all she cared.

Nevertheless, the children seemed to be having it all their own way that day, and the organ-grinders were let loose. Old madame, in her retired corner, could hear the screams, the laughter and the music far more distinctly than she liked. She rocked herself noisily, and hummed "Partant pour la Syrie."

She was straight and slender. Her hair was white, and she wore it in puffs on the temples. Her skin was fair and her eyes blue and cold.

Suddenly she became aware that footsteps were approaching, and threatening to invade her privacy— not only footsteps, but screams! Then two little children, one in hot pursuit of the other, darted wildly around the corner near which she sat.

The child in advance, a pretty little girl, sprang excitedly into Madame Carambeau's lap, and threw her arms convulsively around the old lady's neck. Her companion lightly struck her a "last tag," and ran laughing gleefully away.

The most natural thing for the child to do then would have been to wriggle down from madame's lap, without a "thank you" or a "by your leave," after the manner of small and thoughtless children. But she did not do this. She stayed there, panting and fluttering, like a frightened bird.

Madame was greatly annoyed. She moved as if to put the child away from her, and scolded her sharply for being boisterous and rude. The little one, who did not understand French, was not disturbed by the reprimand, and stayed on in madame's lap. She rested her plump little cheek, that was hot and flushed, against the soft white linen of the old lady's gown.

Her cheek was very hot and very flushed. It was dry, too, and so were her hands. The child's breathing was quick and irregular. Madame was not long in detecting these signs of disturbance.

Though she was a creature of prejudice, she was nevertheless a skillful and accomplished nurse, and a connoisseur in all matters pertaining to health. She prided herself upon this talent, and never lost an opportunity of exercising it. She would have treated an organ-grinder with tender consideration if one had presented himself in the character of an invalid.

Madame's manner toward the little one changed immediately. Her arms and her lap were at once adjusted so as to become the most comfortable of resting places. She rocked very gently to and fro. She fanned the child softly with her palm leaf fan, and sang "Partant pour la Syrie" in a low and agreeable tone.

The child was perfectly content to lie still and prattle a little in that language which madame thought hideous. But the brown eyes were soon swimming in drowsiness, and the little body grew heavy with sleep in madame's clasp.

When the little girl slept Madame Carambeau arose, and treading carefully and deliberately, entered her room, that opened near at hand upon the gallery. The room was large, airy and inviting, with its cool matting upon the floor, and its heavy, old, polished mahogany furniture. Madame, with the child still in her arms, pulled a bell-cord; then she stood waiting, swaying gently back and forth. Presently an old black woman answered the summons. She wore gold hoops in her ears, and a bright bandanna knotted fantastically on her head.

"Louise, turn down the bed," commanded madame. "Place that small, soft pillow below the bolster. Here is a poor little unfortunate creature whom Providence must have driven into my arms." She laid the child carefully down.

"Ah, those Americans! Do they deserve to have children? Understanding as little as they do how to take care of them!" said madame, while Louise was mumbling an accompanying assent that would have been unintelligible to any one unacquainted with the negro patois.

"There, you see, Louise, she is burning up," remarked madame; "she is consumed. Unfasten the little bodice while I lift her. Ah, talk to me of such parents! So stupid as not to perceive a fever like that coming on, but they must dress their child up like a monkey to go play and dance to the music of organ-grinders.

"Haven't you better sense, Louise, than to take off a child's shoe as if you were removing the boot from the leg of a cavalry officer?" Madame would have required fairy fingers to minister to the sick. "Now go to Mamzelle Cécile, and tell her to send me one of those old, soft, thin nightgowns that Gustave wore two summers ago."

When the woman retired, madame busied herself with concocting a cooling pitcher of orange-flower water, and mixing a fresh supply of *eau sédative* with which agreeably to sponge the little invalid.

Madame Lalonde came herself with the old, soft nightgown. She was a pretty, blonde, plump little woman, with the deprecatory air of one whose will has become flaccid from want of use. She was mildly distressed at what her mother had done.

"But, mamma! But, mamma, the child's parents will be sending the carriage for her in a little while. Really, there was no use. Oh dear! oh dear!"

If the bedpost had spoken to Madame Carambeau, she would have paid more attention, for speech from such a source would have been at least surprising if not convincing. Madame Lalonde did not possess the faculty of either surprising or convincing her mother.

"Yes, the little one will be quite comfortable in this," said the old lady, taking the garment from her daughter's irresolute hands.

"But, mamma! What shall I say, what shall I do when they send? Oh, dear; oh, dear!"

"That is your business," replied madame, with

lofty indifference. "My concern is solely with a sick child that happens to be under my roof. I think I know my duty at this time of life, Cécile."

As Madame Lalonde predicted, the carriage soon came, with a stiff English coachman driving it, and a red-cheeked Irish nurse-maid seated inside. Madame would not even permit the maid to see her little charge. She had an original theory that the Irish voice is distressing to the sick.

Madame Lalonde sent the girl away with a long letter of explanation that must have satisfied the parents; for the child was left undisturbed in Madame Carambeau's care. She was a sweet child, gentle and affectionate. And, though she cried and fretted a little throughout the night for her mother, she seemed, after all, to take kindly to madame's gentle nursing. It was not much of a fever that afflicted her, and after two days she was well enough to be sent back to her parents.

Madame, in all her varied experience with the sick, had never before nursed so objectionable a character as an American child. But the trouble was that after the little one went away, she could think of nothing really objectionable against her except the accident of her birth, which was, after all, her misfortune; and her ignorance of the French language, which was not her fault.

But the touch of the caressing baby arms; the pressure of the soft little body in the night; the tones of the voice, and the feeling of the hot lips when the child kissed her, believing herself to be with her mother, were impressions that had sunk through the crust of madame's prejudice and reached her heart.

She often walked the length of the gallery, looking out across the wide, majestic river. Sometimes she trod the mazes of her garden where the solitude was almost that of a tropical jungle. It was during such moments that the seed began to work in her soul—the seed planted by the innocent and undesigning hands of a little child.

The first shoot that it sent forth was Doubt. Madame plucked it away once or twice. But it sprouted again, and with it Mistrust and Dissatisfaction. Then from the heart of the seed, and amid the shoots of Doubt and Misgiving, came the flower of Truth. It was a very beautiful flower, and it bloomed on Christmas morning.

As Madame Carambeau and her daughter were about to enter her carriage on that Christmas morning, to be driven to church, the old lady stopped to give an order to her black coachman, François. François had been driving these ladies every Sunday morning to the French Cathedral for so many years—he had forgotten exactly how many, but ever since he had entered their service, when Madame Lalonde was a little girl. His astonishment may therefore be imagined when Madame Carambeau said to him:

"François, to-day you will drive us to one of the American churches."

"Plait-il, madame?" the negro stammered, doubting the evidence of his hearing.

"I say, you will drive us to one of the American churches. Any one of them," she added, with a sweep of her hand. "I suppose they are all alike," and she followed her daughter into the carriage.

Madame Lalonde's surprise and agitation were painful to see, and they deprived her of the ability to question, even if she had possessed the courage to do so.

François, left to his fancy, drove them to St. Patrick's Church on Camp street. Madame Lalonde looked and felt like the proverbial fish out of its element as they entered the edifice. Madame Carambeau, on the contrary, looked as if she had been attending St. Patrick's Church all her life. She sat with unruffled calm through the long service and through a lengthy English sermon, of which she did not understand a word.

When the mass was ended and they were about to enter the carriage again, Madame Carambeau turned, as she had done before, to the coachman.

"François," she said, coolly, "you will now drive us to the residence of my son, M. Henri Carambeau. No doubt Mamzelle Cécile can inform you where it is," she added, with a sharply penetrating glance that caused Madame Lalonde to wince.

Yes, her daughter Cécile knew, and so did François, for that matter. They drove out St. Charles Avenue—very far out. It was like a strange city to old madame, who had not been in the American quarter since the town had taken on this new and splendid growth.

The morning was a delicious one, soft and mild; and the roses were all in bloom. They were not hidden behind spiked fences. Madame appeared not to notice them, or the beautiful and striking residences that lined the avenue along which they drove. She held a bottle of smelling-salts to her nostrils, as though she were passing through the most unsavory instead of the most beautiful quarter of New Orleans.

Henri's house was a very modern and very handsome one, standing a little distance away from the street. A well-kept lawn, studded with rare and charming plants, surrounded it. The ladies, dismounting, rang the bell, and stood out upon the banquette, waiting for the iron gate to be opened.

A white maid-servant admitted them. Madame did not seem to mind. She handed her a card with all proper ceremony, and followed with her daughter to the house.

Not once did she show a sign of weakness; not even when her son, Henri, came and took her in his arms and sobbed and wept upon her neck as only a warm-hearted Creole could. He was a big, good-looking, honest-faced man, with tender brown eyes like his dead father's and a firm mouth like his mother's.

Young Mrs. Carambeau came, too, her sweet, fresh face transfigured with happiness. She led by the hand her little daughter, the "American child" whom madame had nursed so tenderly a month before, never suspecting the little one to be other than an alien to her.

"What a lucky chance was that fever! What a happy accident!" gurgled Madame Lalonde.

"Cécile, it was no accident, I tell you; it was Providence," spoke madame, reprovingly, and no one contradicted her.

They all drove back together to eat Christmas dinner in the old house by the river. Madame held her little granddaughter upon her lap; her son Henri sat facing her, and beside her was her daughter-in-law.

Henri sat back in the carriage and could not speak. His soul was possessed by a pathetic joy that would not admit of speech. He was going back again to the home where he was born, after a banishment of ten long years.

He would hear again the water beat against the green levee-bank with a sound that was not quite like any other that he could remember. He would sit within the sweet and solemn shadow of the deep and overhanging roof; and roam through the wild, rich solitude of the old garden, where he had played his pranks of boyhood and dreamed his dreams of youth. He would listen to his mother's voice calling him, "mon fils," as it had always done before that day he had had to choose between mother and wife. No; he could not speak.

But his wife chatted much and pleasantly—in a French, however, that must have been trying to old madame to listen to.

"I am so sorry, ma mère," she said, "that our little one does not speak French. It is not my fault, I assure you," and she flushed and hesitated a little. "It—it was Henri who would not permit it."

"That is nothing," replied madame, amiably, drawing the child close to her. "Her grandmother will teach her French; and she will teach her grandmother English. You see, I have no prejudices. I am not like my son. Henri was always a stubborn boy. Heaven only knows how he came by such a character!"

In Sabine
1893

 The sight of a human habitation, even if it was a rude log cabin with a mud chimney at one end, was a very gratifying one to Grégoire.

He had come out of Natchitoches parish, and had been riding a great part of the day through the big lonesome parish of Sabine. He was not following the regular Texas road, but, led by his erratic fancy, was pushing toward the Sabine River by circuitous paths through the rolling pine forests.

As he approached the cabin in the clearing, he discerned behind a palisade of pine saplings an old negro man chopping wood.

"Howdy, Uncle," called out the young fellow, reining his horse. The negro looked up in blank amazement at so unexpected an apparition, but he only answered: "How you do, suh," accompanying his speech by a series of polite nods.

"Who lives yere?"

"Hit 's Mas' Bud Aiken w'at live' heah, suh."

"Well, if Mr. Bud Aiken c'n affo'd to hire a man to chop his wood, I reckon he won't grudge me a bite o' suppa an' a couple hours' res' on his gall'ry. W'at you say, ole man?"

"I say dit Mas' Bud Aiken don't hires me to chop 'ood. Ef I don't chop dis heah, his wife got it to do. Dat w'y I chops 'ood, suh. Go right 'long in, suh; you

g'ine fine Mas' Bud some'eres roun', ef he ain't drunk
an' gone to bed."

Grégoire, glad to stretch his legs, dismounted, and
led his horse into the small inclosure which surrounded
the cabin. An unkempt, vicious-looking little Texas
pony stopped nibbling the stubble there to look mali-
ciously at him and his fine sleek horse, as they passed
by. Back of the hut, and running plumb up against the
pine wood, was a small, ragged specimen of a cotton-
field.

Grégoire was rather undersized, with a square,
well-knit figure, upon which his clothes sat well and
easily. His corduroy trousers were thrust into the legs
of his boots; he wore a blue flannel shirt; his coat was
thrown across the saddle. In his keen black eyes had
come a puzzled expression, and he tugged thoughtfully
at the brown moustache that lightly shaded his upper
lip.

He was trying to recall when and under what circumstances he had before heard the name of Bud
Aiken. But Bud Aiken himself saved Grégoire the trouble of further speculation on the subject. He appeared
suddenly in the small doorway, which his big body
quite filled; and then Grégoire remembered. This was
the disreputable so-called "Texan" who a year ago had
run away with and married Baptiste Choupic's pretty
daughter, 'Tite Reine, yonder on Bayou Pierre, in
Natchitoches parish. A vivid picture of the girl as he
remembered her appeared to him: her trim rounded
figure; her piquant face with its saucy black coquettish
eyes; her little exacting, imperious ways that had ob-
tained for her the nickname of 'Tite Reine, little queen.
Grégoire had known her at the 'Cadian balls that he
sometimes had the hardihood to attend.

These pleasing recollections of 'Tite Reine lent a
warmth that might otherwise have been lacking to Grégoire's manner, when he greeted her husband.

"I hope I fine you well, Mr. Aiken," he exclaimed
cordially, as he approached and extended his hand.

"You find me damn' porely, suh; but you 've got

the better o' me, ef I may so say." He was a big good-looking brute, with a straw-colored "horse-shoe" moustache quite concealing his mouth, and a several days' growth of stubble on his rugged face. He was fond of reiterating that women's admiration had wrecked his life, quite forgetting to mention the early and sustained influence of "Pike's Magnolia" and other brands, and wholly ignoring certain inborn propensities capable of wrecking unaided any ordinary existence. He had been lying down, and looked frouzy and half asleep.

"Ef I may so say, you 've got the better o' me, Mr.—er"—

"Santien, Grégoire Santien. I have the pleasure o' knowin' the lady you married, suh; an' I think I met you befo',—somew'ere o' 'nother," Grégoire added vaguely.

"Oh," drawled Aiken, waking up, "one o' them Red River Sanchuns!" and his face brightened at the prospect before him of enjoying the society of one of the Santien boys. "Mortimer!" he called in ringing chest tones worthy a commander at the head of his troop. The negro had rested his axe and appeared to be listening to their talk, though he was too far to hear what they said.

"Mortimer, come along here an' take my frien' Mr. Sanchun's hoss. Git a move thar, git a move!" Then turning toward the entrance of the cabin he called back through the open door: "Rain!" it was his way of pronouncing 'Tite Reine's name. "Rain!" he cried again peremptorily; and turning to Grégoire: "she 's 'tendin' to some or other housekeepin' truck." 'Tite Reine was back in the yard feeding the solitary pig which they owned, and which Aiken had mysteriously driven up a few days before, saying he had bought it at Many.

Grégoire could hear her calling out as she approached: "I 'm comin', Bud. Yere I come. W'at you want, Bud?" breathlessly, as she appeared in the door frame and looked out upon the narrow sloping gallery where stood the two men. She seemed to Grégoire to have changed a good deal. She was thinner, and her eyes were larger, with an alert, uneasy look in them;

he fancied the startled expression came from seeing him there unexpectedly. She wore cleanly homespun garments, the same she had brought with her from Bayou Pierre; but her shoes were in shreds. She uttered only a low, smothered exclamation when she saw Grégoire.

"Well, is that all you got to say to my frien' Mr. Sanchun? That 's the way with them Cajuns," Aiken offered apologetically to his guest; "ain't got sense enough to know a white man when they see one." Grégoire took her hand.

"I 'm mighty glad to see you, 'Tite Reine," he said from his heart. She had for some reason been unable to speak; now she panted somewhat hysterically:—

"You mus' escuse me, Mista Grégoire. It 's the truth I did n' know you firs', stan'in' up there." A deep flush had supplanted the former pallor of her face, and her eyes shone with tears and ill-concealed excitement.

"I thought you all lived yonda in Grant," remarked Grégoire carelessly, making talk for the purpose of diverting Aiken's attention away from his wife's evident embarrassment, which he himself was at a loss to understand.

"Why, we did live a right smart while in Grant; but Grant ain't no parish to make a livin' in. Then I tried Winn and Caddo a spell; they was n't no better. But I tell you, suh, Sabine 's a damn' sight worse than any of 'em. Why, a man can't git a drink o' whiskey here without going out of the parish fer it, or across into Texas. I 'm fixin' to sell out an' try Vernon."

Bud Aiken's household belongings surely would not count for much in the contemplated "selling out." The one room that constituted his home was extremely bare of furnishing,—a cheap bed, a pine table, and a few chairs, that was all. On a rough shelf were some paper parcels representing the larder. The mud daubing had fallen out here and there from between the logs of the cabin; and into the largest of these apertures had been thrust pieces of ragged bagging and wisps of cotton. A tin basin outside on the gallery offered the only bathing facilities to be seen. Notwithstanding these drawbacks, Grégoire announced his intention of passing the night with Aiken.

"I 'm jus' goin' to ask the privilege o' layin' down yere on yo' gall'ry to-night, Mr. Aiken. My hoss ain't in firs'-class trim; an' a night's res' ain't goin' to hurt him o' me either." He had begun by declaring his intention of pushing on across the Sabine, but an imploring look from 'Tite Reine's eyes had stayed the words upon his lips. Never had he seen in a woman's eyes a look of such heartbroken entreaty. He resolved on the instant to know the meaning of it before setting foot on Texas soil. Grégoire had never learned to steel his heart against a woman's eyes, no matter what language they spoke.

An old patchwork quilt folded double and a moss pillow which 'Tite Reine gave him out on the gallery made a bed that was, after all, not too uncomfortable for a young fellow of rugged habits.

Grégoire slept quite soundly after he laid down upon his improvised bed at nine o'clock. He was awakened toward the middle of the night by some one gently shaking him. It was 'Tite Reine stooping over him; he could see her plainly, for the moon was shining. She had not removed the clothing she had worn during the day; but her feet were bare and looked wonderfully small and white. He arose on his elbow, wide awake at once. "W'y, 'Tite Reine! w'at the devil you mean? w'ere 's yo' husban'?"

"The house kin fall on 'im, 't en goin' wake up Bud w'en he 's sleepin'; he drink' too much." Now that she had aroused Grégoire, she stood up, and sinking her face in her bended arm like a child, began to cry softly. In an instant he was on his feet.

"My God, 'Tite Reine! w'at 's the matta? you got to tell me w'at 's the matta." He could no longer recognize the imperious 'Tite Reine, whose will had been the law in her father's household. He led her to the edge of the low gallery and there they sat down.

Grégoire loved women. He liked their nearness, their atmosphere; the tones of their voices and the things they said; their ways of moving and turning about; the brushing of their garments when they passed him by pleased him. He was fleeing now from the pain that a woman had inflicted upon him. When any over-powering sorrow came to Grégoire he felt a singular longing to cross the Sabine River and lose himself in Texas. He had done this once before when his home, the old Santien place, had gone into the hands of creditors. The sight of 'Tite Reine's distress now moved him painfully.

"W'at is it, 'Tite Reine? tell me w'at it is," he kept asking her. She was attempting to dry her eyes on her coarse sleeve. He drew a handkerchief from his back pocket and dried them for her.

"They all well, yonda?" she asked, haltingly, "my popa? my moma? the chil'en?" Grégoire knew no more of the Baptiste Choupic family than the post beside him. Nevertheless he answered: "They all right well, 'Tite Reine, but they mighty lonesome of you."

"My popa, he got a putty good crop this yea'?"

"He made right smart o' cotton fo' Bayou Pierre."

"He done haul it to the relroad?"

"No, he ain't quite finish pickin'."

"I hope they all ent sole 'Putty Girl'?" she inquired solicitously.

"Well, I should say not! Yo' pa says they ain't ano-tha piece o' hossflesh in the pa'ish he 'd want to swap fo' 'Putty Girl.' " She turned to him with vague but fleeting amazement,—"Putty Girl" was a cow!

The autumn night was heavy about them. The black forest seemed to have drawn nearer; its shadowy depths were filled with the gruesome noises that in-habit a southern forest at night time.

"Ain't you 'fraid sometimes yere, 'Tite Reine?" Grégoire asked, as he felt a light shiver run through him at the weirdness of the scene.

"No," she answered promptly, "I ent 'fred o' nothin' 'cep' Bud."

"Then he treats you mean? I thought so!"

"Mista Grégoire," drawing close to him and whis-pering in his face, "Bud 's killin' me." He clasped her arm, holding her near him, while an expression of profound pity escaped him. "Nobody don' know, 'cep' Unc' Mort'mer," she went on. "I tell you, he beats me; my back an' arms—you ought to see—it's all blue. He would 'a' choke' me to death one day w'en he was drunk, if Unc' Mort'mer had n' make 'im lef go—with his axe ov' his head." Grégoire glanced back over his shoulder toward the room where the man lay sleeping. He was wondering if it would really be a criminal act to go then and there and shoot the top of Bud Aiken's head off. He himself would hardly have considered it a crime, but he was not sure of how others might regard the act.

"That 's w'y I wake you up, to tell you," she continued. "Then sometime' he plague me mos' crazy; he tell me 't ent no preacher, it 's a Texas drummer w'at marry him an' me; an' w'en I don' know w'at way to turn no mo', he say no, it 's a Meth'dis' archbishop, an' keep on laughin' 'bout me, an' I don' know w'at the truth!"

Then again, she told how Bud had induced her to mount the vicious little mustang "Buckeye," knowing that the little brute would n't carry a woman; and how it had amused him to witness her distress and terror when she was thrown to the ground.

"If I would know how to read an' write, an' had some pencil an' paper, it 's long 'go I would wrote to my popa. But it 's no pos'office, it 's no relroad,—nothin' in Sabine. An' you know, Mista Grégoire, Bud say he 's goin' carry me yonda to Vernon an' fu'ther off yet,—'way yonda, an' he 's goin' turn me loose. Oh, don' leave me yere, Mista Grégoire! don' leave me behine you!" she entreated, breaking once more into sobs.

" 'Tite Reine," he answered, "do you think I 'm such a low-down scound'el as to leave you yere with that"—He finished the sentence mentally, not wishing to offend the ears of 'Tite Reine.

They talked on a good while after that. She would not return to the room where her husband lay; the nearness of a friend had already emboldened her to inward revolt. Grégoire induced her to lie down and rest upon the quilt that she had given to him for a bed. She did so, and broken down by fatigue was soon fast asleep.

He stayed seated on the edge of the gallery and began to smoke cigarettes which he rolled himself of périque tobacco. He might have gone in and shared Bud Aiken's bed, but preferred to stay there near 'Tite Reine. He watched the two horses, tramping slowly about the lot, cropping the dewy wet tufts of grass.

Grégoire smoked on. He only stopped when the moon sank down behind the pine-trees, and the long deep shadow reached out and enveloped him. Then he could no longer see and follow the filmy smoke from his cigarette, and he threw it away. Sleep was pressing heavily upon him. He stretched himself full length upon the rough bare boards of the gallery and slept until day-break.

Bud Aiken's satisfaction was very genuine when he learned that Grégoire proposed spending the day and another night with him. He had already recognized in the young creole a spirit not altogether uncongenial to his own.

'Tite Reine cooked breakfast for them. She made coffee; of course there was no milk to add to it, but there was sugar. From a meal bag that stood in the corner of the room she took a measure of meal, and with it made a pone of corn bread. She fried slices of salt pork. Then Bud sent her into the field to pick cotton with old Uncle Mortimer. The negro's cabin was the counterpart of their own, but stood quite a distance away hidden in the woods. He and Aiken worked the crop on shares.

Early in the day Bud produced a grimy pack of cards from behind a parcel of sugar on the shelf. Grégoire threw the cards into the fire and replaced them with a spic and span new "deck" that he took from his saddlebags. He also brought forth from the same receptacle a bottle of whiskey, which he presented to his host, saying that he himself had no further use for it, as he had "sworn off" since day before yesterday, when he had made a fool of himself in Cloutierville.

They sat at the pine table smoking and playing cards all the morning, only desisting when 'Tite Reine came to serve them with the gumbo-filé that she had come out of the field to cook at noon. She could afford to treat a guest to chicken gumbo, for she owned a half dozen chickens that Uncle Mortimer had presented to her at various times. There were only two spoons, and 'Tite Reine had to wait till the men had finished before eating her soup. She waited for Grégoire's spoon, though her husband was the first to get through. It was a very childish whim.

In the afternoon she picked cotton again; and the men played cards, smoked, and Bud drank.

It was a very long time since Bud Aiken had enjoyed himself so well, and since he had encountered so sympathetic and appreciative a listener to the story of his eventful career. The story of 'Tite Reine's fall from the horse he told with much spirit, mimicking quite skillfully the way in which she had complained of never being permitted "to teck a li'le pleasure," whereupon he had kindly suggested horseback riding. Grégoire enjoyed the story amazingly, which encouraged Aiken to relate many more of a similiar character. As the afternoon wore on, all formality of address between the two had disappeared: they were "Bud" and "Grégoire" to each other, and Grégoire had delighted Aiken's soul by promising to spend a week with him. 'Tite Reine was also touched by the spirit of recklessness in the air; it moved her to fry two chickens for supper. She fried them deliciously in bacon fat. After supper she again arranged Grégoire's bed out on the gallery.

The night fell calm and beautiful, with the delicious odor of the pines floating upon the air. But the three did not sit up to enjoy it. Before the stroke of nine, Aiken had already fallen upon his bed unconscious of everything about him in the heavy drunken sleep that would hold him fast through the night. It even clutched him more relentlessly than usual, thanks to Grégoire's free gift of whiskey.

The sun was high when he awoke. He lifted his voice and called imperiously for 'Tite Reine, wondering that the coffee-pot was not on the hearth, and marveling still more that he did not hear her voice in quick response with its, "I 'm comin,' Bud. Yere I come." He called again and again. Then he arose and looked out through the back door to see if she were picking cotton in the field, but she was not there. He dragged himself to the front entrance. Grégoire's bed was still on the gallery, but the young fellow was nowhere to be seen.

Uncle Mortimer had come into the yard, not to cut wood this time, but to pick up the axe which was his own property, and lift it to his shoulder.

"Mortimer," called out Aiken, "whur 's my wife?" at the same time advancing toward the negro. Mortimer stood still, waiting for him. "Whur 's my wife an' that Frenchman? Speak out, I say, before I send you to h—l."

Uncle Mortimer never had feared Bud Aiken; and with the trusty axe upon his shoulder, he felt a double hardihood in the man's presence. The old fellow passed the back of his black, knotty hand unctuously over his lips, as though he relished in advance the words that were about to pass them. He spoke carefully and deliberately:

"Miss Reine," he said, "I reckon she mus' of done struck Natchitoches pa'ish sometime to'ard de middle o' de night, on dat 'ar swif' hoss o' Mr. Sanchun's."

Aiken uttered a terrific oath. "Saddle up Buckeye," he yelled, "before I count twenty, or I 'll rip the black hide off yer. Quick, thar! Thur aint' nothin' fourfooted top o' this earth that Buckeye can't run down." Uncle Mortimer scratched his head dubiously, as he answered:—

"Yas, Mas' Bud, but you see, Mr. Sanchun, he done cross de Sabine befo' sun-up on Buckeye."

Tante Cat'rinette
1894

It happened just as every one had predicted. Tante Cat'rinette was beside herself with rage and indignation when she learned that the town authorities had for some reason condemned her house and intended to demolish it.

"Dat house w'at Vieumaite gi' me his own se'f, out his own mout', w'en he gi' me my freedom! All wrote down en règle befo' de cote! Bon dieu Seigneur, w'at dey talkin' 'bout!"

Tante Cat'rinette stood in the doorway of her home, resting a gaunt black hand against the jamb. In the other hand she held her corncob pipe. She was a tall, large-boned woman of a pronounced Congo type. The house in question had been substantial enough in its time. It contained four rooms: the lower two of brick, the upper ones of adobe. A dilapidated gallery projected from the upper story and slanted over the narrow banquette, to the peril of passers-by.

"I don't think I ever heard why the property was given to you in the first place, Tante Cat'rinette," observed Lawyer Paxton, who had stopped in passing, as so many others did, to talk the matter over with the old negress. The affair was attracting some attention in town, and its development was being watched with a good deal of interest. Tante Cat'rinette asked nothing better than to satisfy the lawyer's curiosity.

"Vieumaite all time say Cat'rinette wort' gole to 'im; de way I make dem nigga' walk chalk. But," she

138

continued, with recovered seriousness, "w'en I nuss 'is li'le gal w'at all de doctor' 'low it 's goin' die, an' I make it well, me, den Vieumaite, he can't do 'nough, him. He name' dat li'le gal Cat'rine fo' me. Das Miss Kitty w'at marry Miché Raymond yon' by Gran' Eco'. Den he gi' me my freedom; he got plenty slave', him; one don' count in his pocket. An' he gi' me dat house w'at I'm stan'in' in de do'; he got plenty house' an' lan', him. Now dey want pay me t'ousan' dolla', w'at I don' axen' fo', an' tu'n me out dat house! I waitin' fo' 'em, Miché Paxtone," and a wicked gleam shot into the woman's small, dusky eyes. "I got my axe grine fine. Fus' man w'at touch Cat'rinette fo' tu'n her out dat house, he git 'is head bus' like I bus' a gode."

"Dat's nice day, ainty, Miché Paxtone? Fine wedda fo' dry my close." Upon the gallery above hung an array of shirts, which gleamed white in the sunshine, and flapped in the rippling breeze.

The spectacle of Tante Cat'rinette defying the authorities was one which offered much diversion to the children of the neighborhood. They played numberless pranks at her expense; daily serving upon her fictitious notices purporting to be to the last degree official. One youngster, in a moment of inspiration, composed a couplet, which they recited, sang, shouted at all hours, beneath her windows.

"Tante Cat'rinette, she go in town;
    W'en she come back, her house pull' down."

So ran the production. She heard it many times during the day, but, far from offending her, she accepted it as a warning,—a prediction, as it were,—and she took heed not to offer to fate the conditions for its fulfillment. She no longer quitted her house even for a moment, so great was her fear and so firm her belief that the town authorities were lying in wait to possess themselves of it. She would not cross the street to visit a neighbor. She waylaid passers-by and pressed them into service to do her errands and small shopping. She grew distrustful and suspicious, ever on the alert to

scent a plot in the most innocent endeavor to induce
her to leave the house.

One morning, as Tante Cat'rinette was hanging out
her latest batch of washing, Eusèbe, a "free mulatto"
from Red River, stopped his pony beneath her gallery.

"Hé, Tante Cat'rinette!" he called up to her.

She turned to the railing just as she was, in her
bare arms and neck that gleamed ebony-like against the
unbleached cotton of her chemise. A coarse skirt was
fastened about her waist, and a string of many-colored
beads knotted around her throat. She held her smoking
pipe between her yellow teeth.

"How you all come on, Miché Eusèbe?" she questioned, pleasantly.

"We all middlin', Tante Cat'rinette. But Miss
Kitty, she putty bad off out yon'a. I see Mista Raymond
dis mo'nin' w'en I pass by his house; he say look like
de feva don' wan' to quit 'er. She been axen fo' you
all t'rough de night. He 'low he reckon I betta tell you.
Nice wedda we got fo' plantin', Tante Cat'rinette."

"Nice wedda fo' lies, Miché Eusèbe," and she spat
contemptuously down upon the banquette. She turned
away without noticing the man further, and proceeded
to hang one of Lawyer Paxton's fine linen shirts upon
the line.

"She been axen' fo' you all t'rough de night."

Somehow Tante Cat'rinette could not get that refrain out of her head. She would not willingly believe
that Eusèbe had spoken the truth, but—"She been
axen fo' you all t'rough de night—all t'rough de night."
The words kept ringing in her ears, as she came and
went about her daily tasks. But by degrees she dismissed Eusèbe and his message from her mind. It was
Miss Kitty's voice that she could hear in fancy following
her, calling out through the night, "W'ere Tante Cat'rinette? W'y Tante Cat'rinette don' come? W'y she don'
come—w'y she don' come?"

All day the woman muttered and mumbled to herself in her Creole patois; invoking council of "Vieumaite," as she always did in her troubles. Tante

Cat'rinette's religion was peculiarly her own; she turned to heaven with her grievances, it is true, but she felt that there was no one in Paradise with whom she was quite so well acquainted as with "Vieumaite."

Late in the afternoon she went and stood on her doorstep, and looked uneasily and anxiously out upon the almost deserted street. When a little girl came walking by,—a sweet child with a frank and innocent face, upon whose word she knew she could rely,—Tante Cat'rinette invited her to enter.

"Come yere see Tante Cat'rinette, Lolo. It's long time you en't come see Tante Cat'rine; you gittin' proud." She made the little one sit down, and offered her a couple of cookies, which the child accepted with pretty avidity.

"You putty good li'le gal, you, Lolo. You keep on go confession all de time?"

"Oh, yes. I'm goin' make my firs' communion firs' of May, Tante Cat'rinette." A dog-eared catechism was sticking out of Lolo's apron pocket.

"Das right; be good li'le gal. Mine yo' maman ev'-t'ing she say; an' neva tell no story. It's nuttin' bad in dis worl' like tellin' lies. You know Eusèbe?"

"Eusèbe?"

"Yas; dat li'le ole Red River free m'latto. Uh, uh! dat one man w'at kin tell lies, yas! He come tell me Miss Kitty down sick yon'a. You ev' yeard such big story like dat, Lolo?"

The child looked a little bewildered, but she answered promptly, " 'Tain't no story, Tante Cat'rinette. I yeard papa sayin', dinner time, Mr. Raymond sen' fo' Dr. Chalon. An' Dr. Chalon says he ain't got time to go yonda. An' papa says it's because Dr. Chalon on'y want to go w'ere it's rich people; an' he's 'fraid Mista Raymond ain' goin' pay 'im."

Tante Cat'rinette admired the little girl's pretty gingham dress, and asked her who had ironed it. She stroked her brown curls, and talked of all manner of things quite foreign to the subject of Eusèbe and his wicked propensity for telling lies.

She was not restless as she had been during the early part of the day, and she no longer mumbled and muttered as she had been doing over her work.

At night she lighted her coal-oil lamp, and placed it near a window where its light could be seen from the street through the half-closed shutters. Then she sat herself down, erect and motionless, in a chair.

When it was near upon midnight, Tante Cat'rinette arose, and looked cautiously, very cautiously, out of the door. Her house lay in the line of deep shadow that extended along the street. The other side was bathed in the pale light of the declining moon. The night was agreeably mild, profoundly still, but pregnant with the subtle quivering life of early spring. The earth seemed asleep and breathing,—a scent-laden breath that blew in soft puffs against Tante Cat'rinette's face as she emerged from the house. She closed and locked her door noiselessly; then she crept slowly away, treading softly, stealthily as a cat, in the deep shadow.

There were but few people abroad at that hour. Once she ran upon a gay party of ladies and gentlemen who had been spending the evening over cards and anisette. They did not notice Tante Cat'rinette almost effacing herself against the black wall of the cathedral. She breathed freely and ventured from her retreat only when they had disappeared from view. Once a man saw her quite plainly, as she darted across a narrow strip of moonlight. But Tante Cat'rinette need not have gasped with fright as she did. He was too drunk to know if she were a thing of flesh, or only one of the fantastic, maddening shadows that the moon was casting across his path to bewilder him. When she reached the outskirts of the town, and had to cross the broad piece of open country which stretched out toward the pine wood, an almost paralyzing terror came over her. But she crouched low, and hurried through the marsh and weeds, avoiding the open road. She could have been mistaken for one of the beasts browsing there where she passed.

But once in the Grand Ecore road that lay through the pine wood, she felt secure and free to move as she pleased. Tante Cat'rinette straightened herself, stiffened herself in fact, and unconsciously assuming the attitude of the professional sprinter, she sped rapidly beneath the Gothic interlacing branches of the pines. She talked constantly to herself as she went, and to the animate and inanimate objects around her. But her speech, far from intelligent, was hardly intelligible.

She addressed herself to the moon, which she apostrophized as an impertinent busybody spying upon her actions. She pictured all manner of troublesome animals, snakes, rabbits, frogs, pursuing her, but she defied them to catch Cat'rinette, who was hurrying toward Miss Kitty. "Pa capab trapé Cat'rinette, vouzot; mo pé couri vite coté Miss Kitty." She called up to a mocking-bird warbling upon a lofty limb of a pine tree, asking why it cried out so, and threatening to secure it and put it into a cage. "Ca to pé crié comme ça, ti céléra? Arete, mo trapé zozos la, mo mété li dan ain bon lacage." Indeed, Tante Cat'rinette seemed on very familiar terms with the night, with the forest, and with all the flying, creeping, crawling things that inhabit it. At the speed with which she traveled she soon had covered the few miles of wooded road, and before long had reached her destination.

The sleeping-room of Miss Kitty opened upon the long outside gallery, as did all the rooms of the unpretentious frame house which was her home. The place could hardly be called a plantation; it was too small for that. Nevertheless Raymond was trying to plant; trying to teach school between times, in the end room; and sometimes, when he found himself in a tight place, trying to clerk for Mr. Jacobs over in Campte, across Red River.

Tante Cat'rinette mounted the creaking steps, crossed the gallery, and entered Miss Kitty's room as though she were returning to it after a few moments' absence. There was a lamp burning dimly upon the high mantelpiece. Raymond had evidently not been to bed; he was in shirt sleeves, rocking the baby's cradle. It was the same mahogany cradle which had held Miss Kitty thirty-five years before, when Tante Cat'rinette had rocked it. The cradle had been bought then to match the bed,—that big, beautiful bed on which Miss Kitty lay now in a restless half slumber. There was a fine French clock on the mantel, still telling the hours as it had told them years ago. But there were no carpets or rugs on the floors. There was no servant in the house.

Raymond uttered an exclamation of amazement when he saw Tante Cat'rinette enter.

"How you do, Miché Raymond?" she said, quietly. "I yeard Miss Kitty been sick; Eusèbe tell me dat dis mo'nin'."

She moved toward the bed as lightly as though shod with velvet, and seated herself there. Miss Kitty's hand lay outside the coverlid; a shapely hand, which her few days of illness and rest had not yet softened. The negress laid her own black hand upon it. At the touch Miss Kitty instinctively turned her palm upward.

"It's Tante Cat'rinette!" she exclaimed, with a note of satisfaction in her feeble voice. "W'en did you come, Tante Cat'rinette? They all said you wouldn' come."

"I'm goin' come ev'y night, cher coeur, ev'y night tell you be well. Tante Cat'rinette can't come daytime no mo'."

"Raymond tole me about it. They doin' you mighty mean in town, Tante Cat'rinette."

"Nev' mine, ti chou. I know how take care dat w'at Vieumaite gi' me. You go sleep now. Cat'rinette goin' set yere an' mine you. She goin' make you well like she all time do. We don' wan' no céléra doctor. We drive 'em out wid a stick, dey come roun' yere."

Miss Kitty was soon sleeping more restfully than she had done since her illness began. Raymond had finally succeeded in quieting the baby, and he tiptoed into the adjoining room, where the other children lay, to snatch a few hours of much-needed rest for himself. Cat'rinette sat faithfully beside her charge, administering at intervals to the sick woman's wants.

But the thought of regaining her home before day-break, and of the urgent necessity for doing so, did not leave Tante Cat'rinette's mind for an instant.

In the profound darkness, the deep stillness of the night that comes before dawn, she was walking again through the woods, on her way back to town.

The mocking-birds were asleep, and so were the frogs and the snakes; and the moon was gone, and so was the breeze. She walked now in utter silence but for the heavy guttural breathing that accompanied her rapid footsteps. She walked with a desperate determination along the road, every foot of which was familiar to her.

When she at last emerged from the woods, the earth about her was faintly, very faintly, beginning to reveal itself in the tremulous, gray, uncertain light of approaching day. She staggered and plunged onward with beating pulses quickened by fear.

A sudden turn, and Tante Cat'rinette stood facing the river. She stopped abruptly, as if at command of some unseen power that forced her. For an instant she pressed a black hand against her tired, burning eyes, and stared fixedly ahead of her.

Tante Cat'rinette had always believed that Paradise was up there overhead where the sun and stars and moon are, and that "Vieumaite" inhabited that region of splendor. She never for a moment doubted this. It would be difficult, perhaps unsatisfying, to explain why Tante Cat'rinette, on that particular morning, when a vision of the rising day broke suddenly upon her, should have believed that she stood in face of a heavenly revelation. But why not, after all? Since she talked so familiarly herself to the unseen, why should it not respond to her when the time came?

Across the narrow, quivering line of water, the delicate budding branches of young trees were limned black against the gold, orange,—what word is there to tell the color of that morning sky! And steeped in the splendor of it hung one pale star; there was not another in the whole heaven.

Tante Cat'rinette stood with her eyes fixed intently

upon that star, which held her like a hypnotic spell. She stammered breathlessly:

"Mo pé couté, Vieumaite. Cat'rinette pé couté." (I am listening, Vieumaite. Cat'rinette hears you.)

She stayed there motionless upon the brink of the river till the star melted into the brightness of the day and became part of it.

When Tante Cat'rinette entered Miss Kitty's room for the second time, the aspect of things had changed somewhat. Miss Kitty was with much difficulty holding the baby while Raymond mixed a saucer of food for the little one. Their oldest daughter, a child of twelve, had come into the room with an apronful of chips from the woodpile, and was striving to start a fire on the hearth, to make the morning coffee. The room seemed bare and almost squalid in the daylight.

"Well, yere Tante Cat'rinette come back," she said, quietly announcing herself.

They could not well understand why she was back; but it was good to have her there, and they did not question.

She took the baby from its mother, and, seating herself, began to feed it from the saucer which Raymond placed beside her on a chair.

"Yas," she said, "Cat'rinette goin' stay; dis time she en't nev' goin' 'way no mo'."

Husband and wife looked at each other with surprised, questioning eyes.

"Miché Raymond," remarked the woman, turning her head up to him with a certain comical shrewdness in her glance, "if somebody want len' you t'ousan' dolla', w'at you goin' say? Even if it's ole nigga 'oman?"

The man's face flushed with sudden emotion. "I would say that person was our bes' frien', Tante Cat'rinette. An'," he added, with a smile, "I would give her a mortgage on the place, of co'se, to secu' her f'om loss."

"Das right," agreed the woman practically. "Den Cat'rinette goin' len' you t'ousan' dolla'. Dat w'at Vieumaite give her, dat b'long to her; don' b'long to nobody else. An' we go yon'a to town, Miché Raymond, you an' me. You care me befo' Miché Paxtone. I want 'im fo' put down in writin' befo' de cote dat w'at Cat'rinette got, it fo' Miss Kitty w'en I be dead."

Miss Kitty was crying softly in the depths of her pillow.

"I en't got no head fo' all dat, me," laughed Tante Cat'rinette, good humoredly, as she held a spoonful of pap up to the baby's eager lips. "It's Vieumaite tell me all dat clair an' plain dis mo'nin', w'en I comin' 'long de Gran' Eco' road."

A Dresden Lady in Dixie
1894

Madame Valtour had been in the sitting-room some time before she noticed the absence of the Dresden china figure from the corner of the mantel-piece, where it had stood for years. Aside from the intrinsic value of the piece, there were some very sad and tender memories associated with it. A baby's lips that were now forever still had loved once to kiss the pointed "pitty 'ady"; and the baby arms had often held it in a close and smothered embrace.

Madame Valtour gave a rapid, startled glance around the room, to see perchance if it had been misplaced; but she failed to discover it.

Viny, the house-maid, when summoned, remembered having carefully dusted it that morning, and was rather indignantly positive that she had not broken the thing to bits and secreted the pieces.

"Who has been in the room during my absence?" questioned Madame Valtour, with asperity. Viny abandoned herself to a moment's reflection.

"Pa-Jeff comed in yere wid de mail—" If she had said St. Peter came in with the mail, the fact would have had as little bearing on the case from Madame Valtour's point of view.

Pa-Jeff's uprightness and honesty were so long and firmly established as to have become proverbial on the plantation. He had not served the family faithfully since boyhood and been all through the war with "old Marse

Valtour" to descend at his time of life to tampering with
household bric-a-brac.

"Has any one else been here?" Madame Valtour
naturally inquired.

"On'y Agapie w'at brung you some Creole aiggs. I
tole 'er to sot 'em down in de hall. I don' know she
comed in de settin'-room o' not."

Yes, there they were; eight, fresh "Creole eggs"
reposing on the muslin in the sewing basket. Viny herself had been seated on the gallery brushing her mistress' gowns during the hours of that lady's absence,
and could think of no one else having penetrated to the
sitting-room.

Madame Valtour did not entertain the thought that
Agapie had stolen the relic. Her worst fear was, that
the girl, finding herself alone in the room, had handled
the frail bit of porcelain and inadvertently broken it.

Agapie came often to the house to play with the
children and amuse them—she loved nothing better.
Indeed, no other spot known to her on earth so closely
embodied her confused idea of paradise, as this home
with its atmosphere of love, comfort and good cheer.
She was, herself, a cheery bit of humanity, overflowing
with kind impulses and animal spirits.

Madame Valtour recalled the fact that Agapie had
often admired this Dresden figure (but what had she
not admired!); and she remembered having heard the
girl's assurance that if ever she became possessed of
"fo' bits" to spend as she liked, she would have some
one buy her just such a china doll in town or in the
city.

Before night, the fact that the Dresden lady had
strayed from her proud eminence on the sitting-room
mantel, became, through Viny's indiscreet babbling,
pretty well known on the place.

The following morning Madame Valtour crossed the
field and went over to the Bedauts' cabin. The cabins on
the plantation were not grouped; but each stood isolated upon the section of land which its occupants cultivated. Pa-Jeff's cabin was the only one near enough to
the Bedauts to admit of neighborly intercourse.

Seraphine Bedaut was sitting on her small gallery, stringing red peppers, when Madame Valtour approached.

"I'm so distressed, Madame Bedaut," began the planter's wife, abruptly. But the 'Cadian woman arose politely and interrupted, offering her visitor a chair.

"Come in, set down, Ma'me Valtour."

"No, no; it's only for a moment. You know, Madame Bedaut, yesterday when I returned from making a visit, I found that an ornament was missing from my sitting-room mantel-piece. It's a thing I prize very, very much—" with sudden tears filling her eyes—"and I would not willingly part with it for many times its value." Seraphine Bedaut was listening, with her mouth partly open, looking, in truth, stupidly puzzled.

"No one entered the room during my absence," continued Madame Valtour, "but Agapie." Seraphine's mouth snapped like a steel trap and her black eyes gleamed with a flash of anger.

"You wan' say Agapie stole some'in' in yo' house!" she cried out in a shrill voice, tremulous from passion.

"No; oh no! I'm sure Agapie is an honest girl and we all love her; but you know how children are. It was a small Dresden figure. She may have handled and broken the thing and perhaps is afraid to say so. She may have thoughtlessly misplaced it; oh, I don't know what! I want to ask if she saw it."

"Come in; you got to come in, Ma'me Valtour," stubbornly insisted Seraphine, leading the way into the cabin. "I sen' 'er to de house yistiddy wid some Creole aiggs," she went on in her rasping voice, "like I all time do, because you all say you can't eat dem sto' aiggs no mo'. Yere de basket w'at I sen' 'em in," reaching for an Indian basket which hung against the wall—and which was partly filled with cotton seed.

"Oh, never mind," interrupted Madame Valtour, now thoroughly distressed at witnessing the woman's agitation.

"Ah, bien non. I got to show you Agapie en't no mo' thief 'an yo' own child'en is." She led the way into the adjoining room of the hut.

"Yere all her things w'at she 'muse herse'f wid,"

continued Seraphine, pointing to a soapbox which stood on the floor just beneath the open window. The box was filled with an indescribable assortment of odds and ends, mostly doll-rags. A catechism and a blue-backed speller poked dog-eared corners from out of the confusion; for the Valtour children were making heroic and patient efforts toward Agapie's training.

Seraphine cast herself upon her knees before the box and dived her thin brown hands among its contents. "I wan' show you; I goin' show you," she kept repeating excitedly. Madame Valtour was standing beside her.

Suddenly the woman drew forth from among the rags, the Dresden lady, as dapper, sound, and smiling as ever. Seraphine's hand shook so violently that she was in danger of letting the image fall to the floor. Madame Valtour reached out and took it very quietly from her. Then Seraphine rose tremblingly to her feet and broke into a sob that was pitiful to hear.

Agapie was approaching the cabin. She was a chubby girl of twelve. She walked with bare, callous feet over the rough ground and bare-headed under the hot sun. Her thick, short, black hair covered her head like a mane. She had been dancing along the path, but slackened her pace upon catching sight of the two women who had returned to the gallery. But when she perceived that her mother was crying she darted impetuously forward. In an instant she had her arms around her mother's neck, clinging so tenaciously in her youthful strength as to make the frail woman totter.

Agapie had seen the Dresden figure in Madame Valtour's possession and at once guessed the whole accusation.

"It en't so! I tell you, maman, it en't so! I neva touch' it. Stop cryin'; stop cryin'!" and she began to cry most piteously herself.

"But Agapie, we fine it in yo' box," moaned Seraphine through her sobs.

"Then somebody put it there. Can't you see somebody put it there? 'Ten't so, I tell you."

The scene was extremely painful to Madame Valtour. Whatever she might tell these two later, for the time she felt herself powerless to say anything befitting, and she walked away. But she turned to remark, with a hardness of expression and intention which she seldom displayed: "No one will know of this through me. But, Agapie, you must not come into my house again; on account of the children; I could not allow it."

As she walked away she could hear Agapie comforting her mother with renewed protestations of innocence.

Pa-Jeff began to fail visibly that year. No wonder, considering his great age, which he computed to be about one hundred. It was, in fact, some ten years less than that, but a good old age all the same. It was seldom that he got out into the field; and then, never to do any heavy work—only a little light hoeing. There were days when the "misery" doubled him up and nailed him down to his chair so that he could not set foot beyond the door of his cabin. He would sit there courting the sunshine and blinking, as he gazed across the fields with the patience of the savage.

The Bedauts seemed to know almost instinctively when Pa-Jeff was sick. Agapie would shade her eyes and look searchingly towards the old man's cabin.

"I don' see Pa-Jeff this mo'nin'," or "Pa-Jeff en't open his winda," or "I didn' see no smoke yet yonda to Pa-Jeff's." And in a little while the girl would be over there with a pail of soup or coffee, or whatever there was at hand which she thought the old negro might fancy. She had lost all the color out of her cheeks and was pining like a sick bird.

She often sat on the steps of the gallery and talked with the old man while she waited for him to finish his soup from her tin pail.

"I tell you, Pa-Jeff, it's neva been no thief in the Bedaut family. My pa say he couldn' hole up his head if he think I been a thief, me. An' maman say it would make her sick in bed, she don' know she could ever git up. Sosthène tell me the chil'en been cryin' fo' me up yonda. Li'le Lulu cry so hard M'sieur Valtour want sen' afta me, an' Ma'me Valtour say no."

And with this, Agapie flung herself at length upon the gallery with her face buried in her arms, and began to cry so hysterically as seriously to alarm Pa-Jeff. It was well he had finished his soup, for he could not have eaten another mouthful.

"Hole up yo' head, chile. God save us! W'at you kiarrin' on dat away?" he exclaimed in great distress. "You gwine to take a fit? Hole up yo' head."

Agapie rose slowly to her feet, and drying her eyes upon the sleeve of her "josie," reached out for the tin bucket. Pa-Jeff handed it to her, but without relinquishing his hold upon it.

"War hit you w'at tuck it?" he questioned in a whisper. "I isn' gwine tell; you knows I isn' gwine tell." She only shook her head, attempting to draw the pail forcibly away from the old man.

"Le' me go, Pa-Jeff. W'at you doin'! Gi' me my bucket!"

He kept his old blinking eyes fastened for a while questioningly upon her disturbed and tear-stained face. Then he let her go and she turned and ran swiftly away towards her home.

He sat very still watching her disappear; only his furrowed old face twitched convulsively, moved by an unaccustomed train of reasoning that was at work in him.

"She w'ite, I is black," he muttered calculatingly. "She young, I is ole; sho I is ole. She good to Pa-Jeff like I her own kin an' color." This line of thought seemed to possess him to the exclusion of every other. Late in the night he was still muttering.

"Sho I is ole. She good to Pa-Jeff, yas."

A few days later, when Pa-Jeff happened to be feeling comparatively well, he presented himself at the house just as the family had assembled at their early dinner. Looking up suddenly, Monsieur Valtour was astonished to see him standing there in the room near the open door. He leaned upon his cane and his grizzled head was bowed upon his breast. There was general satisfaction expressed at seeing Pa-Jeff on his legs once more.

"Why, old man, I'm glad to see you out again," exclaimed the planter, cordially, pouring a glass of wine, which he instructed Viny to hand to the old fellow. Pa-Jeff accepted the glass and set it solemnly down upon a small table near by.

"Marse Albert," he said, "I is come heah to-day fo' to make a statement of de rights an' de wrongs w'at is done hang heavy on my soul dis heah long time. Arter you heahs me an' de missus heahs me an' de chillun an' ev'body, den ef you says: 'Pa-Jeff you kin tech yo' lips to dat glass o' wine,' all well an' right.'"

His manner was impressive and caused the family to exchange surprised and troubled glances. Foreseeing that his recital might be long, a chair was offered to him, but he declined it.

"One day," he began, "w'en I ben hoein' de madam's flower bed close to de fence, Sosthène he ride up, he say: 'Heah, Pa-Jeff, heah de mail.' I takes de mail f'om 'im an' I calls out to Viny wa't settin' on de gallery: 'Heah Marse Albert's mail, gal; come git it.'

"But Viny she answer, pert-like—des like Viny: 'You is got two laigs, Pa-Jeff, des well as me.' I ain't no han' fo' disputin' wid gals, so I brace up an' I come 'long to de house an' goes on in dat settin'-room dah, naix' to de dinin'-room. I lays dat mail down on Marse Albert's table; den I looks roun'.

"Ev'thing do look putty, sho! De lace cu'tains was a-flappin' an' de flowers was a-smellin' sweet, an' de pictures a-settin' back on de wall. I keep on lookin' roun'. To reckly my eye hit fall on de li'le gal w'at al'ays sets on de een' o' de mantel-shelf. She do look mighty sassy dat day, wid 'er toe a-stickin' out, des so; an' holdin' her skirt des dat away; an' lookin' at me wid her head twis'.

"I laff out. Viny mus' heahed me. I say, 'g'long 'way f'om dah, gal.' She keep on smilin'. I reaches out my han'. Den Satan an' de good Sperrit, dey begins to wrastle in me. De Sperrit say: 'You ole fool-nigga, you; mine w'at you about.' Satan keep on shovin' my han'—des so—keep on shovin'. Satan he mighty powerful dat day, an' he win de fight. I kiar dat li'le trick home in my pocket."

Pa-Jeff lowered his head for a moment in bitter confusion. His hearers were moved with distressful astonishment. They would have had him stop the recital right there, but Pa-Jeff resumed, with an effort:

"Come dat night I heah tell how dat li'le trick, wo'th heap money; how madam, she cryin' 'cause her li'le blessed lamb was use' to play wid dat, an' kiar-on ov' it. Den I git scared. I say, 'w'at I gwine do?' An' up jump Satan an' de Sperrit a-wrastlin' again.

"De Sperrit say; 'Kiar hit back whar it come f'om, Pa-Jeff.' Satan 'low: 'Fling it in de bayeh, you ole fool.' De Sperrit say: 'You won't fling dat in de bayeh, whar de madam kain't neva sot eyes on hit no mo'?' Den Satan he kine give in; he 'low he plumb sick o' disputin' so long; tell me go hide it some 'eres whar dey nachelly gwine fine it. Satan he win dat fight.

"Des w'en de day g'ine break, I creeps out an' goes 'long de fiel' road. I pass by Ma'me Bedaut's house. I riclic how dey says li'le Bedaut gal ben in de sittin'-room, too, day befo'. De winda war open. Ev'body sleepin'. I tres' in my head, des like a dog w'at shame hisse'f. I sees dat box o' rags befo' my eyes; an' I drops dat li'le imp'dence 'mongst dem rags.

"Mebby yo' all t'ink Satan an' de Sperrit lef' me 'lone, arter dat?" continued Pa-Jeff, straightening himself from the relaxed position in which his members seemed to have settled.

"No, suh; dey ben desputin' straight 'long. Las' night dey come nigh onto en'in' me up. De Sperrit say: 'Come 'long, I gittin' tired dis heah, you g'long up yonda an' tell de truf an' shame de devil.' Satan 'low: 'Stay whar you is; you heah me!' Dey clutches me. Dey twis'es an' twines me. Dey dashes me down an' jerks me up. But de Sperrit he win dat fight in de en', an' heah I is, mist'ess, master, chillun'; heah I is."

Years later Pa-Jeff was still telling the story of his temptation and fall. The negroes especially seemed never to tire of hearing him relate it. He enlarged greatly upon the theme as he went, adding new and dramatic features which gave fresh interest to its every telling.

Agapie grew up to deserve the confidence and favors of the family. She redoubled her acts of kindness toward Pa-Jeff; but somehow she could not look into his face again.

Yet she need not have feared. Long before the end came, poor old Pa-Jeff, confused, bewildered, believed the story himself as firmly as those who had heard him tell it over and over for so many years.

Regret
1894

Mamzelle Aurélie possessed a good strong figure, ruddy cheeks, hair that was changing from brown to gray, and a determined eye. She wore a man's hat about the farm, and an old blue army overcoat when it was cold, and sometimes topboots.

Mamzelle Aurélie had never thought of marrying. She had never been in love. At the age of twenty she had received a proposal, which she had promptly declined, and at the age of fifty she had not yet lived to regret it.

So she was quite alone in the world, except for her dog Ponto, and the negroes who lived in her cabins and worked her crops, and the fowls, a few cows, a couple of mules, her gun (with which she shot chicken-hawks), and her religion.

One morning Mamzelle Aurélie stood upon her gallery, contemplating, with arms akimbo, a small band of very small children who, to all intents and purposes, might have fallen from the clouds, so unexpected and bewildering was their coming, and so unwelcome. They were the children of her nearest neighbor, Odile, who was not such a near neighbor, after all.

The young woman had appeared but five minutes before, accompanied by these four children. In her arms she carried little Elodie; she dragged Ti Nomme by an unwilling hand; while Marcéline and Marcélette followed with irresolute steps.

Her face was red and disfigured from tears and excitement. She had been summoned to a neighboring parish by the dangerous illness of her mother; her husband was away in Texas—it seemed to her a million miles away; and Valsin was waiting with the mule-cart to drive her to the station.

"It's no question, Mamzelle Aurélie; you jus' got to keep those youngsters fo' me tell I come back. Dieu sait, I would n' botha you with 'em if it was any otha way to do! Make 'em mine you, Mamzelle Aurélie; don' spare 'em. Me, there, I'm half crazy between the chil'ren, an' Léon not home, an' maybe not even to fine po' maman alive encore!"—a harrowing possibility which drove Odile to take a final hasty and convulsive leave of her disconsolate family.

She left them crowded into the narrow strip of shade on the porch of the long, low house; the white sunlight was beating in on the white old boards; some chickens were scratching in the grass at the foot of the steps, and one had boldly mounted, and was stepping heavily, solemnly, and aimlessly across the gallery. There was a pleasant odor of pinks in the air, and the sound of negroes' laughter was coming across the flowering cotton-field.

Mamzelle Aurélie stood contemplating the children. She looked with a critical eye upon Marcéline, who had been left staggering beneath the weight of the chubby Elodie. She surveyed with the same calculating air Marcélette mingling her silent tears with the audible grief and rebellion of Ti Nomme. During those few contemplative moments she was collecting herself, determining upon a line of action which should be identical with a line of duty. She began by feeding them.

If Mamzelle Aurélie's responsibilities might have begun and ended there, they could easily have been dismissed; for her larder was amply provided against an emergency of this nature. But little children are not little pigs; they require and demand attentions which were wholly unexpected by Mamzelle Aurélie, and which she was ill prepared to give.

She was, indeed, very inapt in her management of

Odile's children during the first few days. How could she know that Marcélette always wept when spoken to in a loud and commanding tone of voice? It was a peculiarity of Marcélette's. She became acquainted with Ti Nomme's passion for flowers only when he had plucked all the choicest gardenias and pinks for the apparent purpose of critically studying their botanical construction.

" 'Tain't enough to tell 'im, Mamzelle Aurélie," Marcéline instructed her; "you got to tie 'im in a chair. It's w'at maman all time do w'en he's bad: she tie 'im in a chair." The chair in which Mamzelle Aurélie tied Ti Nomme was roomy and comfortable, and he seized the opportunity to take a nap in it, the afternoon being warm.

At night, when she ordered them one and all to bed as she would have shooed the chickens into the hen-house, they stayed uncomprehending before her. What about the little white nightgowns that had to be taken from the pillow-slip in which they were brought over, and shaken by some strong hand till they snapped like ox-whips? What about the tub of water which had to be brought and set in the middle of the floor, in which the little tired, dusty, sunbrowned feet had every one to be washed sweet and clean? And it made Marcéline and Marcélette laugh merrily—the idea that Mamzelle Aurélie should for a moment have believed that Ti Nomme could fall asleep without being told the story of *Croque-mitaine* or *Loup-garou*, or both; or that Elodie could fall asleep at all without being rocked and sung to.

"I tell you, Aunt Ruby," Mamzelle Aurélie informed her cook in confidence; "me, I'd rather manage a dozen plantation' than fo' chil'ren. It's terrassent! Bonté! Don't talk to me about chil'ren!"

" 'Tain' ispected sich as you would know airy thing 'bout 'em, Mamzelle Aurélie. I see dat plainly yistiddy w'en I spy dat li'le chile playin' wid yo' baskit o' keys. You don' know dat makes chillun grow up hard-headed, to play wid keys? Des like it make 'em teeth hard to look in a lookin'-glass. Them's the things you got to know in the raisin' an' manigement o' chillun."

Mamzelle Aurélie certainly did not pretend or aspire to such subtle and far-reaching knowledge on the subject as Aunt Ruby possessed, who had "raised five an' bared (buried) six" in her day. She was glad enough to learn a few little mother-tricks to serve the moment's need.

Ti Nomme's sticky fingers compelled her to unearth white aprons that she had not worn for years, and she had to accustom herself to his moist kisses—the expressions of an affectionate and exuberant nature. She got down her sewing-basket, which she seldom used, from the top shelf of the armoire, and placed it within the ready and easy reach which torn slips and buttonless waists demanded. It took her some days to become accustomed to the laughing, the crying, the chattering that echoed through the house and around it all day long. And it was not the first or the second night that she could sleep comfortably with little Elodie's hot, plump body pressed close against her, and the little one's warm breath beating her cheek like the fanning of a bird's wing.

But at the end of two weeks Mamzelle Aurélie had grown quite used to these things, and she no longer complained.

It was also at the end of two weeks that Mamzelle Aurélie, one evening, looking away toward the crib where the cattle were being fed, saw Valsin's blue cart turning the bend of the road. Odile sat beside the mulatto, upright and alert. As they drew near, the young woman's beaming face indicated that her homecoming was a happy one.

But this coming, unannounced and unexpected, threw Mamzelle Aurélie into a flutter that was almost agitation. The children had to be gathered. Where was Ti Nomme? Yonder in the shed, putting an edge on his knife at the grindstone. And Marcéline and Marcélette? Cutting and fashioning doll-rags in the corner of the gallery. As for Elodie, she was safe enough in Mamzelle Aurélie's arms; and she had screamed with delight at sight of the familiar blue cart which was bringing her mother back to her.

The excitement was all over, and they were gone. How still it was when they were gone! Mamzelle Aurélie stood upon the gallery, looking and listening. She could no longer see the cart; the red sunset and the blue-gray twilight had together flung a purple mist across the fields and road that hid it from her view. She could no longer hear the wheezing and creaking of its wheels. But she could still faintly hear the shrill, glad voices of the children.

She turned into the house. There was much work awaiting her, for the children had left a sad disorder behind them; but she did not at once set about the task of righting it. Mamzelle Aurélie seated herself beside the table. She gave one slow glance through the room, into which the evening shadows were creeping and deepening around her solitary figure. She let her head fall down upon her bended arm, and began to cry. Oh, but she cried! Not softly, as women often do. She cried like a man, with sobs that seemed to tear her very soul. She did not notice Ponto licking her hand.

Ozème's Holiday
1894

Ozème often wondered why there was not a special dispensation of providence to do away with the necessity for work. There seemed to him so much created for man's enjoyment in this world, and so little time and opportunity to profit by it. To sit and do nothing but breathe was a pleasure to Ozème; but to sit in the company of a few choice companions, including a sprinkling of ladies, was even a greater delight; and the joy which a day's hunting or fishing or picnicking afforded him is hardly to be described. Yet he was by no means indolent. He worked faithfully on the plantation the whole year long, in a sort of methodical way; but when the time came around for his annual week's holiday, there was no holding him back. It was often decidedly inconvenient for the planter that Ozème usually chose to take his holiday during some very busy season of the year.

He started out one morning in the beginning of October. He had borrowed Mr. Laballière's buckboard and Padue's old gray mare, and a harness from the negro Sévérin. He wore a light blue suit which had been sent all the way from St. Louis, and which had cost him ten dollars; he had paid almost as much again for his boots; and his hat was a broad-rimmed gray felt which he had no cause to be ashamed of. When Ozème went "broading," he dressed—well, regardless of cost. His eyes were blue and mild; his hair was light, and he wore it rather long; he was clean shaven, and really did not look his thirty-five years.

Ozème had laid his plans weeks beforehand. He was going visiting along Cane River; the mere contemplation filled him with pleasure. He counted upon reaching Fédeaus' about noon, and he would stop and dine there. Perhaps they would ask him to stay all night. He really did not hold to staying all night, and was not decided to accept if they did ask him. There were only the two old people, and he rather fancied the notion of pushing on to Beltrans', where he would stay a night, or even two, if urged. He was quite sure that there would be something agreeable going on at Beltrans', with all those young people—perhaps a fish-fry, or possibly a ball!

Of course he would have to give a day to Tante Sophie and another to Cousine Victoire; but none to the St. Annes unless entreated—after St. Anne reproaching him last year with being a fainéant for broading at such a season! At Cloutierville, where he would linger as long as possible, he meant to turn and retrace his course, zigzagging back and forth across Cane River so as to take in the Duplans, the Velcours, and others that he could not at the moment recall. A week seemed to Ozème a very, very little while in which to crowd so much pleasure.

There were steam-gins at work; he could hear them whistling far and near. On both sides of the river the fields were white with cotton, and everybody in the world seemed busy but Ozème. This reflection did not distress or disturb him in the least; he pursued his way at peace with himself and his surroundings.

At Lamérie's cross-roads store, where he stopped to buy a cigar, he learned that there was no use heading for Fédeaus', as the two old people had gone to town for a lengthy visit, and the house was locked up. It was at Fédeaus' that Ozème had intended to dine.

He sat in the buckboard, given up to a moment or two of reflection. The result was that he turned away from the river, and entered the road that led between two fields back to the woods and into the heart of the country. He had determined upon taking a short cut to the Beltrans' plantation, and on the way he meant to keep an eye open for old Aunt Tildy's cabin, which he knew lay in some remote part of this cut-off. He remembered that Aunt Tildy could cook an excellent meal if she had the material at hand. He would induce her to fry him a chicken, drip a cup of coffee, and turn him out a pone of corn-bread, which he thought would be sumptuous enough fare for the occasion.

Aunt Tildy dwelt in the not unusual log cabin, of one room, with its chimney of mud and stone, and its shallow gallery formed by the jutting of the roof. In close proximity to the cabin was a small cotton-field, which from a long distance looked like a field of snow. The cotton was bursting and overflowing foam-like from bolls on the drying stalk. On the lower branches it was hanging ragged and tattered, and much of it had already fallen to the ground. There were a few chinaberry-trees in the yard before the hut, and under one of them an ancient and rusty-looking mule was eating corn from a wood trough. Some common little Creole chickens were scratching about the mule's feet and snatching at the grains of corn that occasionally fell from the trough.

Aunt Tildy was hobbling across the yard when Ozème drew up before the gate. One hand was confined in a sling; in the other she carried a tin pan, which she let fall noisily to the ground when she recognized him. She was broad, black, and misshapen, with her body bent forward almost at an acute angle. She wore a blue cottonade of large plaids, and a bandana awkwardly twisted around her head.

"Good God A'mighty, man! Whar you come from?" was her startled exclamation at beholding him.

"F'om home, Aunt Tildy; w'ere else do you expec'?" replied Ozème, dismounting composedly.

He had not seen the old woman for several years—since she was cooking in town for the family with which he boarded at the time. She had washed and ironed for him, atrociously, it is true, but her intentions were beyond reproach if her washing was not. She had also been clumsily attentive to him during a spell of illness. He had paid her with an occasional bandana, a calico dress, or a checked apron, and they had always considered the account between themselves square, with no sentimental feeling of gratitude remaining on either side.

"I like to know," remarked Ozème, as he took the gray mare from the shafts, and led her up to the trough where the mule was—"I like to know w'at you mean by makin' a crop like that an' then lettin' it go to was'e? Who you reckon's goin' to pick that cotton? You think maybe the angels goin' to come down an' pick it fo' you, an' gin it an' press it, an' then give you ten cents a poun' fo' it, hein?"

"Ef de Lord don' pick it, I don' know who gwine pick it, Mista Ozème. I tell you, me an' Sandy we wuk dat crap day in an' day out; it's him done de mos' of it."

"Sandy? That little—"

"He ain' dat li'le Sandy no mo' w'at you rec'lec's; he 'mos' a man, an' he wuk like a man now. He wuk mo' 'an fittin' fo' his strenk, an' now he layin' in dah sick—God A'mighty knows how sick. An' me wid a risin' twell I bleeged to walk de flo' o' nights, an' don' know ef I ain' gwine to lose de han' atter all."

"W'y, in the name o' conscience, you don' hire somebody to pick?"

"Whar I got money to hire? An' you knows well as me ev'y chick an' chile is pickin' roun' on de plantations an' gittin' good pay."

The whole outlook appeared to Ozème very depressing, and even menacing, to his personal comfort and peace of mind. He foresaw no prospect of dinner unless he should cook it himself. And there was that Sandy—he remembered well the little scamp of eight, always at his grandmother's heels when she was cooking or washing. Of course he would have to go in and look at the boy, and no doubt dive into his traveling-bag for quinine, without which he never traveled.

Sandy was indeed very ill, consumed with fever. He lay on a cot covered up with a faded patchwork quilt. His eyes were half closed, and he was muttering and rambling on about hoeing and bedding and cleaning and thinning out the cotton; he was hauling it to the gin, wrangling about weight and bagging and ties and the price offered per pound. That bale or two of cotton had not only sent Sandy to bed, but had pursued him there, holding him through his fevered dreams, and threatening to end him. Ozème would never have known the black boy, he was so tall, so thin, and seemingly so wasted, lying there in bed.

"See yere, Aunt Tildy," said Ozème, after he had, as was usual with him when in doubt, abandoned himself to a little reflection; "between us—you an' me— we got to manage to kill an' cook one o' those chickens I see scratchin' out yonda, fo' I'm jus' about starved. I reckon you ain't got any quinine in the house? No; I didn't suppose an instant you had. Well, I'm goin' to give Sandy a good dose o' quinine to-night, an' I'm goin' stay an' see how that'll work on 'im. But sun-up, min' you, I mus' get out o' yere."

Ozème had spent more comfortable nights than the one passed in Aunt Tildy's bed, which she considerately abandoned to him.

In the morning Sandy's fever was somewhat abated, but had not taken a decided enough turn to justify Ozème in quitting him before noon, unless he was willing "to feel like a dog," as he told himself. He appeared before Aunt Tildy stripped to the undershirt, and wearing his second-best pair of trousers.

"That's a nice pickle o' fish you got me in, ol' woman. I guarantee, nex' time I go abroad, 'tain't me that'll take any cut-off. W'ere's that cotton-basket an' cotton-sack o' yo's?"

"I knowed it!" chanted Aunt Tildy—"I knowed de Lord war gwine sen' somebody to holp me out. He war n' gwine let de crap was'e after he give Sandy an' me de strenk to make hit. De Lord gwine shove you 'long de row, Mista Ozème. De lord gwine give you plenty mo' fingers an' han's to pick dat cotton nimble an' clean."

"Neva you min' w'at the Lord's goin' to do; go get

me that cotton-sack. An' you put that poultice like I tol'
you on yo' han', an' set down there an' watch Sandy. It
looks like you are 'bout as helpless as a' ol' cow tangled
up in a potato-vine."

Ozème had not picked cotton for many years, and
he took to it a little awkwardly at first; but by the time
he had reached the end of the first row the old dexter-
ity of youth had come back to his hands, which flew
rapidly back and forth with the motion of a weaver's
shuttle; and his ten fingers became really nimble in
clutching the cotton from its dry shell. By noon he had
gathered about fifty pounds. Sandy was not then quite
so well as he had promised to be, and Ozème con-
cluded to stay that day and one more night. If the boy
were no better in the morning, he would go off in
search of a doctor for him, and he himself would continue on down to Tante Sophie's; the Beltrans' was out
of the question now.

Sandy hardly needed a doctor in the morning.
Ozème's doctoring was beginning to tell favorably; but
he would have considered it criminal indifference and
negligence to go away and leave the boy to Aunt Tildy's
awkward ministrations just at the critical moment when
there was a turn for the better; so he stayed that day
out, and picked his hundred and fifty pounds.

On the third day it looked like rain, and a heavy
rain just then would mean a heavy loss to Aunt Tildy
and Sandy, and Ozème again went to the field, this
time urging Aunt Tildy with him to do what she might
with her one good hand.

"Aunt Tildy," called out Ozème to the bent old
woman moving ahead of him between the white rows
of cotton, "if the Lord gets me safe out o' this ditch, 't
ain't to-morro' I'll fall in anotha with my eyes open, I
bet you."

"Keep along, Mista Ozème; don' grumble, don'
stumble; de Lord's a-watchin' you. Look at yo' Aunt
Tildy; she doin' mo' wid her one han' 'an you doin' wid
yo' two, man. Keep right along, honey. Watch dat cotton how it fallin' in yo' Aunt Tildy's bag."

"I am watchin' you, ol' woman; you don' fool me.

You got to work that han' o' yo's spryer than you doin',
or I'll take the rawhide. You done fo'got w'at the rawhide tas'e like, I reckon"—a reminder which amused
Aunt Tildy so powerfully that her big negro-laugh resounded over the whole cotton-patch, and even caused
Sandy, who heard it, to turn in his bed.

The weather was still threatening on the suc-
ceeding day, and a sort of dogged determination or
characteristic desire to see his undertakings carried to
a satisfactory completion urged Ozème to continue his
efforts to drag Aunt Tildy out of the mire into which
circumstances seemed to have thrust her.

One night the rain did come, and began to beat
softly on the roof of the old cabin. Sandy opened his
eyes, which were no longer brilliant with the fever
flame. "Granny," he whispered, "de rain! Des listen,
granny; de rain a-comin', an' I ain' pick dat cotton yit.
W'at time it is? Gi' me my pants—I got to go—"

"You lay whar you is, chile alive. Dat cotton put
aside clean and dry. Me an' de Lord an' Mista Ozème
done pick dat cotton."

Ozème drove away in the morning looking quite
as spick and span as the day he left home in his blue
suit and his light felt drawn a little over his eyes.

"You want to take care o' that boy," he instructed
Aunt Tildy at parting, "an' get 'im on his feet. An', let
me tell you, the nex' time I start out to broad, if you
see me passin' in this yere cut-off, put on yo' specs an'
look at me good, because it won't be me; it'll be my
ghos', ol' woman."

Indeed, Ozème, for some reason or other, felt
quite shamefaced as he drove back to the plantation.
When he emerged from the lane which he had entered
the week before, and turned into the river road, Lamérie, standing in the store door, shouted out:

"Hé, Ozème! you had good times yonda? I bet you
danced holes in the sole of them new boots."

"Don't talk, Lamérie!" was Ozème's rather ambig-
uous reply, as he flourished the remainder of a whip
over the old gray mare's sway-back, urging her to a
gentle trot.

When he reached home, Bodé, one of Padue's boys, who was assisting him to unhitch, remarked:

"How come you didn' go yonda down de coas' like you said, Mista Ozème? Nobody didn' see you in Cloutierville, an' Mailitte say you neva cross' de twenty-fo'-mile ferry, an' nobody didn' see you no place."

Ozème returned, after his customary moment of reflection:

"You see, it's 'mos' always the same thing on Cane riva, my boy; a man get tired o' that à la fin. This time I went back in the woods, 'way yonda in the Fédeau cut-off; kin' o' campin' an' roughin' like, you might say. I tell you, it was sport, Bodé."

Odalie Misses Mass
1895

Odalie sprang down from the mulecart, shook out her white skirts, and firmly grasping her parasol, which was blue to correspond with her sash, entered Aunt Pinky's gate and proceeded towards the old woman's cabin. She was a thick-waisted young thing who walked with a firm tread and carried her head with a determined poise. Her straight brown hair had been rolled up over night in papillotes, and the artificial curls stood out in clusters, stiff and uncompromising beneath the rim of her white chip hat. Her mother, sister and brother remained seated in the cart before the gate.

It was the fifteenth of August, the great feast of the Assumption, so generally observed in the Catholic parishes of Louisiana. The Chotard family were on their way to mass, and Odalie had insisted upon stopping to "show herself" to her old friend and protegée, Aunt Pinky.

The helpless, shrivelled old negress sat in the depths of a large, rudely-fashioned chair. A loosely hanging unbleached cotton gown enveloped her mite of a figure. What was visible of her hair beneath the bandana turban, looked like white sheep's wool. She wore round, silver-rimmed spectacles, which gave her an air of wisdom and respectability, and she held in her hand the branch of a hickory sapling, with which she kept mosquitoes and flies at bay, and even chickens

170

and pigs that sometimes penetrated the heart of her domain.

Odalie walked straight up to the old woman and kissed her on the cheek.

"Well, Aunt Pinky, yere I am," she announced with evident self-complacency, turning herself slowly and stiffly around like a mechanical dummy. In one hand she held her prayer-book, fan and handkerchief, in the other the blue parasol, still open; and on her plump hands were blue cotton mitts. Aunt Pinky beamed and chuckled; Odalie hardly expected her to be able to do more.

"Now you saw me," the child continued. "I reckon you satisfied. I mus' go; I ain't got a minute to was'e." But at the threshold she turned to inquire, bluntly:

"W'ere's Pug?"

"Pug," replied Aunt Pinky, in her tremulous old-woman's voice. "She's gone to chu'ch; done gone; she done gone," nodding her head in seeming approval of Pug's action.

"To church!" echoed Odalie with a look of consternation settling in her round eyes.

"She gone to chu'ch," reiterated Aunt Pinky. "Say she kain't miss chu'ch on de fifteent'; de debble gwine pester her twell jedgment, she miss chu'ch on de fifteent'."

Odalie's plump cheeks fairly quivered with indignation and she stamped her foot. She looked up and down the long, dusty road that skirted the river. Nothing was to be seen save the blue cart with its dejected looking mule and patient occupants. She walked to the end of the gallery and called out to a negro boy whose black bullet-head showed up in bold relief against the white of the cotton patch:

"He, Baptiste! w'ere's yo' ma? Ask yo' ma if she can't come set with Aunt Pinky."

"Mammy, she gone to chu'ch," screamed Baptiste in answer.

"Bonté! w'at's taken you all darkies with yo' 'church' to-day? You come along yere Baptiste an' set

with Aunt Pinky. That Pug! I'm goin' to make yo' ma
wear her out fo' that trick of hers—leavin' Aunt Pinky
like that."

But at the first intimation of what was wanted of
him, Baptiste dipped below the cotton like a fish beneath water, leaving no sight nor sound of himself to
answer Odalie's repeated calls. Her mother and sister
were beginning to show signs of impatience.

"But, I can't go," she cried out to them. "It's nobody to stay with Aunt Pinky. I can't leave Aunt Pinky
like that, to fall out of her chair, maybe, like she already fell out once."

"You goin' to miss mass on the fifteenth, you, Odalie! W'at you thinkin' about?" came in shrill rebuke
from her sister. But her mother offering no objection,
the boy lost not a moment in starting the mule forward
at a brisk trot. She watched them disappear in a cloud
of dust; and turning with a déjected, almost tearful
countenance, re-entered the room.

Aunt Pinky seemed to accept her reappearance as
a matter of course; and even evinced no surprise at
seeing her remove her hat and mitts, which she laid
carefully, almost religiously, on the bed, together with
her book, fan and handkerchief.

Then Odalie went and seated herself some distance
from the old woman in her own small, low rocking-
chair. She rocked herself furiously, making a great clatter with the rockers over the wide, uneven boards of
the cabin floor; and she looked out through the open
door.

"Puggy, she done gone to chu'ch; done gone. Say
de debble gwine pester her twell jedgment—"

"You done tole me that, Aunt Pinky; neva mine;
don't le's talk about it."

Aunt Pinky thus rebuked, settled back into silence
and Odalie continued to rock and stare out of the door.

Once she arose, and taking the hickory branch
from Aunt Pinky's nerveless hand, made a bold and
sudden charge upon a little pig that seemed bent upon
keeping her company. She pursued him with flying

heels and loud cries as far as the road. She came back flushed and breathless and her curls hanging rather limp around her face; she began again to rock herself and gaze silently out of the door.

"You gwine make yo' fus' c'mmunion?"

This seemingly sober inquiry on the part of Aunt Pinky at once shattered Odalie's ill-humor and dispelled every shadow of it. She leaned back and laughed with wild abandonment.

"Mais w'at you thinkin' about, Aunt Pinky? How you don't remember I made my firs' communion las' year, with this same dress w'at maman let out the tuck," holding up the altered skirt for Aunt Pinky's inspection. "An' with this same petticoat w'at maman added this ruffle an' crochet' edge; excep' I had a w'ite sash."

These evidences proved beyond question convincing and seemed to satisfy Aunt Pinky. Odalie rocked as furiously as ever, but she sang now, and the swaying chair had worked its way nearer to the old woman.

"You gwine git mar'ied?"

"I declare, Aunt Pinky," said Odalie, when she had ceased laughing and was wiping her eyes, "I declare, sometime' I think you gittin' plumb foolish. How you expec' me to git married w'en I'm on'y thirteen?"

Evidently Aunt Pinky did not know why or how she expected anything so preposterous; Odalie's holiday attire that filled her with contemplative rapture, had doubtless incited her to these vagaries.

The child now drew her chair quite close to the old woman's knee after she had gone out to the rear of the cabin to get herself some water and had brought a drink to Aunt Pinky in the gourd dipper.

There was a strong, hot breeze blowing from the river, and it swept fitfully and in gusts through the cabin, bringing with it the weedy smell of cacti that grew thick on the bank, and occasionally a shower of reddish dust from the road. Odalie for a while was greatly occupied in keeping in place her filmy skirt, which every gust of wind swelled balloon-like about her

knees. Aunt Pinky's little black, scrawny hand had
found its way among the droopy curls, and strayed often
caressingly to the child's plump neck and shoulders.

"You riclics, honey, dat day yo' granpappy say it
wur pinchin' times an' he reckin he bleege to sell Yallah
Tom an' Susan an' Pinky? Don' know how come he
think 'bout Pinky, 'less caze he sees me playin' an'
trapsin' roun' wid you alls, day in an' out. I riclics yit
how you tu'n w'ite like milk an' fling yo' arms roun'
li'le black Pinky; an' you cries out you don' wan' no
saddle-mar'; you don' wan' no silk dresses and fing'
rings an' sich; an' don' wan' no idication; des wants
Pinky. An' you cries an' screams an' kicks, an' 'low you
gwine kill fus' pusson w'at dar come an' buy Pinky an'
kiars her off. You riclics dat, honey?"

Odalie had grown accustomed to these flights of
fancy on the part of her old friend; she liked to humor
her as she chose to sometimes humor very small children; so she was quite used to impersonating one
dearly beloved but impetuous, "Paulette," who seemed
to have held her place in old Pinky's heart and imagination through all the years of her suffering life.

"I rec'lec' like it was yesterday, Aunt Pinky. How
I scream an' kick an' maman gave me some med'cine;
an' how you scream an' kick an' Susan took you down
to the quarters an' give you 'twenty'."

"Das so, honey; des like you says," chuckled Aunt
Pinky. "But you don' riclic dat time you cotch Pinky
cryin' down in de holler behine de gin; an' you say you
gwine give me 'twenty' ef I don' tell you wa't I cryin'
'bout?"

"I rec'lec' like it happen'd to-day, Aunt Pinky. You
been cryin' because you want to marry Hiram, ole Mr.
Benitou's servant."

"Das true like you says, Miss Paulette; an' you
goes home an' cries and kiars on an' won' eat, an' breaks
dishes, an' pesters yo' gran'pap 'tell he bleedge to buy
Hi'um f'om de Benitous."

"Don't talk, Aunt Pink! I can see all that jus' as
plain!" responded Odalie sympathetically, yet in truth

she took but a languid interest in these reminiscences which she had listened to so often before.

She leaned her flushed cheek against Aunt Pinky's knee.

The air was rippling now, and hot and caressing. There was the hum of bumble bees outside; and busy mud-daubers kept flying in and out through the door. Some chickens had penetrated to the very threshold in their aimless roamings, and the little pig was approaching more cautiously. Sleep was fast overtaking the child, but she could still hear through her drowsiness the familiar tones of Aunt Pinky's voice.

"But Hi'um, he done gone; he nuva come back; an' Yallah Tom nuva come back; an' ole Marster an' de chillun—all gone—nuva come back. Nobody nuva come back to Pinky 'cep you, my honey. You ain' gwine 'way f'om Pinky no mo', is you, Miss Paulette?"

"Don' fret, Aunt Pinky—I'm goin'—to stay with—you."

"No pussun nuva come back 'cep' you."

Odalie was fast asleep. Aunt Pinky was asleep with her head leaning back on her chair and her fingers thrust into the mass of tangled brown hair that swept across her lap. The chickens and little pig walked fearlessly in and out. The sunlight crept close up to the cabin door and stole away again.

Odalie awoke with a start. Her mother was standing over her arousing her from sleep. She sprang up and rubbed her eyes. "Oh, I been asleep!" she exclaimed. The cart was standing in the road waiting. "An' Aunt Pinky, she's asleep, too."

"Yes, chérie, Aunt Pinky is asleep," replied her mother, leading Odalie away. But she spoke low and trod softly as gentle-souled women do, in the presence of the dead.

Dead Men's Shoes
1895

It never occurred to any person to wonder what would befall Gilma now that "le vieux Gamiche" was dead. After the burial people went their several ways, some to talk over the old man and his eccentricities, others to forget him before nightfall, and others to wonder what would become of his very nice property, the hundred-acre farm on which he had lived for thirty years, and on which he had just died at the age of seventy.

If Gilma had been a child, more than one motherly heart would have gone out to him. This one and that one would have bethought them of carrying him home with them; to concern themselves with his present comfort, if not his future welfare. But Gilma was not a child. He was a strapping fellow of nineteen, measuring six feet in his stockings, and as strong as any healthy youth need be. For ten years he had lived there on the plantation with Monsieur Gamiche; and he seemed now to have been the only one with tears to shed at the old man's funeral.

Gamiche's relatives had come down from Caddo in a wagon the day after his death, and had settled themselves in his house. There was Septime, his nephew, a cripple, so horribly afflicted that it was distressing to look at him. And there was Septime's widowed sister, Ma'me Brozé, with her two little girls. They had remained at the house during the burial, and Gilma found them still there upon his return.

The young man went at once to his room to seek a moment's repose. He had lost much sleep during Monsieur Gamiche's illness; yet, he was in fact more worn by the mental than the bodily strain of the past week.

But when he entered his room, there was something so changed in its aspect that it seemed no longer to belong to him. In place of his own apparel which he had left hanging on the row of pegs, there were a few shabby little garments and two battered straw hats, the property of the Brozé children. The bureau drawers were empty, there was not a vestige of anything belonging to him remaining in the room. His first impression was that Ma'me Brozé had been changing things around and had assigned him to some other room.

But Gilma understood the situation better when he discovered every scrap of his personal effects piled up on a bench outside the door, on the back or "false" gallery. His boots and shoes were under the bench, while coats, trousers and underwear were heaped in an indiscriminate mass together.

The blood mounted to his swarthy face and made him look for the moment like an Indian. He had never thought of this. He did not know what he had been thinking of; but he felt that he ought to have been prepared for anything; and it was his own fault if he was not. But it hurt. This spot was "home" to him against the rest of the world. Every tree, every shrub was a friend; he knew every patch in the fences; and the little old house, gray and weather-beaten, that had been the shelter of his youth, he loved as only few can love inanimate things. A great enmity arose in him against Ma'me Brozé. She was walking about the yard, with her nose in the air, and a shabby black dress trailing behind her. She held the little girls by the hand.

Gilma could think of nothing better to do than to mount his horse and ride away—anywhere. The horse was a spirited animal of great value. Monsieur Gamiche had named him "Jupiter" on account of his proud bearing, and Gilma had nicknamed him "Jupe," which seemed to him more endearing and expressive of his great attachment to the fine creature. With the bitter resentment of youth, he felt that "Jupe" was the only friend remaining to him on earth.

He had thrust a few pieces of clothing in his saddlebags and had requested Ma'me Brozé, with assumed indifference, to put his remaining effects in a place of safety until he should be able to send for them.

As he rode around by the front of the house, Septime, who sat on the gallery all doubled up in his uncle Gamiche's big chair, called out:

"Hé, Gilma! w'ere you boun' fo'?"

"I'm goin' away," replied Gilma, curtly, reining his horse.

"That's all right; but I reckon you might jus' as well leave that hoss behine you."

"The hoss is mine," returned Gilma, as quickly as he would have returned a blow.

"We'll see 'bout that li'le later, my frien'. I reckon you jus' well turn 'im loose."

Gilma had no more intention of giving up his horse than he had of parting with his own right hand. But Monsieur Gamiche had taught him prudence and respect for the law. He did not wish to invite disagreeable complications. So, controlling his temper by a supreme effort, Gilma dismounted, unsaddled the horse then and there, and led it back to the stable. But as he started to leave the place on foot, he stopped to say to Septime:

"You know, Mr. Septime, that hoss is mine; I can collec' a hundred aff'davits to prove it. I'll bring them yere in a few days with a statement f'om a lawyer; an' I'll expec' the hoss an' saddle to be turned over to me in good condition."

"That's all right. We'll see 'bout that. Won't you stay fo' dinna?"

"No, I thank you, suh; Ma'me Brozé already ask' me." And Gilma strode away, down the beaten footpath that led across the sloping grassplot toward the outer road.

A definite destination and a settled purpose ahead of him seemed to have revived his flagging energies of an hour before. It was with no trace of fatigue that he stepped out bravely along the wagon-road that skirted the bayou.

It was early spring, and the cotton had already a good stand. In some places the negroes were hoeing. Gilma stopped alongside the rail fence and called to an old negress who was plying her hoe at no great distance.

"Hello, Aunt Hal'fax! see yere."

She turned, and immediately quitted her work to go and join him, bringing her hoe with her across her shoulder. She was largeboned and very black. She was dressed in the deshabille of the field.

"I wish you'd come up to yo' cabin with me a minute, Aunt Hally," he said; "I want to get an aff'davit f'om you."

She understood, after a fashion, what an affidavit was; but she couldn't see the good of it.

"I ain't got no aff'davis, boy; you g'long an' don' pesta me."

"'Twon't take you any time, Aunt Hal'fax. I jus' want you to put yo' mark to a statement I'm goin' to write to the effec' that my hoss, Jupe, is my own prop'-ty; that you know it, an' willin' to swear to it."

"Who say Jupe don' b'long to you?" she questioned cautiously, leaning on her hoe.

He motioned toward the house.

"Who? Mista Septime and them?"

"Yes."

"Well, I reckon!" she exclaimed, sympathetically.

"That's it," Gilma went on; "an' nex' thing they'll be sayin' yo' ole mule, Policy, don't b'long to you."

She started violently.

"Who say so?"

"Nobody. But I say, nex' thing, that' w'at they'll be sayin'."

She began to move along the inside of the fence, and he turned to keep pace with her, walking on the grassy edge of the road.

"I'll jus' write the aff'davit, Aunt Hally, an' all you got to do"—

"You know des well as me dat mule mine. I done paid ole Mista Gamiche fo' 'im in good cotton; dat year you falled outen de puckhorn tree; an' he write it down hisse'f in his 'count book."

Gilma did not linger a moment after obtaining the desired statement from Aunt Halifax. With the first of those "hundred affidavits" that he hoped to secure, safe in his pocket, he struck out across the country, seeking the shortest way to town.

Aunt Halifax stayed in the cabin door.

" 'Relius," she shouted to a little black boy out in the road, "does you see Pol'cy anywhar? G'long, see ef he 'roun' de ben'. Wouldn' s'prise me ef he broke de fence an' got in yo' pa's corn ag'in." And, shading her eyes to scan the surrounding country, she muttered, uneasily: "Whar dat mule?"

The following morning Gilma entered town and proceeded at once to Lawyer Paxton's office. He had no difficulty in obtaining the testimony of blacks and whites regarding his ownership of the horse; but he wanted to make his claim as secure as possible by consulting the lawyer and returning to the plantation armed with unassailable evidence.

The lawyer's office was a plain little room opening upon the street. Nobody was there, but the door was open; and Gilma entered and took a seat at the bare round table and waited. It was not long before the lawyer came in; he had been in conversation with some one across the street.

"Good-morning, Mr. Pax'on," said Gilma, rising.

The lawyer knew his face well enough, but could not place him, and only returned: "Good-morning, sir—good-morning."

"I come to see you," began Gilma plunging at once into business, and drawing his handful of nondescript affidavits from his pocket, "about a matter of prope'ty, about regaining possession of my hoss that Mr. Septime, ole Mr. Gamiche's nephew, is holdin' f'om me yonder."

The lawyer took the papers and, adjusting his eyeglasses, began to look them through.

"Yes, yes," he said; "I see."

"Since Mr. Gamiche died on Tuesday"—began Gilma.

"Gamiche died!" repeated Lawyer Paxton, with astonishment. "Why, you don't mean to tell me that vieux Gamiche is dead? Well, well, I hadn't heard of it; I just returned from Shreveport this morning. So le vieux Gamiche is dead, is he? And you say you want to get possession of a horse. What did you say your name was?" Drawing a pencil from his pocket.

"Gilma Germain is my name, suh."

"Gilma Germain," repeated the lawyer, a little meditatively, scanning his visitor closely. "Yes, I recall your face now. You are the young fellow whom le vieux Gamiche took to live with him some ten or twelve years ago."

"Ten years ago las' November, suh."

Lawyer Paxton arose and went to his safe, from which, after unlocking it, he took a legal-looking document that he proceeded to read carefully through to himself.

"Well, Mr. Germain, I reckon there won't be any trouble about regaining possession of the horse," laughed Lawyer Paxton. "I'm pleased to inform you, my dear sir, that our old friend, Gamiche, has made you sole heir to his property; that is, his plantation, including live stock, farming implements, machinery, household effects, etc. Quite a pretty piece of property," he proclaimed leisurely, seating himself comfortably for a long talk. "And I may add, a pretty piece of luck, Mr. Germain, for a young fellow just starting out in life; nothing but to step into a dead man's shoes! A great chance—great chance. Do you know, sir, the moment you mentioned your name, it came back to me like a flash, how le vieux Gamiche came in here one day, about three years ago, and wanted to make his will"—And the loquacious lawyer went on with his reminiscences and interesting bits of information, of which Gilma heard scarcely a word.

He was stunned, drunk, with the sudden joy of possession; the thought of what seemed to him great wealth, all his own—his own! It seemed as if a hundred different sensations were holding him at once, and as if a thousand intentions crowded upon him. He felt like another being who would have to readjust himself to the new conditions, presenting themselves so unexpectedly. The narrow confines of the office were stifling, and it seemed as if the lawyer's flow of talk would never stop. Gilma arose abruptly, and with a half-uttered apology, plunged from the room into the outer air.

Two days later Gilma stopped again before Aunt Halifax's cabin, on his way back to the plantation. He was walking as before, having declined to avail himself of any one of the several offers of a mount that had been tendered him in town and on the way. A rumor of Gilma's great good fortune had preceded him, and Aunt Halifax greeted him with an almost triumphal shout as he approached.

"God knows you desarve it, Mista Gilma! De Lord knows you does, suh! Come in an' res' yo'se'f, suh. You, 'Relius! git out dis heah cabin; crowdin' up dat away!" She wiped off the best chair available and offered it to Gilma.

He was glad to rest himself and glad to accept Aunt Halifax's proffer of a cup of coffee, which she was in the act of dripping before a small fire. He sat as far as he could from the fire, for the day was warm; he mopped his face, and fanned himself with his broadrimmed hat.

"I des' can't he'p laughin' w'en I thinks 'bout it," said the old woman, fairly shaking, as she leaned over the hearth. "I wakes up in de night, even, an' has to laugh."

"How's that, Aunt Hal'fax," asked Gilma, almost tempted to laugh himself at he knew not what.

"G'long, Mista Gilma! like you don' know! It's w'en I thinks 'bout Septime an' them like I gwine see 'em in dat wagon to-mor' mo'nin', on' dey way back to Caddo. Oh, lawsy!"

"That isn' so ver' funny, Aunt Hal'fax," returned

Gilma, feeling himself ill at ease as he accepted the
cup of coffee which she presented to him with much
ceremony on a platter. "I feel pretty sorry for Septime,
myse'f."

"I reckon he know now who Jupe b'long to," she
went on, ignoring his expression of sympathy; "no need
to tell him who Pol'cy b'long to, nuther. An' I tell you,
Mista Gilma," she went on. leaning upon the table
without seating herself, "dey gwine back to hard times
in Caddo. I heah tell dey nuva gits 'nough to eat,
yonda. Septime, he can't do nuttin' 'cep' set still all
twis' up like a sarpint. An' Ma'me Brozé, she do some
kine sewin'; but don't look like she got sense 'nough to
do dat halfway. An' dem li'le gals, dey 'bleege to run
bar'foot mos' all las' winta', twell dat li'les' gal, she got
her heel plum fros' bit, so dey tells me. Oh, lawsy!
How dey gwin look to-mor', all trapsin' back to Caddo!"

Gilma had never found Aunt Halifax's company so
intensely disagreeable as at that moment. He thanked
her for the coffee, and went away so suddenly as to
startle her. But her good humor never flagged. She
called out to him from the doorway:

"Oh, Mista Gilma! You reckon dey knows who
Pol'cy b'longs to now?"

He somehow did not feel quite prepared to face
Septime; and he lingered along the road. He even
stopped a while to rest, apparently, under the shade of
a huge cottonwood tree that overhung the bayou. From
the very first, a subtle uneasiness, a self-dissatisfaction
had mingled with his elation, and he was trying to discover what it meant.

To begin with, the straightforwardness of his own
nature had inwardly resented the sudden change in the
bearing of most people toward himself. He was trying
to recall, too, something which the lawyer had said; a
little phrase, out of that multitude of words, that had
fallen in his consciousness. It had stayed there, generat-
ing a little festering sore place that was beginning to
make itself irritatingly felt. What was it, that little
phrase? Something about—in his excitement he had
only half heard it—something about dead men's shoes.

The exuberant health and strength of his big body; the courage, virility, endurance of his whole nature revolted against the expression in itself, and the meaning which it conveyed to him. Dead men's shoes! Were they not for such afflicted beings as Septime? as that helpless, dependent woman up there? as those two little ones, with their poorly fed, poorly clad bodies and sweet, appealing eyes? Yet he could not determine how he would act and what he would say to them.

But there was no room left in his heart for hesitancy when he came to face the group. Septime was still crouched in his uncle's chair; he seemed never to have left it since the day of the funeral. Ma'me Brozé had been crying, and so had the children—out of sympathy, perhaps.

"Mr. Septime," said Gilma, approaching, "I brought those aff'davits about the hoss. I hope you about made up yo' mind to turn it over without further trouble."

Septime was trembling, bewildered, almost speechless.

"W'at you mean?" he faltered, looking up with a shifting, sideward glance. "The whole place b'longs to you. You tryin' to make a fool out o' me?"

"Fo' me," returned Gilma, "the place can stay with Mr. Gamiche's own flesh an' blood. I'll see Mr. Pax'on again an' make that according to the law. But I want my hoss."

Gilma took something besides his horse—a picture of le vieux Gamiche, which had stood on his mantelpiece. He thrust it into his pocket. He also took his old benefactor's walking-stick and a gun.

As he rode out of the gate, mounted upon his well-beloved "Jupe," the faithful dog following, Gilma felt as if he had awakened from an intoxicating but depressing dream.

A Night in Acadie
1896

There was nothing to do on the plantation so Telèsphore, having a few dollars in his pocket, thought he would go down and spend Sunday in the vicinity of Marksville.

There was really nothing more to do in the vicinity of Marksville than in the neighborhood of his own small farm; but Elvina would not be down there, nor Amaranthe, nor any of Ma'me Valtour's daughters to harass him with doubt, to torture him with indecision, to turn his very soul into a weather-cock for love's fair winds to play with.

Telèsphore at twenty-eight had long felt the need of a wife. His home without one was like an empty temple in which there is no altar, no offering. So keenly did he realize the necessity that a dozen times at least during the past year he had been on the point of proposing marriage to almost as many different young women of the neighborhood. Therein lay the difficulty, the trouble which Telèsphore experienced in making up his mind. Elvina's eyes were beautiful and had often tempted him to the verge of a declaration. But her skin was over swarthy for a wife; and her movements were slow and heavy; he doubted she had Indian blood, and we all know what Indian blood is for treachery. Amaranthe presented in her person none of these obstacles to matrimony. If her eyes were not so handsome as Elvina's, her skin was fine, and being slender to a fault, she moved swiftly about her household affairs, or when

185

she walked the country lanes in going to church or to the store. Telèsphore had once reached the point of believing that Amaranthe would make him an excellent wife. He had even started out one day with the intention of declaring himself, when, as the god of chance would have it, Ma'me Valtour espied him passing in the road and enticed him to enter and partake of coffee and "baignés." He would have been a man of stone to have resisted, or to have remained insensible to the charms and accomplishments of the Valtour girls. Finally there was Ganache's widow, seductive rather than handsome, with a good bit of property in her own right. While Telèsphore was considering his chances of happiness or even success with Ganache's widow, she married a younger man.

From these embarrassing conditions, Telèsphore sometimes felt himself forced to escape; to change his environment for a day or two and thereby gain a few new insights by shifting his point of view.

It was Saturday morning that he decided to spend Sunday in the vicinity of Marksville, and the same afternoon found him waiting at the country station for the south-bound train.

He was a robust young fellow with good, strong features and a somewhat determined expression—despite his vacillations in the choice of a wife. He was dressed rather carefully in navy-blue "store clothes" that fitted well because anything would have fitted Telèsphore. He had been freshly shaved and trimmed and carried an umbrella. He wore—a little tilted over one eye—a straw hat in preference to the conventional gray felt; for no other reason than that his uncle Telèsphore would have worn a felt, and a battered one at that. His whole conduct of life had been planned on lines in direct contradistinction to those of his uncle Telèsphore, whom he was thought in early youth to greatly resemble. The elder Telèsphore could not read nor write, therefore the younger had made it the object of his existence to acquire these accomplishments. The uncle pursued the avocations of hunting, fishing and moss-picking; employments which the nephew held in detestation. And as for carrying an umbrella, "Nonc" Telèsphore would have walked the length of the parish in a deluge before he would have so much as thought of one. In short, Telèsphore, by advisedly shaping his course in direct opposition to that of his uncle, managed to lead a rather orderly, industrious, and respectable existence.

It was a little warm for April but the car was not uncomfortably crowded and Telèsphore was fortunate enough to secure the last available window-seat on the shady side. He was not too familiar with railway travel, his expeditions being usually made on horse-back or in a buggy, and the short trip promised to interest him.

There was no one present whom he knew well enough to speak to: the district attorney, whom he knew by sight, a French priest from Natchitoches and a few faces that were familiar only because they were native.

But he did not greatly care to speak to anyone. There was a fair stand of cotton and corn in the fields and Telèsphore gathered satisfaction in silent contemplation of the crops, comparing them with his own.

It was toward the close of his journey that a young girl boarded the train. There had been girls getting on and off at intervals and it was perhaps because of the bustle attending her arrival that this one attracted Telèsphore's attention.

She called good-bye to her father from the platform and waved good-bye to him through the dusty, sun-lit window pane after entering, for she was compelled to seat herself on the sunny side. She seemed inwardly excited and preoccupied save for the attention which she lavished upon a large parcel that she carried religiously and laid reverentially down upon the seat before her.

She was neither tall nor short, nor stout nor slender; nor was she beautiful, nor was she plain. She wore a figured lawn, cut a little low in the back, that exposed a round, soft nuque with a few little clinging circlets of soft, brown hair. Her hat was of white straw, cocked up on the side with a bunch of pansies, and she wore gray lisle-thread gloves. The girl seemed very warm and kept mopping her face. She vainly sought her fan, then she fanned herself with her handkerchief, and finally made an attempt to open the window. She might as well have tried to move the banks of Red river.

Telèsphore had been unconsciously watching her the whole time and perceiving her straight he arose and went to her assistance. But the window could not be opened. When he had grown red in the face and wasted an amount of energy that would have driven the plow for a day, he offered her his seat on the shady side. She demurred—there would be no room for the bundle. He suggested that the bundle be left where it was and agreed to assist her in keeping an eye upon it. She accepted Telèsphore's place at the shady window and he seated himself beside her.

He wondered if she would speak to him. He feared she might have mistaken him for a Western drummer, in which event he knew that she would not; for the women of the country caution their daughters against speaking to strangers on the trains. But the girl was not one to mistake an Acadian farmer for a Western traveling man. She was not born in Avoyelles parish for nothing.

"I wouldn' want anything to happen to it," she said.

"It's all right w'ere it is," he assured her, following the direction of her glance, that was fastened upon the bundle.

"The las' time I came over to Foché's ball I got caught in the rain on my way up to my cousin's house, an' my dress! J' vous réponds! it was a sight. Li'le mo', I would miss the ball. As it was, the dress looked like I'd wo' it weeks without doin'-up."

"No fear of rain to-day," he reassured her, glancing out at the sky, "but you can have my umbrella if it does rain; you jus' as well take it as not."

"Oh, no! I wrap' the dress roun' in toile-cirée this time. You goin' to Foché's ball? Didn' I meet you once yonda on Bayou Derbanne? Looks like I know yo' face. You mus' come f'om Natchitoches pa'ish."

"My cousins, the Fédeau family, live yonda. Me, I live on my own place in Rapides since '92."

He wondered if she would follow up her inquiry relative to Foché's ball. If she did, he was ready with an answer, for he had decided to go to the ball. But her thoughts evidently wandered from the subject and were occupied with matters that did not concern him, for she turned away and gazed silently out of the window.

It was not a village; it was not even a hamlet at which they descended. The station was set down upon the edge of a cotton field. Near at hand was the post office and store; there was a section house; there were a few cabins at wide intervals, and one in the distance the girl informed him was the home of her cousin, Jules Trodon. There lay a good bit of road before them and she did not hesitate to accept Telèsphore's offer to bear her bundle on the way.

She carried herself boldly and stepped out freely and easily, like a negress. There was an absence of reserve in her manner; yet there was no lack of womanliness. She had the air of a young person accustomed to decide for herself and for those about her.

"You said yo' name was Fédeau?" she asked, looking squarely at Telèsphore. Her eyes were penetrating—not sharply penetrating, but earnest and dark, and a little searching. He noticed that they were handsome eyes; not so large as Elvina's, but finer in their expression. They started to walk down the track before turning into the lane leading to Trodon's house. The sun was sinking and the air was fresh and invigorating by contrast with the stifling atmosphere of the train.

"You said yo' name was Fédeau?" she asked.

"No," he returned. "My name is Telèsphore Baquette."

"An' my name; it's Zaïda Trodon. It looks like you ought to know me; I don' know w'y."

"It looks that way to me, somehow," he replied. They were satisfied to recognize this feeling—almost conviction—of pre-acquaintance, without trying to penetrate its cause.

By the time they reached Trodon's house he knew that she lived over on Bayou de Glaize with her parents and a number of younger brothers and sisters. It was rather dull where they lived and she often came to lend a hand when her cousin's wife got tangled in domestic complications; or, as she was doing now, when Foché's Saturday ball promised to be unusually important and brilliant. There would be people there even from Marksville, she thought; there were often gentlemen from Alexandria. Telèsphore was as unreserved as she, and they appeared like old acquaintances when they reached Trodon's gate.

Trodon's wife was standing on the gallery with a baby in her arms, watching for Zaïda; and four little bare-footed children were sitting in a row on the step, also waiting; but terrified and struck motionless and dumb at sight of a stranger. He opened the gate for the girl but stayed outside himself. Zaïda presented him formally to her cousin's wife, who insisted upon his entering.

"Ah, b'en, pour ça! you got to come in. It's any sense you goin' to walk yonda to Foché's! Ti Jules, run call yo' pa." As if Ti Jules could have run or walked even, or moved a muscle!

But Telèsphore was firm. He drew forth his silver watch and looked at it in a business-like fashion. He always carried a watch; his uncle Telèsphore always told the time by the sun, or by instinct, like an animal. He was quite determined to walk on to Foché's, a couple of miles away, where he expected to secure supper and a lodging, as well as the pleasing distraction of the ball.

"Well, I reckon I see you all to-night," he uttered in cheerful anticipation as he moved away.

"You'll see Zaïda; yes, an' Jules," called out Trodon's wife good-humoredly. "Me, I got no time to fool with balls, J' vous réponds! with all them chil'ren."

"He's good-lookin'; yes," she exclaimed, when Telèsphore was out of ear-shot. "An' dressed! it's like a prince. I didn' know you knew any Baquettes, you, Zaïda."

"It's strange you don' know 'em yo' se'f, cousine."

Well, there had been no question from Ma'me Trodon, so why should there be an answer from Zaïda?

Telèsphore wondered as he walked why he had not accepted the invitation to enter. He was not regretting it; he was simply wondering what could have induced him to decline. For it surely would have been agreeable to sit there on the gallery waiting while Zaïda prepared herself for the dance; to have partaken of supper with the family and afterward accompanied them to Foché's. The whole situation was so novel, and had presented itself so unexpectedly that Telèsphore wished in reality to become acquainted with it, accustomed to it. He wanted to view it from this side and that in comparison with other, familiar situations. The girl had impressed him—affected him in some way; but in some new, unusual way, not as the others always had. He could not recall details of her personality as he could recall such details of Amaranthe or the Valtours, of any of them. When Telèsphore tried to think of her he could not think at all. He seemed to have absorbed her in some way and his brain was not so occupied with her as his senses were. At that moment he was looking forward to the ball; there was no doubt about that. Afterwards, he did not know what he would look forward to; he did not care; afterward made no difference. If he had expected the crash of doom to come after the dance at Foché's, he would only have smiled in his thankfulness that it was not to come before.

There was the same scene every Saturday at Foché's! A scene to have aroused the guardians of the peace in a locality where such commodities abound. And all on account of the mammoth pot of gumbo that bubbled, bubbled, bubbled out in the open air. Foché in shirt-sleeves, fat, red and enraged, swore and reviled, and stormed at old black Douté for her extravagance. He called her every kind of a name of every kind of animal that suggested itself to his lurid imagination. And every fresh invective that he fired at her she hurled it back at him while into the pot went the chickens and the pans-full of minced ham, and the fists-full of onion and sage and piment rouge and piment vert. If he wanted her to cook for pigs he had only to say so. She knew how to cook for pigs and she knew how to cook for people of les Avoyelles.

The gumbo smelled good, and Telèsphore would have liked a taste of it. Douté was dragging from the fire a stick of wood that Foché had officiously thrust beneath the simmering pot, and she muttered as she hurled it smouldering to one side:

"Vaux mieux y s'mêle ces affairs, lui; si non!" But she was all courtesy as she dipped a steaming plate for Telèsphore; though she assured him it would not be fit for a Christian or a gentleman to taste till midnight.

Telèsphore having brushed, "spruced" and refreshed himself, strolled about, taking a view of the surroundings. The house, big, bulky and weather-beaten, consisted chiefly of galleries in every stage of decrepitude and dilapidation. There were a few china-berry trees and a spreading live oak in the yard. Along the edge of the fence, a good distance away, was a line of gnarled and distorted mulberry trees; and it was there, out in the road, that the people who came to the ball tied their ponies, their wagons and carts.

Dusk was beginning to fall and Telèsphore, looking out across the prairie, could see them coming from all directions. The little Creole ponies galloping in a line looked like hobby horses in the faint distance; the mule-carts were like toy wagons. Zaïda might be among those people approaching, flying, crawling ahead of the darkness that was creeping out of the far wood. He hoped so, but he did not believe so; she would hardly have had time to dress.

Foché was noisily lighting lamps, with the assistance of an inoffensive mulatto boy whom he intended in the morning to butcher, to cut into sections, to pack and salt down in a barrel, like the Colfax woman did to her old husband—a fitting destiny for so stupid a pig as the mulatto boy. The negro musicians had arrived: two fiddlers and an accordion player, and they were drinking whiskey from a black quart bottle which was passed socially from one to the other. The musicians

were really never at their best till the quart bottle had
been consumed.

The girls who came in wagons and on ponies from
a distance wore, for the most part, calico dresses and
sun-bonnets. Their finery they brought along in pillow-
slips or pinned up in sheets and towels. With these
they at once retired to an upper room; later to appear
be-ribboned and be-furbelowed; their faces masked
with starch powder, but never a touch of rouge.

Most of the guests had assembled when Zaïda arrived—"dashed up" would better express her coming—
in an open, two-seated buckboard, with her cousin
Jules driving. He reined the pony suddenly and viciously before the time-eaten front steps, in order to
produce an impression upon those who were gathered
around. Most of the men had halted their vehicles outside and permitted their women folk to walk up from
the mulberry trees.

But the real, the stunning effect was produced
when Zaïda stepped upon the gallery and threw aside
her light shawl in the full glare of half a dozen kerosene
lamps. She was white from head to foot—literally, for
her slippers even were white. No one would have believed, let alone suspected, that they were a pair of old
black ones which she had covered with pieces of her
first communion sash. There is no describing her dress,
it was fluffy, like a fresh powder-puff, and stood out.
No wonder she had handled it so reverentially! Her
white fan was covered with spangles that she herself
had sewed all over it; and in her belt and in her brown
hair were thrust small sprays of orange blossom.

Two men leaning against the railing uttered long
whistles expressive equally of wonder and admiration.

"Tiens! t'es pareille comme ain mariée, Zaïda,"
cried out a lady with a baby in her arms. Some young
women tittered and Zaïda fanned herself. The women's
voices were almost without exception shrill and pierc-
ing; the men's, soft and low-pitched.

The girl turned to Telèsphore, as to an old and
valued friend:

"Tiens! c'est vous?" He had hesitated at first to

approach, but at this friendly sign of recognition he
drew eagerly forward and held out his hand. The men
looked at him suspiciously, inwardly resenting his stylish appearance, which they considered intrusive, offensive and demoralizing.

How Zaïda's eyes sparkled now! What very pretty
teeth Zaïda had when she laughed, and what a mouth!
Her lips were a revelation, a promise; something to
carry away and remember in the night and grow hungry
thinking of next day. Strictly speaking, they may not
have been quite all that; but in any event, that is the
way Telèsphore thought about them. He began to take
account of her appearance: her nose, her eyes, her hair.
And when she left him to go in and dance her first
dance with cousin Jules, he leaned up against a post
and thought of them: nose, eyes, hair, ears, lips and
round, soft throat.

Later it was like Bedlam.

The musicians had warmed up and were scraping
away indoors and calling the figures. Feet were pounding through the dance; dust was flying. The women's
voices were piped high and mingled discordantly, like
the confused, shrill clatter of waking birds, while the
men laughed boisterously. But if some one had only
thought of gagging Foché, there would have been less
noise. His good humor permeated everywhere, like an
atmosphere. He was louder than all the noise; he was
more visible than the dust. He called the young mulatto (destined for the knife) "my boy" and sent him
flying hither and thither. He beamed upon Douté as
he tasted the gumbo and congratulated her: "C'est toi
qui s'y connais, ma fille! 'cré tonnerre!"

Telèsphore danced with Zaïda and then he leaned
out against the post; then he danced with Zaïda, and
then he leaned against the post. The mothers of the
other girls decided that he had the manners of a pig.

It was time to dance again with Zaïda and he went
in search of her. He was carrying her shawl, which she
had given him to hold.

"W'at time is it?" she asked him when he had

found and secured her. They were under one of the
kerosene lamps on the front gallery and he drew forth
his silver watch. She seemed to be still laboring under
some suppressed excitement that he had noticed
before.

"It's fo'teen minutes pas' twelve," he told her
exactly.

"I wish you'd fine out w'ere Jules is. Go look yonda
in the card-room if he's there, an' come tell me." Jules
had danced with all the prettiest girls. She knew it was
his custom after accomplishing this agreeable feat, to
retire to the card-room.

"You'll wait yere till I come back?" he asked.

"I'll wait yere; you go on." She waited but drew
back a little into the shadow. Telèsphore lost no time.

"Yes, he's yonda playin' cards with Foché an' some
others I don' know," he reported when he had discovered her in the shadow. There had been a spasm of
alarm when he did not at once see her where he had
left her under the lamp.

"Does he look—look like he's fixed yonda fo'
good?"

"He's got his coat off. Looks like he's fixed pretty
comf'table fo' the nex' hour or two."

"Gi' me my shawl."

"You cole?" offering to put it around her.

"No, I ain't cole." She drew the shawl about her
shoulders and turned as if to leave him. But a sudden
generous impulse seemed to move her, and she added:

"Come along yonda with me."

They descended the few rickety steps that led
down to the yard. He followed rather than accompanied
her across the beaten and trampled sward. Those who
saw them thought they had gone out to take the air.
The beams of light that slanted out from the house
were fitful and uncertain, deepening the shadows. The
embers under the empty gumbo-pot glared red in the
darkness. There was a sound of quiet voices coming
from under the trees.

Zaïda, closely accompanied by Telèsphore, went

out where the vehicles and horses were fastened to the fence. She stepped carefully and held up her skirts as if dreading the least speck of dew or of dust.

"Unhitch Jules' ho'se an' buggy there an' turn 'em 'roun' this way, please." He did as instructed, first backing the pony, then leading it out to where she stood in the half-made road.

"You goin' home?" he asked her, "betta let me water the pony."

"Neva mine." She mounted and seating herself grasped the reins. "No, I ain't goin' home," she added. He, too, was holding the reins gathered in one hand across the pony's back.

"W'ere you goin'?" he demanded.

"Neva you mine w'ere I'm goin'."

"You ain't goin' anyw'ere this time o' night by yo'se'f?"

"W'at you reckon I'm 'fraid of?" she laughed. "Turn loose that ho'se," at the same time urging the animal forward. The little brute started away with a bound and Telèsphore, also with a bound, sprang into the buckboard and seated himself beside Zaïda.

"You ain't goin' anyw'ere this time o' night by yo'se'f." It was not a question now, but an assertion, and there was no denying it. There was even no disputing it, and Zaïda recognizing the fact drove on in silence.

There is no animal that moves so swiftly across a 'Cadian prairie as the little Creole pony. This one did not run nor trot; he seemed to reach out in galloping bounds. The buckboard creaked, bounced, jolted and swayed. Zaïda clutched at her shawl while Telèsphore drew his straw hat further down over his right eye and offered to drive. But he did not know the road and she would not let him. They had soon reached the woods.

If there is any animal that can creep more slowly through a wooded road than the little Creole pony, that animal has not yet been discovered in Acadie. This particular animal seemed to be appalled by the darkness of the forest and filled with dejection. His head drooped and he lifted his feet as if each hoof were

weighted with a thousand pounds of lead. Any one unacquainted with the peculiarities of the breed would
sometimes have fancied that he was standing still. But
Zaïda and Telèsphore knew better. Zaïda uttered a
deep sigh as she slackened her hold on the reins and
Telèsphore, lifting his hat, let it swing from the back
of his head.

"How you don' ask me w'ere I'm goin'?" she said
finally. These were the first words she had spoken since
refusing his offer to drive.

"Oh, it don' make any diff'ence w'ere you goin'."

"Then if it don' make any diff'ence w'ere I'm goin',
I jus' as well tell you." She hesitated, however. He
seemed to have no curiosity and did not urge her.

"I'm goin' to get married," she said.

He uttered some kind of an exclamation; it was
nothing articulate—more like the tone of an animal that
gets a sudden knife thrust. And now he felt how dark
the forest was. An instant before it had seemed a sweet,
black paradise; better than any heaven he had ever
heard of.

"W'y can't you get married at home?" This was not
the first thing that occurred to him to say, but this was
the first thing he said.

"Ah, b'en oui! with perfec' mules fo' a father an'
mother! it's good enough to talk."

"W'y couldn' he come an' get you? W'at kine of a
scoun'el is that to let you go through the woods at
night by yo'se'f?"

"You betta wait till you know who you talkin'
about. He didn' come an' get me because he knows I
ain't 'fraid; an' because he's got too much pride to ride
in Jules Trodon's buckboard afta he done been put out
o' Jules Trodon's house."

"W'at's his name an' w'ere you goin' to fine 'im?"

"Yonda on the other side the woods up at ole Wat
Gibson's—a kine of justice of the peace or something.
Anyhow he's goin' to marry us. An' afta we done married those têtes-de-mulets yonda on bayou de Glaize
can say w'at they want."

"W'at's his name?"

"André Pascal."

The name meant nothing to Telèsphore. For all he knew, André Pascal might be one of the shining lights of Avoyelles; but he doubted it.

"You betta turn 'roun'," he said. It was an unselfish impulse that prompted the suggestion. It was the thought of this girl married to a man whom even Jules Trodon would not suffer to enter his house.

"I done give my word," she answered.

"W'at's the matta with 'im? W'y don't yo' father and mother want you to marry 'im?"

"W'y? Because it's always the same tune! W'en a man's down eve'ybody's got stones to throw at 'im. They say he's lazy. A man that will walk from St. Landry plumb to Rapides lookin' fo' work; an' they call that lazy! Then, somebody's been spreadin' yonda on the Bayou that he drinks. I don' b'lieve it. I neva saw 'im drinkin', me. Anyway, he won't drink afta he's married to me; he's too fon' of me fo' that. He say he'll blow out his brains if I don' marry 'im."

"I reckon you betta turn roun'."

"No, I done give my word." And they went creeping on through the woods in silence.

"W'at time is it?" she asked after an interval. He lit a match and looked at his watch.

"It's quarta to one. W'at time did he say?"

"I tole 'im I'd come about one o'clock. I knew that was a good time to get away f'om the ball."

She would have hurried a little but the pony could not be induced to do so. He dragged himself, seemingly ready at any moment to give up the breath of life. But once out of the woods he made up for lost time. They were on the open prairie again, and he fairly ripped the air; some flying demon must have changed skins with him.

It was a few minutes of one o'clock when they drew up before Wat Gibson's house. It was not much more than a rude shelter, and in the dim starlight it seemed isolated, as if standing alone in the middle of the black, far-reaching prairie. As they halted at the gate a dog within set up a furious barking; and an old negro who had been smoking his pipe at that ghostly hour, advanced toward them from the shelter of the gallery. Telèsphore descended and helped his companion to alight.

"We want to see Mr. Gibson," spoke up Zaïda. The old fellow had already opened the gate. There was no light in the house.

"Marse Gibson, he yonda to ole Mr. Bodel's playin' kairds. But he neva' stay atter one o'clock. Come in, ma'am; come in, suh; walk right 'long in." He had drawn his own conclusions to explain their appearance. They stood upon the narrow porch waiting while he went inside to light the lamp.

Although the house was small, as it comprised but one room, that room was comparatively a large one. It looked to Telèsphore and Zaïda very large and gloomy when they entered it. The lamp was on a table that stood against the wall, and that held further a rusty looking ink bottle, a pen and an old blank book. A narrow bed was off in the corner. The brick chimney extended into the room and formed a ledge that served as mantel shelf. From the big, low-hanging rafters swung an assortment of fishing tackle, a gun, some discarded articles of clothing and a string of red peppers. The boards of the floor were broad, rough and loosely joined together.

Telèsphore and Zaïda seated themselves on opposite sides of the table and the negro went out to the wood pile to gather chips and pieces of bois-gras with which to kindle a small fire.

It was a little chilly; he supposed the two would want coffee and he knew that Wat Gibson would ask for a cup the first thing on his arrival.

"I wonder w'at's keepin' 'im," muttered Zaïda impatiently. Telèsphore looked at his watch. He had been looking at it at intervals of one minute straight along.

"It's ten minutes pas' one," he said. He offered no further comment.

At twelve minutes past one Zaïda's restlessness again broke into speech.

"I can't imagine, me, w'at's become of André! He

said he'd be yere sho' at one." The old negro was kneeling before the fire that he had kindled, contemplating the cheerful blaze. He rolled his eyes toward Zaïda.

"You talkin' 'bout Mr. André Pascal? No need to look fo' him. Mr. André he b'en down to de P'int all day raisin' Cain."

"That's a lie," said Zaïda. Telèsphore said nothing.

"Tain't no lie, ma'am; he b'en sho raisin' de ole Nick." She looked at him, too contemptuous to reply.

The negro told no lie so far as his bald statement was concerned. He was simply mistaken in his estimate of André Pascal's ability to "raise Cain" during an entire afternoon and evening and still keep a rendezvous with a lady at one o'clock in the morning. For André was even then at hand, as the loud and menacing howl of the dog testified. The negro hastened out to admit him.

André did not enter at once; he stayed a while outside abusing the dog and communicating to the negro his intention of coming out to shoot the animal after he had attended to more pressing business that was awaiting him within.

Zaïda arose, a little flurried and excited when he entered. Telèsphore remained seated.

Pascal was partially sober. There had evidently been an attempt at dressing for the occasion at some early part of the previous day, but such evidences had almost wholly vanished. His linen was soiled and his whole appearance was that of a man who, by an effort, had aroused himself from a debauch. He was a little taller than Telèsphore, and more loosely put together. Most women would have called him a handsomer man. It was easy to imagine that when sober, he might betray by some subtle grace of speech or manner, evidences of gentle blood.

"W'y did you keep me waitin', André? w'en you knew—" she got no further, but backed up against the table and stared at him with earnest, startled eyes.

"Keep you waiting, Zaïda? my dear li'le Zaïdé, how can you say such a thing! I started up yere an hour ago an' that—w'ere's that damned ole Gibson?" He had approached Zaïda with the evident intention of embracing her, but she seized his wrist and held him at arm's length away. In casting his eyes about for old Gibson his glance alighted upon Telèsphore.

The sight of the 'Cadian seemed to fill him with astonishment. He stood back and began to contemplate the young fellow and lose himself in speculation and conjecture before him, as if before some unlabeled wax figure. He turned for information to Zaïda.

"Say, Zaïda, w'at you call this? W'at kine of damn fool you got sitting yere? Who let him in? W'at you reckon he's lookin' fo'? trouble?"

Telèsphore said nothing; he was awaiting his cue from Zaïda.

"André Pascal," she said, "you jus' as well take the do' an' go. You might stan' yere till the day o' judgment on yo' knees befo' me; an' blow out yo' brains if you a mine to. I ain't neva goin' to marry you."

"The hell you ain't!"

He had hardly more than uttered the words when he lay prone on his back. Telèsphore had knocked him down. The blow seemed to complete the process of sobering that had begun in him. He gathered himself together and rose to his feet; in doing so he reached back for his pistol. His hold was not yet steady, however, and the weapon slipped from his grasp and fell to the floor. Zaïda picked it up and laid it on the table behind her. She was going to see fair play.

The brute instinct that drives men at each other's throat was awake and stirring in these two. Each saw in the other a thing to be wiped out of his way—out of existence if need be. Passion and blind rage directed the blows which they dealt, and steeled the tension of muscles and clutch of fingers. They were not skillful blows, however.

The fire blazed cheerily; the kettle which the negro had placed upon the coals was steaming and singing. The man had gone in search of his master. Zaïda had placed the lamp out of harm's way on the high mantel ledge and she leaned back with her hands behind her upon the table.

She did not raise her voice or lift her finger to

stay the combat that was acting before her. She was motionless, and white to the lips; only her eyes seemed to be alive and burning and blazing. At one moment she felt that André must have strangled Telèsphore; but she said nothing. The next instant she could hardly doubt that the blow from Telèsphore's doubled fist could be less than a killing one; but she did nothing.

How the loose boards swayed and creaked beneath the weight of the struggling men! the very old rafters seemed to groan; and she felt that the house shook.

The combat, if fierce, was short, and it ended out on the gallery whither they had staggered through the open door—or one had dragged the other—she could not tell. But she knew when it was over, for there was a long moment of utter stillness. Then she heard one of the men descend the steps and go away, for the gate slammed after him. The other went out to the cistern; the sound of the tin bucket splashing in the water reached her where she stood. He must have been endeavoring to remove traces of the encounter.

Presently Telèsphore entered the room. The elegance of his apparel had been somewhat marred; the men over at the 'Cadian ball would hardly have taken exception now to his appearance.

"W'ere is André?" the girl asked.

"He's gone," said Telèsphore.

She had never changed her position and now when she drew herself up her wrists ached and she rubbed them a little. She was no longer pale; the blood had come back into her cheeks and lips, staining them crimson. She held out her hand to him. He took it gratefully enough, but he did not know what to do with it; that is, he did not know what he might dare to do with it, so he let it drop gently away and went to the fire.

"I reckon we betta be goin', too," she said. He stooped and poured some of the bubbling water from the kettle upon the coffee which the negro had set upon the hearth.

"I'll make a li'le coffee firs'," he proposed, "an' anyhow we betta wait till ole man w'at's-his-name comes back. It wouldn't look well to leave his house that way without some kine of excuse or explanation."

She made no reply, but seated herself submissively beside the table.

Her will, which had been overmastering and aggressive, seemed to have grown numb under the disturbing spell of the past few hours. An illusion had gone from her, and had carried her love with it. The absence of regret revealed this to her. She realized, but could not comprehend it, not knowing that the love had been part of the illusion. She was tired in body and spirit, and it was with a sense of restfulness that she sat all drooping and relaxed and watched Telèsphore make the coffee.

He made enough for them both and a cup for old Wat Gibson when he should come in, and also one for the negro. He supposed the cups, the sugar and spoons were in the safe over there in the corner, and that is where he found them.

When he finally said to Zaïda, "Come, I'm going to take you home now," and drew her shawl around her, pinning it under the chin, she was like a little child and followed whither he led in all confidence.

It was Telèsphore who drove on the way back, and he let the pony cut no capers, but held him to a steady and tempered gait. The girl was still quiet and silent; she was thinking tenderly—a little tearfully of those two old têtes-de-mulets yonder on Bayou de Glaize.

How they crept through the woods! and how dark it was and how still!

"W'at time it is?" whispered Zaïda. Alas! he could not tell her; his watch was broken. But almost for the first time in his life, Telèsphore did not care what time it was.

A Family Affair
1897

The moment that the wagon rattled out of the yard away to the station, Madame Solisainte settled herself into a state of nervous expectancy.

She was superabundantly fat; and her body accommodated itself to the huge chair in which she sat, filling up curves and crevices like water poured into a mould. She was clad in an ample muslin *peignoir* sprigged with brown. Her cheeks were flabby, her mouth thin-lipped and decisive. Her eyes were small, watchful, and at the same time timid. Her brown hair, streaked with gray, was arranged in a bygone fashion, a narrow mesh being drawn back from the centre of the forehead to conceal a bald spot, and the sides plastered down smooth over her small, close ears.

The room in which she sat was large and uncarpeted. There were handsome and massive pieces of furniture decorating the apartment, and a magnificent brass clock stood on the mantelpiece.

Madame Solisainte sat at a back window which overlooked the yard, the brick kitchen—a little removed from the house—and the field road which led down to the negro quarters. She was unable to leave her chair. It was an affair of importance to get her out of bed in the morning, and an equally arduous task to put her back there at night.

It was a sore affliction to the old woman to be thus incapacitated during her latter years, and rendered

unable to watch and control her household affairs. She
was sure that she was being robbed continuously and
on all sides. This conviction was nourished and kept
alive by her confidential servant, Dimple, a very black
girl of sixteen, who trod softly about on her bare feet
and had thereby made herself unpopular in the kitchen
and down at the quarters.

The notion had entered Madame Solisainte's head
to have one of her nieces come up from New Orleans
and stay with her. She thought it would be doing the
niece and her family a great kindness, and would fur-
thermore be an incalculable saving to herself in many
ways, and far cheaper than hiring a housekeeper.

There were four nieces, not too well off, with
whom she was indifferently acquainted. In selecting
one of these to make her home on the plantation she
exercised no choice, leaving that matter to her sister
and the girls, to be settled among them.

It was Bosey who consented to go to her aunt. Her
mother spelled her name Bosé. She herself spelled it
Bosey. But as often as not she was called plain Bose.
It was she who was sent, because, as her mother wrote
to Madame Solisainte, Bosé was a splendid manager, a
most excellent housekeeper, and moreover possessed a
temperament of such rare amiability that none could
help being cheered and enlivened by her presence.

What she did not write was that none of the other
girls would entertain the notion for an instant of making
even a temporary abiding place with their *Tante* Félicie. And Bosey's consent was only wrung from her with
the understanding that the undertaking was purely ex-
perimental, and that she bound herself by no cast-iron
obligations.

Madame Solisainte had sent the wagon to the station for her niece, and was impatiently awaiting its
return.

"It's no sign of the wagon yet, Dimple? You don't
see it? You don't year it coming "

"No'um; 'tain't no sign. De train des 'bout lef' de
station. I yeard it w'istle." Dimple stood on the back
porch beside her mistress' open window. She wore a

calico dress so skimp and inadequate that her growing figure was bursting through the rents and apertures. She was constantly pinning it at the back of the waist with a bent safety-pin which was forever giving way. The task of pinning her dress and biting the old brass safety-pin into shape occupied a great deal of her time.

"It's true," Madame said. "I recommend to Daniel to drive those mule' very slow in this hot weather. They are not strong, those mule'.'"

"He drive 'em slow 'nough long 's he's in the fiel' road!" exclaimed Dimple. "Time he git roun' in de big road whar you kain't see 'im—uh! uh! he make' dem mule' fa'r' lope!"

Madame tightened her lips and blinked her eyes. She rarely replied otherwise to these disclosures of Dimple, but they sank into her soul and festered there.

The cook—in reality a big-boned field hand—came in with pans and pails to get out the things for supper. Madame kept her provisions right there under her nose in a large closet, or cupboard, which she had had built in the side of the room. A small supply of butter was in a jar that stood on the hearth, and the eggs were kept in a basket that hung on a peg near by.

Dimple came in and unlocked the cupboard, taking the keys from her mistress' bag. She gave out a little flour, a little meal, a cupful of coffee, some sugar and a piece of bacon. Four eggs were wanted for a pudding, but Madame thought that two would be enough, finally compromising, however, upon three.

Miss Bosey Brantonniere arrived at her aunt's house with three trunks, a large, circular, tin bathtub, a bundle of umbrellas and sunshades, and a small dog. She was a pretty, energetic-looking girl, with her chin in the air, tastefully dressed in the latest fashion, and dispersing an atmosphere of bustle and importance about her. Daniel had driven her up the field road, depositing her at the back entrance, where Madame, from her window, commanded a complete view of her arrival.

"I thought you would have sent the carriage for me, *Tante* Félicie, but Daniel tells me you have no carriage," said the girl after the first greetings were over. She had had her trunks taken to her room, the tub slipped under the bed, and now she sat fondling the dog and talking to *Tante* Félicie.

The old lady shook her head dismally and her lips curled into a disparaging smile.

"Oh! no, no! The ol' carriage 'as been sol' ages ago to Zéphire Lablatte. It was falling to piece' in the shed. Me—I never stir f'um w'ere you see me; it is good two year' since I 'ave been inside the church, let alone to go *en promenade.*"

"Well, I'm going to take all care and bother off your shoulders, *Tante* Félicie," uttered the girl cheerfully. "I'm going to brighten things up for you, and we'll see how quickly you'll improve. Why, in less than two months I'll have you on your feet, going about as spry as anybody."

Madame was far less hopeful. "My ol' mother was the same," she replied with dejected resignation. "Nothing could 'elp her. She lived many year' like you see me; your mamma mus' 'ave often tol' you."

Mrs. Brantonniere had never related to the girls anything disparaging concerning their Aunt Félicie, but other members of the family had been less considerate, and Bosey had often been told of her aunt's avarice and grasping ways. How she had laid her clutch upon her mother's belongings, taking undisputed possession by the force of audacity alone. The girl could not help thinking it must have been while her grandmother sat so helpless in her huge chair that *Tante* Félicie had made herself mistress of the situation. But she was not one to harbor malice. She felt very sorry for *Tante* Félicie, so afflicted in her childless old age.

Madame lay long awake that night troubled someway over the advent of this niece from New Orleans, who was not precisely what she had expected. She did not like the excess of trunks, the bathtub and the dog, all of which savored of extravagance. Nor did she like the chin in the air, which indicated determination and promised trouble.

Dimple was warned next morning to say nothing

to her mistress concerning a surprise which Miss Bosey had in store for her. This surprise was that, instead of being deposited in her accustomed place at the back window, where she could keep an eye upon her people, Madame was installed at the front-room window that looked out toward the live oaks and along a leafy, sleepy road that was seldom used.

"*Jamais! Jamais!* it will never do! *Pas possible!*" cried out the old lady with helpless excitement when she perceived what was about to be done to her.

"You'll do just as I say, *Tante* Félicie," said Bosey, with sprightly determination. "I'm here to take care of you and make you comfortable, and I'm going to do it. Now, instead of looking out on that hideous back yard, full of dirty little darkies, and pigs and chickens wallowing round, here you have this sweet, peaceful view whenever you look out of the window. Now, here comes Dimple with the magazines and things. Bring them right here, Dimple, and lay them on the table beside Ma'me Félicie. I brought these up from the city expressly for you, *Tante,* and I have a whole trunkful more when you are through with them."

Dimple was entering, staggering with arms full of books and periodicals of all sizes, shapes and colors. The strain of carrying the weight of literature had caused the safety-pin to give way, and Dimple greatly feared it might have fallen and been lost.

"So, *Tante* Félicie, you'll have nothing to do but read and enjoy yourself. Here are some French books mamma sent you, something by Daudet, something by Maupassant and a lot more. Here, let me brighten up your spectacles." She brightened the old lady's glasses with a piece of thin tissue paper which fell from one of the books.

"And now, Madame Solisainte, you give me all the keys! Turn them right over, and I'll go out and make myself thoroughly acquainted with everything." Madame spasmodically clutched the bag that swung to the arm of her chair.

"Oh! a whole bagful!" exclaimed the girl, gently

but firmly disengaging it from her aunt's claw-like fingers. "My, what an undertaking I have before me! Dimple had better show me round this morning until I get thoroughly acquainted. You can knock on the floor with your stick when you want her. Come along, Dimple. Fasten your dress." The girl was scanning the floor for the safety-pin, which she found out in the hall.

During all of Madame Solisainte's days no one had ever spoken to her with the authority which this young woman assumed. She did not know what to make of it. She felt that she should have revolted at once against being thus banished to the front room. She should have spoken out and maintained possession of her keys when demanded, with the spirit of a highway robber, to give them up. She pounded her stick on the floor with loud and sudden energy. Dimple appeared with inquisitive eyes.

"Dimple," said Madame, "tell Miss Bosé to please 'ave the kin'ness an sen' me back my bag of key'."

Dimple vanished and returned almost on the instant.

"Miss Bosey 'low don't you bodda. Des you go on lookin' at de picters. She ain' gwine let nuttin' happen to de keys."

After an uneasy interval Madame recalled the girl.

"Dimple, if you could look in the bag an' bring me my armoire key—you know it—the brass one. Do not let on as though I would want that key in partic'lar."

"De bag hangin' on her arm. She got de string twis' roun' her wris'," reported Dimple presently. Madame Félicie inwardly fumed with impotent rage.

"W'at is she doing, Dimple?" she asked uneasily.

"She got de cubbud do's fling wide open. She standin' on a cha'r lookin' in de corners an' behin' eve'ything."

"Dimple!" called out Bosey from the far room. And away flew Dimple, who had not been so pleasingly agitated since the previous Christmas.

After a little while, of her own accord she stole noiselessly back into the room where Madame Félicie sat in speechless wrath beside the table of books. She closed the door behind her, rolled her eyes, and spoke in a hoarse whisper:

"She done fling 'way de barrel o' meal; 'low it all fill up wid weevils."

"Weevil'!" cried out her mistress.

"Yas'um, weevils; 'low it plumb sp'ilt. 'Low it on'y fitten fo' de chickens an' hogs; 'tain't fitten fo' folks. She done make Dan'el roll it out on de gal'ry."

"Weevil'!" reiterated Madame Félicie, tremulous with suppressed excitement. "Bring me some of that meal in a saucer, Dimple. Don't let on anything."

She and Dimple bent over the cup of meal which the girl brought concealed under her skirt.

"Do you see any weevil', you, Dimple?"

"No'um." Dimple smelled it, and Madame felt the sample of meal and rolled a pinch or two between her fingers. It was lumpy, musty and old.

"She got Susan out dah helpin' her," insinuated Dimple, "an' Sam an' Dan'el; all helpin' her."

"*Bon Dieu!* it won't be a grain of sugar left, a bar of soap—nothing! nothing! Go watch, Dimple. Don't stan' there like a stick."

"She 'low she gwine sen' Susan back to wuk in de fiel'," went on Dimple, heedless of her mistress' admonition. "She 'low Susan don' know how to cook. Susan say she willin' to go back, her. An' Miss Bosey, she ax Dan'el ef he know a fus'-class cook, w'at kin brile chicken an' steak an' make good soup, an' waffles, an' rolls, an' fricassée, an' dessert, an' custud, an sich."

She passed her tongue over a slobbering lip. "Dan'el say his wife Mandy done cook fo' de pa'tic'lest people in town, but she don' wuk cheap 'nough fo' Ma'me Félicie. An' Miss Bosey, she 'low it don' make no odd' 'bout de price, 'long she git hole o' somebody wa't know how to cook."

Madame's fingers worked nervously at the illuminated cover of a magazine. She said nothing. Only tightened her lips and blinked her small eyes.

When Bosey thrust her head in at the door to inquire how "*Tantine*" was getting on, the old lady fumbled at the books with a pretense of having been occupied with looking at them.

"That's right, *Tante* Félicie! You look as comfortable as can be. I wanted to make you a nice glass of lemonade, but Susan tells me there isn't a lemon on the place. I told Fannie's boy to bring up half a box of lemons from Lablatte's store in the handcart. There's nothing healthier than lemonade in summer. And he's going to bring a chunk of ice, too. We'll have to order ice from town after this." She had on a white apron over her gingham dress, and her sleeves were rolled to the elbows.

"I detes' lemonade; it is bad for *mon estomac*," interposed Madame vehemently. "We 'ave no use in the worl' for lemon', an' there is no place vere to keep ice. Tell Fannie's boy never min' about lemon' an' ice."

"Oh, he's gone long ago! And as for the ice, why, Daniel says he can make me me a box lined with sawdust—he made one for Doctor Godfrey. We can keep it under the back porch." And away she went, the embodiment of the thoroughgoing, bustling little housewife. Somewhat past noon, Dimple came in with an air of importance, removed the books, and spread a white damask cloth upon the table. It was like spreading a red cloth before a sullen bull. Madame's eyes glared at the cloth.

"W'ere did you get that?" she asked as if she would have annihilated Dimple on the spot.

"Miss Bosey, she tuck it out de big press; tuck some mo' out; 'low she kain't eat on dat meal-sack w'at we alls calls de table-clot'e." The damask cloth bore the initials of Madame's mother, embroidered in a corner.

"She done kilt two dem young pullets in de *basse-cour*," went on Dimple, like a croaking raven. "Mandy come lopin' up f'om de quarters time Dan'el told 'er. She yonder, rarin' roun' in de kitchen. Dey done sent fo' some sto' lard an' bakin' powders down to Lablatte's. Fannie's boy, he ben totin' all mornin'. De cubbud done look lak a sto'."

"Dimple!" called Bosey in the distance.

When she returned it was with a pompous air, her head uplifted, and stepping carefully like a fat chicken.

She bore a tray weighted with a repast such as she had never before in her life served to Madame Solisainte.

Mandy had outdone herself. She had broiled the breast of a pullet to a turn. She had fried the potatoes after a New Orleans receipt, and had made a pudding of richest ingredients of her own invention which had given her a name in the parish. There were two milky-looking poached eggs, and the biscuits were as light as snowflakes and the color of gold. The forks and spoons were of massive silver, also bearing the initials of Madame's mother. They had been reclaimed from the press with the table linen.

Under this new, strange influence Madame Solisainte seemed to have been deprived of the power of asserting her will. There was an occasional outburst like the flare of a smouldering fire, but she was outwardly timid and submissive. Only when she was alone with her young handmaid did she speak her mind.

Bosey took special care in arranging her aunt's toilet one morning not long after her arrival. She fastened a sheer white 'kerchief (which she found in the press) about the old lady's neck. She powdered her face from her own box of *duvet de cygne;* and she gave her a fine linen handkerchief (which she also found in the press), sprinkling it from the bottle of cologne water which she had brought from New Orleans. She filled the vase upon the table with fresh flowers, and dusted and re-arranged the books there.

Madame had been moving forward the bookmark in the novel to pretend that she was reading it.

These unusual preparations were explained an hour or two later, when Bosey introduced into Madame Solisainte's presence their neighbor, Doctor Godfrey. He was a youngish, good-looking man, with a loud, cheery voice and a superabundance of animal spirits. He seemed to carry about with him the very atmosphere of health and to dispense it broadcast in invisible waves.

"Do you see, *Tante* Félicie, how I think of everything? When I saw, last night, the suffering you endured at being put to bed, I decided that you ought to be under a physician's treatment. So the first thing I did this morning was to send a messenger for Doctor Godfrey, and here he is!"

Madame glared at him as he drew up a chair on the opposite side of the table and began to talk about how long it was since he had seen her.

"I do not need a physician!" she cried in tones of exasperation, looking from one to the other. "All the physician' in the worl' cannot 'elp me. My mother was the same; she try all the physician' of the parish. She went to the 'ot spring', to *la Nouvelle Orleans*, an' she die' at las' in this chair. Nothing will 'elp me."

"That is for me to say, Madame Solisainte," said the Doctor, with cheerful assurance. "It is a good idea of your niece's that you should place yourself under a physician's care. I don't say mine, understand—there are many excellent physicians in the parish—but some one ought to look after you, if it is only to keep you in comfortable condition."

Madame blinked at him under lowered brows. She was thinking of his bill for this visit, and determined that he should not make a second one. She saw ruin staring her in the face, and felt as if she were being borne along on a raging torrent of extravagance to meet it.

Bosey had already explained Madame's symptoms to the Doctor, and he said he would send or bring over a preparation which Madame Solisainte must take night and morning till he saw fit to alter or discontinue it. Then he glanced at the magazines, while he and the girl engaged in a lively conversation across Madame's chair. His eyes sparkled with animation as he looked at Bosey, as fresh and sweet in her pink dimity gown as one of the flowers there on the table.

He came very often, and Madame grew sick with apprehension and uncertainty, unable to distinguish between his professional and social visits. At first she refused to take his medicine until Bosey stood over her one evening with a spoonful, gently but firmly expressing a determination to stand there till morning, if necessary, and Madame consented to swallow the mixture. The Doctor took Bosey out driving in his new buggy behind two fast trotters. The first time, after she had driven away, Madame Félicie charged Dimple to go into Miss Bosey's room and search everywhere for the bag of keys. But they were not to be found.

"She mus' kiard 'em wid 'er. She all time got 'em twis' roun' 'er arm. I believe she sleep wid 'em twis' round' 'er arm," offered Dimple in explanation of her failure.

Unable to find the keys, she turned to examining the young girl's dainty belongings—such as were not under lock. She crept back into Madame Félicie's room, carrying a lace-frilled parasol which she silently held out for Madame's inspection. The lace was simple and inexpensive, but the old woman shuddered at sight of it as if it had been the rarest d'Alençon.

Perceiving the impression created by the gay sunshade, Dimple next brought in a pair of slippers with spangled toes, a fine pair of stockings that hung on the back of a chair, an embroidered petticoat, and finally a silk waist. She brought the articles one by one, with a certain solemnity rendered doubly impressive by her silence.

Dimple was wearing her best dress—a red calico with ruffles and puffed sleeves (Miss Bosey had compelled her to discard the other). As a consequence of this holiday attire Dimple gave herself Sunday airs, and passed her time hanging to the gallery post or doubling her body across the bannister rail.

Bosey grew more and more prolific in devices for her Aunt Félicie's comfort and entertainment. She invited Madame's old friends to visit her, singly and in groups; to spend the day—in some instances several days.

She began to have company herself. The young gentlemen and girls of the parish came from miles around to pay their respects. She was of a hospitable turn, and dispensed iced lemonade on such occasions, and sangaree—Lablatte having ordered a case of red wine from the city. There was constant baking of cakes going on in the kitchen, Daniel's wife surpassing all her former efforts in that direction.

Bosey gave lawn parties, with the Chinese lanterns all festooned among the oaks, with three musicians from the quarters playing the fiddle, the guitar and accordion on the gallery, right under Madame Solisainte's nose. She gave a ball and dressed *Tante* Félicie up for the occasion in a silk *peignoir* which she had had made in the city as a surprise.

The Doctor took Bosey driving or horseback riding every other day. He all but lived at Madame Solisainte's, and was in danger of losing all his practice, till Bosey, in mercy, promised to marry him.

She kept her engagement a secret from *Tante* Félicie, pursuing her avocation of the ministering angel up to the very day of her departure for the city to make preparations for her approaching marriage.

A beatitude, a beneficent joy settled upon Madame when Bosey announced her engagement to the Doctor and her intention to leave the plantation that afternoon.

"Oh! You can't imagine, *Tante* Félicie, how I regret to leave you—just as I was getting things so comfortably and pleasantly settled about you, too. If you want, perhaps Fifine or sister Adèle would come——"

"No! no!" cried Madame in shrill protest. "Nothing of the kin'! I insist, let them stay w'ere they are. I am ole; I am use' to my ways. It is not 'ard for me to be alone. I will not year of it!"

Madame could have sung for very joy as she listened all morning to the bustle of her niece's packing. She even petted doggie in her exuberance, for she had aimed many a blow at him with her stick when he had had the temerity to trust himself alone with her.

The trunks and the bathtub were sent away at noon. The clatter accompanying their departure sounded like sweet music in Madame Solisainte's ears. It was with almost a feeling of affection that she embraced her niece when the girl came and kissed her good-by. The Doctor was going to drive his *fiancée* to the station in his buggy.

He told Madame Félicie that he felt like an archangel. In reality, he looked demented with happiness and excitement. She was as suave as honey to him. She was thinking that in the character of a nephew he would not have the indelicacy to present a bill for professional services.

The Doctor hurried out to turn the horses and to get ready the lap-robe to spread over the knees of his divinity. Bosey looked as dainty as the day she had made her appearance, in the same brown linen gown and jaunty traveling hat. There was a fathomless look in her blue eyes.

"And now, *Tante* Félicie," she said finally, "here is your bag of keys. You will find everything in perfect order, and I hope you will be satisfied. All the purchases have been entered in the book—you will find Lablatte's bills and everything correct. But, by the way, *Tante* Félicie, I want to tell you—I have made an equal division of grandmother's silver and table linen and jewels which I found in the strong box, and sent them to mamma. You know yourself it was only just; mamma had as much right to them as you. So, good-by, *Tante* Félicie. You are quite sure you wouldn't like to have sister Adèle?"

"Voleuse! voleuse! voleuse!" she heard her aunt's voice lifted after her in a shrill scream. It followed her as far as the leafy road beyond the live oaks.

Madame Solisainte trembled with excitement and agitation. She looked into the bag and counted the keys. They were all there.

"Voleuse!" she kept muttering. She was convinced that Bosey had robbed her of everything she possessed. The jewels were gone, she was sure of it—all gone. Her mother's watch and chain; bracelets, rings, earrings, everything gone. All the silver; the table, the bed linen, her mother's clothes—ah! that was why she had brought those three trunks!

Madame Solisainte clutched the brass key and glared at it with eyes wild with apprehension. She pounded her stick upon the floor till the rafters rang. But at that time of the afternoon—the hours between dinner and supper—the yard was deserted. And Dimple, still under the delusion created by the red ruffles

and puffed sleeves, was strolling leisurely toward the
station to see Miss Bosey off.

Madame pounded and called. In her wrath she
overturned the table and sent the books and magazines
flying in all directions. She sat a while a prey to the
most violent agitation, the most turbulent misgivings,
that made the pulses throb in her head and the blood
course through her body as though the devil himself
were at the valve.

"Robbed! Robbed! Robbed!" she repeated. "My
gold; the rings; the necklace! I might have known! Oh!
fool! Ah! *cher maître! pas possible!*"

Her head quivered as with a palsy upon its fat
bulk. She clutched the arm of her chair and attempted
to rise; her effort was fruitless. A second attempt, and
she drew herself a few inches out of the chair and fell
back again. A third effort, in which her whole big body
shook and swayed like a vessel which has sprung a leak,
and Madame Solisainte stood upon her feet.

She grasped the cane there at hand and stood helpless, screaming for Dimple. Then she began to walk—
or rather drag her feet along the floor, slowly and with
painful effort, shaking and leaning heavily upon her
stick.

Madame did not think it strange or miraculous that
she should be moving thus upon her tottering limbs,
which for two years had refused to do their office. Her
whole attention was bent upon reaching the press in
her bedroom across the hall. She clutched the brass
key; she had let all the other keys go, and she said
nothing now but *"Volé, volé, volé!"*

Madame Solisainte managed to reach the room without other assistance than the chairs in her way afforded
her, and the walls along which she propped her body
as she sidled along. Her first thought upon unlocking
the press was for her gold. Yes, there it was, all of it,
in little piles as she had so often arranged it. But half
the silver was gone; half the jewels and table linen.

When the servants began to congregate in the
yard, they discovered Madame Félicie standing upon

the gallery waiting for them. They uttered exclamations of wonder and consternation. Dimple became hysterical, and began to cry and scream out.

"Go an' fin' Richmond," said Madame to Daniel, and without comment or question he hurried off in search of the overseer.

"I will 'ave the law! Ah! *par exemple! pas possible!* to be rob' in that way! I will 'ave the law. Tell Lablatte I will not pay the bills. Mandy, go back to the quarters, an' sen' Susan to the kitchen. Dimple! Go an' carry all those book' an' magazine' up in the attic, an' put on you' other dress. Do not let me fin' you array in those flounce' again! *Pas possible! volé comme ça!* I will 'ave the law!"

The Storm
A Sequel to "At the 'Cadian Ball"
1898

I

The leaves were so still that even Bibi thought it was going to rain. Bobinôt, who was accustomed to converse on terms of perfect equality with his little son, called the child's attention to certain sombre clouds that were rolling with sinister intention from the west, accompanied by a sullen, threatening roar. They were at Friedheimer's store and decided to remain there till the storm had passed. They sat within the door on two empty kegs. Bibi was four years old and looked very wise.

"Mama'll be 'fraid, yes," he suggested with blinking eyes.

"She'll shut the house. Maybe she got Sylvie helpin' her this evenin'," Bobinôt responded reassuringly.

"No; she ent got Sylvie. Sylvie was helpin' her yistiday," piped Bibi.

Bobinôt arose and going across to the counter purchased a can of shrimps, of which Calixta was very fond. Then he returned to his perch on the keg and sat stolidly holding the can of shrimps while the storm burst. It shook the wooden store and seemed to be ripping great furrows in the distant field. Bibi laid his little hand on his father's knee and was not afraid.

II

Calixta, at home, felt no uneasiness for their safety. She sat at a side window sewing furiously on a sewing machine. She was greatly occupied and did not notice the approaching storm. But she felt very warm and often stopped to mop her face on which the perspiration gathered in beads. She unfastened her white sacque at the throat. It began to grow dark, and suddenly realizing the situation she got up hurriedly and went about closing windows and doors.

Out on the small front gallery she had hung Bobinôt's Sunday clothes to air and she hastened out to gather them before the rain fell. As she stepped outside, Alcée Laballière rode in at the gate. She had not seen him very often since her marriage, and never alone. She stood there with Bobinôt's coat in her hands, and the big rain drops began to fall. Alcée rode his horse under the shelter of a side projection where the chickens had huddled and there were plows and a harrow piled up in the corner.

"May I come and wait on your gallery till the storm is over, Calixta?" he asked.

"Come 'long in, M'sieur Alcée."

His voice and her own startled her as if from a trance, and she seized Bobinôt's vest. Alcée, mounting to the porch, grabbed the trousers and snatched Bibi's braided jacket that was about to be carried away by a sudden gust of wind. He expressed an intention to remain outside, but it was soon apparent that he might as well have been out in the open: the water beat in upon the boards in driving sheets, and he went inside, closing the door after him. It was even necessary to put something beneath the door to keep the water out.

"My! what a rain! It's good two years since it rain' like that," exclaimed Calixta as she rolled up a piece of bagging and Alcée helped her to thrust it beneath the crack.

She was a little fuller of figure than five years before when she married; but she had lost nothing of her vivacity. Her blue eyes still retained their melting quality; and her yellow hair, dishevelled by the wind and rain, kinked more stubbornly than ever about her ears and temples.

The rain beat upon the low, shingled roof with a force and clatter that threatened to break an entrance and deluge them there. They were in the dining room—the sitting room—the general utility room. Adjoining was her bed room, with Bibi's couch along side her own. The door stood open, and the room with its white, monumental bed, its closed shutters, looked dim and mysterious.

Alcée flung himself into a rocker and Calixta nervously began to gather up from the floor the lengths of a cotton sheet which she had been sewing.

"If this keeps up, *Dieu sait* if the levees goin' to stan' it!" she exclaimed.

"What have you got to do with the levees?"

"I got enough to do! An' there's Bobinôt with Bibi out in that storm—if he only didn' left Friedheimer's!"

"Let us hope, Calixta, that Bobinôt's got sense enough to come in out of a cyclone."

She went and stood at the window with a greatly disturbed look on her face. She wiped the frame that was clouded with moisture. It was stiflingly hot. Alcée got up and joined her at the window, looking over her shoulder. The rain was coming down in sheets obscuring the view of far-off cabins and enveloping the distant wood in a gray mist. The playing of the lightning was incessant. A bolt struck a tall chinaberry tree at the edge of the field. It filled all visible space with a blinding glare and the crash seemed to invade the very boards they stood upon.

Calixta put her hands to her eyes, and with a cry, staggered backward. Alcée's arm encircled her, and for an instant he drew her close and spasmodically to him.

"*Bonté!*" she cried, releasing herself from his encircling arm and retreating from the window, "the
house'll go next! If I only knew w'ere Bibi was!" She
would not compose herself; she would not be seated.
Alcée clasped her shoulders and looked into her face.
The contact of her warm, palpitating body when he
had unthinkingly drawn her into his arms, had
aroused all the old-time infatuation and desire for her
flesh.

"Calixta," he said, "don't be frightened. Nothing
can happen. The house is too low to be struck, with so
many tall trees standing about. There! aren't you going
to be quiet? say, aren't you?" He pushed her hair back
from her face that was warm and steaming. Her lips
were as red and moist as pomegranate seed. Her white
neck and a glimpse of her full, firm bosom disturbed
him powerfully. As she glanced up at him the fear in
her liquid blue eyes had given place to a drowsy gleam
that unconsciously betrayed a sensuous desire. He
looked down into her eyes and there was nothing for
him to do but to gather her lips in a kiss. It reminded
him of Assumption.

"Do you remember—in Assumption, Calixta?"
he asked in a low voice broken by passion. Oh! she
remembered; for in Assumption he had kissed her
and kissed and kissed her; until his senses would well
nigh fail, and to save her he would resort to a desperate flight. If she was not an immaculate dove in those
days, she was still inviolate; a passionate creature
whose very defenselessness had made her defense,
against which his honor forbade him to prevail.
Now—well, now—her lips seemed in a manner free
to be tasted, as well as her round, white throat and
her whiter breasts.

They did not heed the crashing torrents, and the
roar of the elements made her laugh as she lay in his
arms. She was a revelation in that dim, mysterious
chamber; as white as the couch she lay upon. Her firm,
elastic flesh that was knowing for the first time its birth-
right, was like a creamy lily that the sun invites to

contribute its breath and perfume to the undying life of the world.

The generous abundance of her passion, without guile or trickery, was like a white flame which penetrated and found response in depths of his own sensuous nature that had never yet been reached.

When he touched her breasts they gave themselves up in quivering ecstasy, inviting his lips. Her mouth was a fountain of delight. And when he possessed her, they seemed to swoon together at the very borderland of life's mystery.

He stayed cushioned upon her, breathless, dazed, enervated, with his heart beating like a hammer upon her. With one hand she clasped his head, her lips lightly touching his forehead. The other hand stroked with a soothing rhythm his muscular shoulders.

The growl of the thunder was distant and passing away. The rain beat softly upon the shingles, inviting them to drowsiness and sleep. But they dared not yield.

The rain was over; and the sun was turning the glistening green world into a palace of gems. Calixta, on the gallery, watched Alcée ride away. He turned and smiled at her with a beaming face; and she lifted her pretty chin in the air and laughed aloud.

III

Bobinôt and Bibi, trudging home, stopped without at the cistern to make themselves presentable.

"My! Bibi, w'at will yo' mama say! You ought to be ashame'. You oughtn' put on those good pants. Look at 'em! An' that mud on yo' collar! How you got that mud on yo' collar, Bibi? I never saw such a boy!" Bibi was the picture of pathetic resignation. Bobinôt was the embodiment of serious solicitude as he strove to remove from his own person and his son's the signs of their tramp over heavy roads and through wet fields.

He scraped the mud off Bibi's bare legs and feet with a stick and carefully removed all traces from his heavy brogans. Then, prepared for the worst—the meeting with an over-scrupulous housewife, they entered cautiously at the back door.

Calixta was preparing supper. She had set the table and was dripping coffee at the hearth. She sprang up as they came in.

"Oh, Bobinôt! You back! My! but I was uneasy. W'ere you been during the rain? An' Bibi? he ain't wet? he ain't hurt?" She had clasped Bibi and was kissing him effusively. Bobinôt's explanations and apologies which he had been composing all along the way, died on his lips as Calixta felt him to see if he were dry, and seemed to express nothing but satisfaction at their safe return.

"I brought you some shrimps, Calixta," offered Bobinôt, hauling the can from his ample side pocket and laying it on the table.

"Shrimps! Oh, Bobinôt! you too good fo' anything! and she gave him a smacking kiss on the cheek that resounded. *"J'vous réponds,* we'll have a feas' to night! umph-umph!"

Bobinôt and Bibi began to relax and enjoy themselves, and when the three seated themselves at table they laughed much and so loud that anyone might have heard them as far away as Laballière's.

IV

Alcée Laballière wrote to his wife, Clarisse, that night. It was a loving letter, full of tender solicitude. He told her not to hurry back, but if she and the babies liked it at Biloxi, to stay a month longer. He was getting on nicely; and though he missed them, he was willing to bear the separation a while longer—realizing that their health and pleasure were the first things to be considered.

V

As for Clarisse, she was charmed upon receiving her husband's letter. She and the babies were doing well. The society was agreeable; many of her old friends and acquaintances were at the bay. And the first free breath since her marriage seemed to restore the pleasant liberty of her maiden days. Devoted as she was to her husband, their intimate conjugal life was something which she was more than willing to forego for a while.

So the storm passed and every one was happy.

A Little Country Girl
1899

Ninette was scouring the tin milk-pail with sand and lye-soap, and bringing it to a high polish. She used for that purpose the native scrub-brush, the fibrous root of the palmetto, which she called *latanier*. The long table on which the tins were ranged, stood out in the yard under a mulberry tree. It was there that the pots and kettles were washed, the chickens, the meats and vegetables cut up and prepared for cooking.

Occasionally a drop of water fell with a faint splash on the shining surface of the tin; whereupon Ninette would wipe it away and carrying the corner of her checked apron up to her eyes, she would wipe them and proceed with her task. For the drops were falling from Ninette's eyes; trickling down her cheeks and sometimes dropping from the end of her nose.

It was all because two disagreeable old people, who had long outlived their youth, no longer believed in the circus as a means of cheering the human heart; nor could they see the use of it.

Ninette had not even mentioned the subject to them. Why should she? She might as well have said: "Grandfather and Grandmother, with your permission and a small advance of fifty cents, I should like, after my work is done, to make a visit to one of the distant planets this afternoon."

It was very warm and Ninette's face was red with heat and ill-humor. Her hair was black and straight and kept falling over her face. It was an untidy length; her grandmother having decided to let it grow, about six months before. She was barefooted and her calico skirt reached a little above her thick, brown ankles.

Even the negroes were all going to the circus. Suzan's daughter, who was known as Black-Gal, had lingered beside the table a moment on her way through the yard.

"You ain't gwine to de suckus?" she inquired with condescension.

"No," and bread-pan went bang on the table.

"We all's goin'. Pap an' Mammy an' all us is goin'," with a complacent air and a restful pose against the table.

"Where you all goin' to get the money, I like to know."

"Oh, Mr. Ben advance' Mammy a dollar on de crap; an' Joe, he got six bits lef' f'om las' pickin'; an' pap sole a ole no'count plow to Dennis. We all's goin'.

"Joe say he seed 'em pass yonder back Mr. Ben's lane. Dey a elephant mos' as big as dat corn-crib, walkin' long des like he somebody. An' a whole pa'cel wild critters shet up in a cage. An' all kind o' dogs an' hosses; an' de ladies rarin' an' pitchin' in red skirts all fill' up wid gole an' diamonds.

"We all's goin'. Did you ax yo' gran'ma? How come you don't ax yo' gran'pap?"

"That's my business; 'tain't none o' yo's, Black-Gal. You better be gettin' yonder home, tendin' to yo' work, I think."

"I ain't got no work, 'cep' iron out my pink flounce' dress fo' de suckus." But she took herself off with an air of lofty contempt, swinging her tattered skirts. It was after that that Ninette's tears began to drop and spatter.

Resentment rose and rose within her like a leaven, causing her to ferment with wickedness and to make all manner of diabolical wishes in regard to the circus. The worst of these was that she wished it would rain.

"I hope to goodness it'll po' down rain; po' down

rain; po' down rain!" She uttered the wish with the air of a young Medusa pronouncing a blighting curse.

"I like to see 'em all drippin' wet. Black-Gal with her pink flounces, all drippin' wet." She spoke these wishes in the very presence of her grandfather and grandmother, for they understood not a word of English; and she used that language to express her individual opinion on many occasions.

"What do you say, Ninette?" asked her grandmother. Ninette had brought in the last of the tin pails and was ranging them on a shelf in the kitchen.

"I said I hoped it would rain," she answered, wiping her face and fanning herself with a pie pan as though the oppressive heat had suggested the desire for a change of weather.

"You are a wicked girl," said her grandmother, turning on her, "when you know your grandfather has acres and acres of cotton ready to fall, that the rain would ruin. He's angry enough, too, with every man, woman and child leaving the fields to-day to take themselves off to the village. There ought to be a law to compel them to pick their cotton; those trifling creatures! Ah! it was different in the good old days."

Ninette possessed a sensitive soul, and she believed in miracles. For instance, if she were to go to the circus that afternoon she would consider it a miracle. Hope follows on the heels of Faith. And the white-winged goddess—which is Hope—did not leave her, but prompted her to many little surreptitious acts of preparation in the event of the miracle coming to pass.

She peeped into the clothes-press to see that her gingham dress was where she had folded and left it the Sunday before, after Mass. She inspected her shoes and got out a clean pair of stockings which she hid beneath the pillow. In the tin basin behind the house, she scrubbed her face and neck till they were red as boiled crawfish. And her hair, which was too short to plait, she plastered and tied back with a green ribbon; it stood out in a little bristling, stiff tail.

The noon hour had hardly passed, than an unusual agitation began to be visible throughout the surrounding country. The fields were deserted. People, black and white, began passing along the road in squads and detachments. Ponies were galloping on both sides of the river, carrying two and as many as three, on their backs. Blue and green carts with rampant mules; top-buggies and no-top buggies; family carriages that groaned with age and decrepitude; heavy wagons filled with piccaninnies made a passing procession that nothing short of a circus in town could have accounted for.

Grandfather Bézeau was too angry to look at it. He retired to the hall, where he sat gloomily reading a two-weeks-old paper. He looked about ninety years old; he was in reality, not more than seventy.

Grandmother Bézeau stayed out on the gallery, apparently to cast ridicule and contempt upon the heedless and extravagant multitude; in reality, to satisfy a womanly curiosity and a natural interest in the affairs of her neighbors.

As for Ninette, she found it difficult to keep her attention fixed upon her task of shelling peas and her inward supplications that something might happen.

Something *did* happen. Jules Perrault, with a family load in his big farm-wagon, stopped before their gate. He handed the reins to one of the children and he, himself, got down and came up to the gallery where Ninette and her grandmother were sitting.

"What's this! what's this!" he cried out in French, "Ninette not going to the circus? not even ready to go?"

"*Par exemple!*" exclaimed the old lady, looking daggers over her spectacles. She was binding the leg of a wounded chicken that squawked and fluttered with terror.

" '*Par exemple*' or no '*par exemple*' she's going and she's going with me; and her grandfather will give her the money. Run in, little one; get ready; make haste, we shall be late." She looked appealingly at her grandmother who said nothing, being ashamed to say what she felt in the face of her neighbor, Perrault, of whom she stood a little in awe. Ninette, taking silence for consent, darted into the house to get ready.

And when she came out, wonder of wonders! There was her grandfather taking his purse from his pocket. He was drawing it out slowly and painfully, with a hideous grimace, as though it were some vital organ that he was extracting. What arguments could Mons. Perrault have used! They were surely convincing. Ninette had heard them in wordy discussion as she nervously laced her shoes; dabbed her face with flour; hooked the gingham dress; and balanced upon her head a straw "flat" whose roses looked as though they had stayed out over night in a frost.

But no triumphant queen on her throne could have presented a more beaming and joyful countenance than did Ninette when she ascended and seated herself in the big wagon in the midst of the Perrault family. She at once took the baby from Mme. Perrault and held it and felt supremely happy.

The more the wagon jolted and bounced, the more did it convey to her a sense of reality; and less did it seem like a dream. They passed Black-Gal and her family in the road, trudging ankle-deep in dust. Fortunately the girl was barefooted; though the pink flounces were all there, and she carried a green parasol. Her mother was *semi-décolletée* and her father wore a heavy winter coat; while Joe had secured piecemeal, a species of cakewalk costume for the occasion. It was with a feeling of lofty disdain that Ninette passed and left the Black-Gal family in a cloud of dust.

Even after they reached the circus grounds, which were just outside the village, Ninette continued to carry the baby. She would willingly have carried three babies, had such a thing been possible. The infant took a wild and noisy interest in the merry-go-round with its hurdy-gurdy accompaniment. Oh! that she had had more money! that she might have mounted one of those flying horses and gone spinning round in a whirl of ecstasy!

There were side-shows, too. She would have liked to see the lady who weighed six hundred pounds and the gentleman who tipped the scales at fifty. She would have wanted to peep in at the curious monster, captured after a desperate struggle in the wilds of Africa. Its picture, in red and green on the flapping canvas, was surely not like anything she had ever seen or even heard of.

The lemonade was tempting: the pop-corn, the peanuts, the oranges were delights that she might only gaze upon and sigh for. Mons. Perrault took them straight to the big tent, bought the tickets and entered.

Ninette's pulses were thumping with excitement. She sniffed the air, heavy with the smell of saw-dust and animals, and it lingered in her nostrils like some delicious odor. Sure enough! There was the elephant which Black-Gal had described. A chain was about his ponderous leg and he kept reaching out his trunk for tempting morsels. The wild creatures were all there in cages, and the people walked solemnly around, looking at them; awed by the unfamiliarity of the scene.

Ninette never forgot that she had the baby in her arms. She talked to it, and it listened and looked with round, staring eyes. Later on she felt as if she were a person of distinction assisting at some royal pageant when the be-spangled Knights and Ladies in plumes and flowing robes went prancing round on their beautiful horses.

The people all sat on the circus benches and Ninette's feet hung down, because an irritable old lady objected to having them thrust into the small of her back. Mme. Perrault offered to take the baby, but Ninette clung to it. It was something to which she might communicate her excitement. She squeezed it spasmodically when her emotions became uncontrollable.

"Oh! *bébé*! I believe I'm goin' to split my sides! Oh, la! la! if gran'ma could see that, I know she'd laugh herse'f sick." It was none other than the clown who was producing this agreeable impression upon Ninette. She had only to look at his chalky face to go into contortions of mirth.

No one had noticed a gathering obscurity, and the ominous growl of thunder made every one start with disappointment or apprehension. A flash and a second clap, that was like a crash, followed. It came just as the ring-master was cracking his whip with a "hip-la! hip-la!" at the bareback rider, and the clown was standing on his head. There was a sinister roar; a terrific stroke of the wind; the center pole swayed and snapped; the great canvas swelled and beat the air with bellowing resistance.

Pandemonium reigned. In the confusion Ninette found herself down beneath piled up benches. Still clutching the baby, she proceeded to crawl out of an opening in the canvas. She stayed huddled up against the fallen tent, thinking her end had come, while the baby shrieked lustily.

The rain poured in sheets. The cries and howls of the frightened animals were like unearthly sounds. Men called and shouted; children screamed; women went into hysterics and the negroes were having fits.

Ninette got on her knees and prayed God to keep her and the baby and everyone from injury and to take them safely home. It was thus that Mons. Perrault discovered her and the baby, half covered by the fallen tent.

She did not seem to recover from the shock. Days afterward, Ninette was going about in a most unhappy frame of mind, with a wretched look upon her face. She was often discovered in tears.

When her condition began to grow monotonous and depressing, her grandmother insisted upon knowing the cause of it. Then it was that she confessed her wickedness and claimed the guilt of having caused the terrible catastrophe at the circus.

It was her fault that a horse had been killed; it was her fault if an old gentleman had had a collar-bone broken and a lady an arm dislocated. She was the cause of several persons having been thrown into fits and hysterics. All her fault! She it was who had called the rain down upon their heads and thus had she been punished!

It was a very delicate matter for grandmother Bézeau to pronounce upon—far too delicate. So the next day she went and explained it all to the priest and got him to come over and talk to Ninette.

The girl was at the table under the mulberry tree peeling potatoes when the priest arrived. He was a jolly little man who did not like to take things too seriously. So he advanced over the short, tufted grass, bowing low to the ground and making deep salutations with his hat.

"I am overwhelmed," he said, "at finding myself in the presence of the wonderful Magician! who has but to call upon the rain and down it comes. She whistles for the wind and—there it is! Pray, what weather will you give us this afternoon, fair Sorceress?"

Then he became serious and frowning, straightened himself and rapped his stick upon the table.

"What foolishness is this I hear? look at me; look at me!" for she was covering her face, "and who are you, I should like to know, that you dare think you can control the elements!"

Well, they made a great deal of fuss of Ninette and she felt ashamed.

But Mons. Perrault came over; he understood best of all. He took grandmother and grandfather aside and told them the girl was morbid from staying so much with old people, and never associating with those of her own age. He was very impressive and convincing. He frightened them, for he hinted vaguely at terrible consequences to the child's intellect.

He must have touched their hearts, for they both consented to let her go to a birthday party over at his house the following day. Grandfather Bézeau even declared that *if it was necessary* he would contribute towards providing her with a suitable toilet for the occasion.

The Gentleman from New Orleans
1900

Mr. and Mrs. Thomas Bénoîte, commonly known as Mr. and Mrs. Buddie Bénoîte, were so devoted a couple it seemed an unusual pity that anything so sombre as a cloud should ever shadow their domestic serenity. That is what Sophronie would have said if she had put her thoughts into words. It grieved her beyond measure whenever this amiable couple, for example, got upon the subject of Mrs. Buddie's family, a family which, having strongly objected, with some reason, to the marriage in the first place, would in the second place have gladly forgiven and forgotten when things turned out so happily.

But Buddie Bénoîte was neither forgiving nor forgetting, and had a sinister way of oiling his shot gun after a too emphatic conversation regarding family ties and obligations. There were minor differences too, upon the training of the children and the treatment of domestic animals which were not serious and furnished zest to what might otherwise have been too colorless an existence.

There hung no cloud however over this engaging family the morning they started off to the barbecue in Mr. Buddie's big spring wagon. He, his wife, three small children, a couple of neighbors and a huge hemper were as much of a load as the mules could be expected to draw. Mr. Buddie was good looking,

234

energetic, a little too stout and blustering; characteristics which were overemphasized by contrast with his wife, too faded for her years and showing a certain lack of self assertion which her husband regarded as the perfection of womanliness. But one and all beamed happy anticipation as they drove away with noisy clatter.

The morning was still fresh; the sun had not yet dried the dew that shone like a silvery frost on the spears of grass and rested like a mantle of gems on the hardy rose bushes. Sophronie stood shading her eyes and watching them till they were out of sight. She bore not the slightest ill will at being left behind. She was good-natured, and reflected that some one had to stay and watch the premises. To be sure there was old Aunt Crissy, rather the worse for rheumatism. But with the best intentions in the world, what was to prevent Aunt Crissy, if left alone, from setting fire to the house with a coal from her pipe?

No, Sophronie did not complain, but cherished a sense of importance after they were gone. So many things to remember! and so inconsiderate of them to expect her to remember them all! She was not to forget the milk, the calves, the chickens, the dogs. She was to remember to lay the sheets to bleach; to remember if Mr. Sneckbauer from New Orleans stopped in passing, to be polite and to apologize for Mr. Buddie's absence. Mr. Sneckbauer was a commercial representative making the parish rounds and he was due any moment of any day that week.

Sophronie rattled the keys and bustled around at a great rate. She made up the beds and threw things about on the sunny galleries to air. Aunt Crissy was quite impressed:—" 'Tain't right," she grumbled, "leave a nice, pert gal like you behine an' take demse'fs off to de barb'cue des so. "

"Oh, well; every dog its day, Aunt Crissy," said Sophronie pounding a pillow into shape; "my turn 'll come some these times. 'Tain't much fun anyhow to go to a barbecue in a wagon with a lot of chil'ren an' ol' people."

"I know w'at you studyin' 'bout," laughed Aunt Crissy; "you got yo' mine sot on settin' up 'side a nice young man behine a fas' trotter like in Kaintuck yonda."

"You losin' yo' time, Aunt Crissy. Go sit down an' shell those peas. I'll have you here on my han's cryin' misery before you get through."

Aunt Crissy reluctantly retired, deploring Sophronie's unwillingness to profit by so excellent an opportunity for cheerful conversation.

Pitty-pot, pitty-pat went Sophronie's little feet. Now she was flying down to the yard shooing the chickens; again she was dragging the pillows in out of the sun. Swish, swash! went the broom over the bare floors. Bing, bang! opening windows; closing shutters. Clitter, clatter! filling water jars and buckets at the cistern. It's a pity there was no one more appreciative than Aunt Crissy and the ducks to witness such a display of comeliness and youthful energy.

"She mus' a' walked ten miles sence dey gone," grumbled the old woman shelling the peas with her knotty fingers. "W'at you gwine have fo' dinner, Miss Phrony?" she called out.

"I'll jus' take some milk an' something cold, Aunt Crissy. You got yo' bacon an' greens. I don't want to bother with dinner."

It was nearly noon when Sophronie, freshened up, neat as a pin in her blue calico, seated herself to her sewing within the shade of the gallery. But the tribulations of this young housewife were seemingly endless. From afar she had seen a buggy coming down the long, country road. She gazed at it with the natural speculation of the country girl, never dreaming that it would stop there at the gate.

But stop it did. The buggy was old and weather worn. The horse, while an honest enough looking animal, would never have carried off the blue ribbon at a horse show. A thin, blond man in a long linen duster and a soft gray hat got down and divided his attention between his horse and a brace of dogs that viciously challenged his presence.

"Oh, my!" wailed Sophronie; "the gentleman from

New Orleans! An' I can't even remember his name to save me. W'y couldn't he waited till tomorrow! You! Jet! *Passez!* Maje! Go back there! Come in, suh; they won't touch you; don't be afraid."

He opened the gate and came forward with a long, slow stride; pulling at his straggling, straw-colored beard.

"Please come in, suh; come right in. Brother Buddie was expecting you all week. It's too bad; they gone since mornin' to the barbecue."

"Family all gone?" he asked with a slow, bashful drawl, seating himself with an uneasy look.

"Yes, the chil'ren an' all. But you make yo'se'f at home."

He pushed back his broad hat, tilted his chair and crossed his legs; nevertheless he did not appear at ease. Sophronie, after the formalities of his reception were over, felt it would be a relief to him if she excused herself and went away to see about preparing some dinner for him.

"He's come, Aunt Crissy; the gentleman from New Orleans. Here, take a glass of fresh water to him an' come back quick as yo' ol' legs'll bring you."

Nothing could have been more welcome to Aunt Crissy than this pleasing distraction. She pinned a clean kerchief about her neck, gave an extra twist to her bandana and started out to the guest with a cool glass of sparkling water on a tray. She was almost bent double, exaggerating her infirmities as was her custom on special occasions. The gentleman from New Orleans thanked her, wiped his beard on a red cotton handkerchief that he abstracted from the depths of the linen duster, and relapsed into silence.

She eyed him closely while he drank. On her way back to the kitchen she passed through the rooms turning the keys on the closet doors and putting small articles of value out of sight.

Sophronie was already busy with the chicken which had been prepared for the evening meal when Aunt Crissy returned to the kitchen.

"W'at he said 'is name was?" she asked bluntly.

"Oh! I didn't ask him, Aunt Crissy. Here, pour some water on the peas. He knows we know his name; I wasn't goin' to let on I'd forgotten it. Watch the chicken w'ile I go set the table. An' I think I better get out a bottle of wine. Brother Buddie wouldn't be pleased if we didn't treat 'im right."

"W'at he said 'is name was?"

"You enough to try the patience of a saint, Aunt Crissy!"

"Don' look to me like a gemman f'om Noo O'leans."

"Oh! you know so many gentlemen from New Orleans an' from Shreveport an' Baton Rouge an' New York! You can tell one from the other if any body can!"

Aunt Crissy at this pointed rebuke considered all responsibility removed and set stolidly about watching the bubbling pots, while Sophronie busied herself in the dining room, spreading out the very best of everything.

The gentleman from New Orleans laid his felt hat down on the floor beside him when he seated himself at table. He still wore the linen duster because he had no coat beneath it, and he still seemed shy and reluctant to talk.

"You reckon they'll be home before night?" he asked. It was the third time he had put the same question to Sophronie.

"Yes indeed. They wouldn't think of stayin' out with the chil'ren after dark. He'p yo'se'f to mo' wine, suh; it's good wine; it was made in the parish on Mr. Billy Botton's place. Not good as you get in New Orleans, of course, but it's good wine."

"Let's see; there's two children, ain't there?"

"Three. The las' little boy is jus' a year ol'. They beautiful chil'ren, an' jus' as good! The ol'es' boy's got a will of his own, though; he takes after brother Buddie." Later she suggested, with the purpose of discovering whether he intended to stay or not: "If you decide to wait you can put yo' buggy in the shed." The respectable horse had already been provided for.

"Well, I reckon I'll wait s'long as I came this far."

"You can take a walk over the place," prompted Sophronie. "Brother Buddie's put in a new press; an' he's got some o' the fines' cotton fo' miles aroun', down the far end o' the field."

She was delighted to find that her suggestion met with approval. Though a healthy and energetic girl, the strain of entertaining this difficult visitor was beginning to tell on her nerves. She had offered him papers to read which he never looked at. She gave him books with the same result. Conversation was too one-sided to please even a talkative young person.

It was with intense relief that she saw him take his way down the field path, followed by the dogs that had made friends. The linen duster flapped like a skirt about his ankles, and he looked with some show of interest from side to side. Aunt Crissy's gaze followed him with smouldering disapproval. But she washed the dishes in silence and when through, sat in grim silence smoking her pipe on the bench outside the kitchen door.

Sophronie retreated to her room, drew the shutters and lay down to take a nap. She certainly needed the rest.

"Now, if he comes back too soon," she thought with a certain reckless desperation, "he'll have to entertain himself the best he can."

It was not yet dark when the barbecue party came back, thoroughly tired and disheartened, except Mr. Buddie whose spirits seemed to be not in the least impaired. His wife's face was white and drawn, with the premature lines brought strongly out by fatigue. Her pale hair fell on either side in wisps, and she offered altogether a pathetic picture, struggling with the fretful children. The wagon went on, to convey the two neighbors to their home, and the Bénoîte family struggled to the house, Sophronie who had been on the watch, carrying the baby.

"The gentleman from New Orleans is here," she announced to her brother.

"Mr. Sneckbauer! w'en did he come?"

"This mornin'. I gave him dinner. He went out to take a walk an' he hasn't come back yet."

"My, my! did you receive him well?" questioned Mr. Buddie with evident anxiety; "did you give him a good dinner and did Sam put up his buggy? Mr. Sneckbauer's here, Millie," to his wife, "go primp up a little an' fix up the chil'ren. You showed him to his room, Phronie? Did Crissy see that he had everything he needed?"

"Yes, I invited him to make himse'f comfortable, but he didn't seem to want anything in particular. He's been gone a long time; I'll reckon he'll soon be back."

Mr. Buddie performed quite a bit of toilet on his own account, anxious that the family should make a good impression upon Mr. Sneckbauer. His little daughter who was the idol of his heart, toddled after his every step as he came and went about the room, clinging to his legs, hanging to his loosened suspenders. The two were inseparable friends; and when Mr. Buddie had put the last touch by getting into a spic and span blue linen coat, he gathered the importunate little one up in his arms and tenderly brushed the curls away from her dimpled face.

"He's coming, brother Buddie," said Sophronie thrusting her head in at the door. "Sister Millie's out on the back gallery; hurry up!"

When Mr. Buddie reached the gallery he saw the tall, lean figure approaching, already close at hand. Mrs. Buddie stood pale and apparently stricken with some powerful emotion. Then she uttered a cry, and as if possessed of wings, she was down the steps, had crossed the short bit of sward and the next instant she was lost in the arms of the stranger and was sobbing with the utter abandon of a child. He lifted her small person bodily from the ground and for a moment she was quite enfolded in the flapping duster.

"Bud Bénoîte," began the visitor without preliminary, "I know it's common talk you got your shotgun fixed for the first Parkins that steps foot on your land. I respected your wishes; I never feared your gun; now blaze away. I was bound to see my daughter if I had

to die for it." Mrs. Buddie had never relinquished her
clutch about his neck with her face buried upon his
shoulder.

The scene was so unexpected to Buddie Bénoîte
that it found him wholly unprepared. He could find no
words. The wrath which he had always expected would
blaze up at sight of a Parkins, was somehow dispelled
by factors that he had not considered. The sight of
his wife's great emotion was a painful revelation. The
realization that the tie which united those two clinging
to each other out there was the same that bound his
own to the cherished baby in his arms, was an overwhelming realization. His impulses were not slow. He
hastened forward and held out his hand to his wife's
father.

Sophronie had sunk into a chair. She was astounded
at her mistake, and trying to comprehend it. She feared
at first she had committed a crime. A moment later she
began to believe she had brilliantly managed a difficult
situation.

"Her mother's failing pretty smart," went on Parkins, caressing Mrs. Buddie's cheek but showing not
half so much emotion now as Mr. Buddie who was
frankly shedding tears. "She couldn't stand the trip
from Winn; but she felt the same as me; we'd got to
see Millie; we couldn't stand it no longer; neither could
her brothers. The last words she says was, 'Si Parkins
you fetch my girl to me if you got to bring her across
Bud Bénoîte's dead body; if we wait any longer it might
be too late.'"

Mr. Buddie in his entire change of sentiment felt
like placing a pistol in Mr. Parkins' hand and requesting
that gentleman to use him as a target. But he happily
realized that there is a limit even to belated courtesy.

Aunt Crissy was trying to make herself heard; she
had hobbled around from the front of the house:
"Marse Buddie, oh, Marse Buddie; de gen'man f'om
Noo O'leans is roun' at de front gate."

And there he was, Mr. Sneckbauer, in a finely
varnished buggy drawn by two bays that shone with
health and good grooming; a young darky driving him;

a tightly packed suit case strapped behind; himself, dapper, wide awake, affable.

But Mr. Sneckbauer was not the guest of honor that night at Mr. Buddie's table, notwithstanding the fresh and pleasing atmosphere which his presence brought with it.

Sophronie was delighted to think the one cloud over the domestic paradise had been removed. She could not help regretting, however, that the gentleman from New Orleans and the gentleman from Winn had not reversed the order of their coming. What a charming day she might have spent in providing hospitality to so agreeable a personage! She avoided Aunt Crissy's eye. There was a triumphant light in it which interpreted meant: "I know a gentleman when I see one."

"Yo' father can drive you an' the baby in his buggy," said Mr. Buddie after supper with the air of arranging for a second barbecue. "I'll take the other chil'ren with me in the light wagon."

His wife looked up with startled enquiry.

"To Winn," he replied; "we'll start in the mornin'."

Sophronie wondered if she were again going to be left behind, and began to feel a little discouraged.

THE COMPLETE WORKS IN 29 VOLUMES
Edited, with Introductions by David Bevington
•Forewords by Joseph Papp

- □ ANTONY AND CLEOPATRA 21289-3 $2.95
- □ AS YOU LIKE IT 21290-7 $2.50
- □ THE COMEDY OF ERRORS 21291-5 $2.95
- □ HAMLET 21292-3 $2.95
- □ HENRY IV, PART ONE 21293-1 $2.50
- □ HENRY IV, PART TWO 21294-X $2.95
- □ HENRY V 21295-8 $3.50
- □ JULIUS CAESAR 21296-6 $1.95
- □ KING LEAR 21297-4 $2.95
- □ MACBETH 21298-2 $2.95
- □ THE MERCHANT OF VENICE 21299-0 $2.25
- □ A MIDSUMMER NIGHT'S DREAM 21300-8 $2.95
- □ MUCH ADO ABOUT NOTHING 21301-6 $2.95
- □ OTHELLO 21302-4 $3.50
- □ RICHARD II 21303-2 $2.50
- □ RICHARD III 21304-0 $2.75
- □ ROMEO AND JULIET 21305-9 $2.95
- □ THE TAMING OF THE SHREW 21306-7 $2.50
- □ THE TEMPEST 21307-5 $2.25

- □ TWELFTH NIGHT 21308-3 $2.75
- □ FOUR COMEDIES 21281-8 $4.95
  (The Taming of the Shrew, A Midsummer Night's Dream, The Merchant of Venice, and Twelfth Night)
- □ THREE EARLY COMEDIES 21282-6 $4.95
  (Love's Labor's Lost, The Two Gentlemen of Verona, and The Merry Wives of Windsor)
- □ FOUR TRAGEDIES 21283-4 $4.95
  (Hamlet, Othello, King Lear, and Macbeth)
- □ THREE CLASSICAL TRAGEDIES 21284-2 $4.95
  (Titus Andronicus, Timon of Athens, and Coriolanus)
- □ HENRY VI, PARTS ONE, TWO, and THREE 21285-0 $4.95
- □ KING JOHN and HENRY VIII 21286-9 $4.95
- □ MEASURE FOR MEASURE, ALL'S WELL THAT ENDS WELL, and TROILUS AND CRESSIDA 21287-7 $4.95
- □ THE LATE ROMANCES 21288-5 $4.95
  (Pericles, Cymbeline, The Winter's Tale, and The Tempest)
- □ THE POEMS 21309-1 $4.95

Bantam Classics bring you the world's greatest literature—books that have stood the test of time—at specially low prices. These beautifully designed books will be proud additions to your bookshelf. You'll want all these time-tested classics for your own reading pleasure.

Titles by Mark Twain:

☐ 21079-3	**ADVENTURES OF HUCKLEBERRY FINN**	$2.25
☐ 21128-5	**ADVENTURES OF TOM SAWYER**	$2.25
☐ 21195-1	**COMPLETE SHORT STORIES**	$5.95
☐ 21143-9	**A CONNECTICUT YANKEE IN KING ARTHUR'S COURT**	$2.95
☐ 21349-0	**LIFE ON THE MISSISSIPPI**	$2.50
☐ 21256-7	**THE PRINCE AND THE PAUPER**	$2.25
☐ 21158-7	**PUDD'NHEAD WILSON**	$2.25

Other Great Classics:

☐ 21274-5	**BILLY BUDD** Herman Melville	$2.95
☐ 21311-3	**MOBY DICK** Herman Melville	$2.95
☐ 21233-8	**THE CALL OF THE WILD & WHITE FANG** Jack London	$2.95
☐ 21011-4	**THE RED BADGE OF COURAGE** Stephen Crane	$1.95
☐ 21350-4	**THE COUNT OF MONTE CRISTO** Alexander Dumas	$4.95